OUREGANO

After the Empire:
The Francophone World and
Postcolonial France

Series Editor
Valérie Orlando, Illinois Wesleyan University

Advisory Board
Robert Bernasconi, Memphis University; Alec Hargreaves, Florida State University; Chima Korieh, Rowan University; Françoise Lionnet, UCLA; Obioma Nnaemeka, Indiana University; Kamal Salhi, University of Leeds; Tracy D. Sharpley-Whiting, Hamilton College; Frank Ukadike, Tulane University

See www.lexingtonbooks.com/series for the series description and a complete list of published titles.

Recent and Forthcoming Titles
French Civilization and Its Discontents: Nationalism, Colonialism, Race, edited by Tyler Stovall and Georges Van Den Abbeele

After the Deluge: New Perspectives on Postwar French Intellectual and Cultural History, edited by Julian Bourg, afterword by François Dosse

Remnants of Empire in Algeria and Vietnam: Women, Words, and War, by Pamela A. Pears

Packaging Post/Coloniality: The Manufacture of Literary Identity in the Francophone World, by Richard Watts

The Production of the Muslim Woman: Negotiating Text, History, and Ideology, by Lamia Ben Youssef Zayzafoon

France and "Indochina": Cultural Representations, edited by Kathryn Robson and Jennifer Yee

Against the Postcolonial: "Francophone" Writers at the Ends of French Empire, by Richard Serrano

Youth Mobilization in Vichy Indochina and Its Legacies, 1940 to 1970, by Anne Raffin

Afrique sur Seine: A New Generation of African Writers in Paris, by Odile Cazenave

Memory, Empire, and Postcolonialism: Legacies of French Colonialism, edited by Alec G. Hargreaves

Ouregano: A Novel, by Paule Constant, translated and annotated by Margot Miller, and introduced by Claudine Fisher

OUREGANO

A Novel

Paule Constant

Translated and Annotated by **Margot Miller**

Introduction by **Claudine Fisher**

LEXINGTON BOOKS

A Division of
ROWMAN & LITTLEFIELD PUBLISHERS, INC.
Lanham • Boulder • New York • Toronto • Oxford

LEXINGTON BOOKS

A division of Rowman & Littlefield Publishers, Inc.
A wholly owned subsidiary of The Rowman & Littlefield Publishing Group, Inc.
4501 Forbes Boulevard, Suite 200
Lanham, MD 20706

PO Box 317
Oxford
OX2 9RU, UK

British Library Cataloguing in Publication Information Available

Library of Congress Cataloging-in-Publication Data

Constant, Paule, 1944–
    Ouregano : A Novel / Paule Constant ; translation and notes by Margot Miller ; with
an introduction by Claudine Fisher.
        p. cm.
    ISBN 0-7391-1065-9 (alk. paper)—ISBN 0-7391-1066-7 (pbk. : alk. paper)
    1. Europeans—Africa—Fiction. 2. Race relations—Fiction. 3. Kenya—Fiction.
I. Title.
PR6015.U92 C43 2005
823'.912dc—22   2005043059

Printed in the United States of America

♾™ The paper used in this publication meets the minimum requirements of American
National Standard for Information Sciences—Permanence of Paper for Printed Library
Materials, ANSI/NISO Z39.48–1992.

Translator's Preface

Margot Miller

I was first drawn to Paule Constant in 1998 when I heard Brigitte Pichot-Burkette talking about OUREGANO. I was immediately interested because of the setting in 1950s Francophone Africa. I had been a Peace Corps volunteer in West Africa, on the edge of the desert. As Pichot-Burkette described colonial society in the novel, I knew that I had lived in the same world, albeit twenty years later, in the 1970s. When Brigitte described Tiffany and her mother, Matilde, I recognized this relationship as well. Nearly everyone I have met who has been drawn to Constant's work has felt an echo, either in the characters or in the themes, of something they have known. Constant's is a world that calls to readers from the depths of despair, offering transformation and hope in spite of its lack of happy endings. Her novels or, rather, her characters quickly became the focus as well as the vehicle for my Ph.D. dissertation and provided me with a way to say some things that went beyond the purview of that project, allowing me to develop both personally and as a writer.

I began translating OUREGANO because I wanted to make more of Constant's work available to Anglophone readers.[1] I have made a number of choices as a result of my own evolution and the evolution of the translation.[2] One of the most important is that I have chosen to leave out most of the quotation marks American readers might wish for because there are few if any in the original and because I wanted to keep Con-

---

1. For background on Constant and the context of her work, see Claudine Fisher's introduction.

2. Certain passages used in the revised version of the dissertation, which came out in book form in 2003 (*In Search of Shelter*, see bibliography), have been amended here, and anyone seeking to cite an English translation of OURE-GANO should use this version rather than that one.

stant's style as much as possible. The effect preserves the density of the work, its presentation of the fog in which Tiffany lives. The free indirect discourse that blends with direct discourse is key to Constant's style in all her novels. I have tried to feel my way into the voices of her characters, and the reader will, I am hopeful, be able to follow the changes from one to another. At times, it seems that nothing is happening, and, indeed, this void, this emptiness, is central to Tiffany's experience as much as it is to the experience of the adult characters.

I have also chosen to include a number of footnotes to explain terms and references to readers unfamiliar with colonial or postcolonial Francophone Africa, and I have changed the punctuation of many of her sentences, originally strung together by commas or semi-colons, thereby facilitating the reading for those unfamiliar with French punctuation and syntax.

OUREGANO (pronounced "ooh-ray-gah-no," with equal accent on all syllables), is the name of a fictional town at the margin of what is specified only as Central Africa. The name recalls for French speakers the word *ouragan* (hurricane) with all the irredeemable violence and destructive chaos of the tropical storms originating in the moist winds rising over Equatorial Africa. (OUREGANO has nothing at all to do with the herb "oregano," which will come immediately to mind to most English-speaking readers.) It always appears in the text in small capitals, which serve to underscore the force of both its meaning and the experience it conveys. The town has a subtropical climate (between savanna and forest), a small administrative station, a mission, a primary school, and a hospital with a leper colony. The novel tells the story of this insignificant, ingrown, hierarchical, colonial outpost during the early 1950s.

Tiffany Murano and her parents fly into this abandoned bit of the bush where her father is to take over the hospital as its chief medical officer. Bitter, sometimes hilariously funny, and achingly sad, this novel, traces not only seven-year-old Tiffany's development of a sense of memory, identity, and loss but serves as a massive critique of colonialism both in the political reality of its setting and in the interpersonal contacts between adults and children and between the colonizers and the colonized. Its free indirect narration slips easily into the consciousness of each of the characters and out again to show what they are made of. Each of the adults is in some sense as much a prisoner in this place as Tiffany. Each is either living in the hope of finding something that seemed impossible in France or fleeing circumstances that have made him or her unpopular elsewhere. The white French hold the highest positions in this society, from the administrator to the judge, the doctor, the schoolteachers, an ex-patriot entrepreneur, and a jack-of-all-trades who is also a criminal on the run. Beneath them, also in descending order, are the members of the Dutch mission (white but not French), a single African doctor at the hospital, and finally the prisoners and the other indigenous peoples, including the lepers. Not one of them is free.

Constant's fiction is rich in mythical references. One in particular, which most American readers might miss if it were not included here, is interesting from both the perspective of interpretation and translation. It is central to the way Constant depicts women trapped in stereotypes, including Matilde and Elise, who are unable to find any kind of meaning in their lives. Each can be seen as representing one aspect of the legendary aquatic fairy of Celtic origin found in folklore of the Jura region of France and Switzerland.[3] The *Vouivre*, part snake and part bird, bears a remarkable resemblance to the biblical character Lilith, Adam's first wife and therefore the incarnation of Woman before Eve followed as her more docile replacement. Both the *Vouivre* and Lilith are said to be at once a terrible, child-eating mother and a *femme fatale*. Matilde, an indifferent mother, embodies the disappointed vanity of the *femme fatale* symbolized by the snake image, whose terrible power is similar to that of the Medusa. The *Vouivre* carries her enigmatic force in a carbuncle, a garnet-like stone she wears on her forehead but sets aside to enter the water; she is only exposed and defenseless when she is bathing. Tiffany perceives Matilde's vulnerability when she sees her mother in the shower and afterwards in the transformation back into the hardness of her red-orange lipstick and painted-on eyebrows (21). Later, Alexandrou describes Matilde as *"La mère Murano qui roulait des escarboucles comme une biche aux abois."* The *escarboucles* refer to this ruby-red carbunculus in a French expression that conveys the fire of a dark, angry

---

3. See also, Marcel Aymé, *La Vouivre*, Paris: Gallimard, 1945; and *La Vouivre*, 100 min., Cameras Continentales Films/Filma A2/Gaumont/Nymphéa France Films, 1989.

look often associated with mothers exerting control over their children. I have translated this as "flashing her fiery eyes" (114). Elise, unable to have children, incorporates the child-eating sterility figured in the bird of prey feared by traditional Jewish women when they give birth as the curse of Lilith, who will come and eat their babies. After her miscarriage, Elise is brutally vindictive in her relentless pursuit of Tiffany.

Paule Constant is a disturbing, anti-colonial, and feminist writer who insists on the value of female characters to express the human condition rather than solely as representative of what might be considered the particular condition of female existence. *OUREGANO* (1980), together with *Balta* (1983) and *White Spirit* (1989) form what is called the "Africa Trilogy" and *OUREGANO*, *Propriété privée*, and *Balta* form the "Tiffany Trilogy" overlapping in Balzacian style as to time and in the reappearance of certain characters. In all of Constant's novels the main characters seek a space of intimacy and safety, a space of desire associated with the Mother, who is always absent. The space of the story turns out to be an arena in which loss and unspeakable terror expel the main character into an exile of desperate solitude.

I very much hope that readers will enjoy *OUREGANO* and that, although painful at times, it will nonetheless compel them to look for Constant's other novels, thereby enlarging her English-speaking readership. I especially wish to thank Isabelle Harpey, Sheila Turek, and Jennifer Willging for their comments on the translation and my family for their "non-specialist" readings. I also thank Betsy Wing, Madeleine Cottenet-Hage, Gill Rye, and Camilla Curran for readings of early portions and for their encouragement. I thank Claudine Fisher for her comprehensive and informative introduction to Paule Constant and her work. I also thank Valerie Orlando, the *After the Empire* series editor, and Serena Leigh Krombach, Lexington Books' editorial director and senior editor, for their enthusiasm for this project, which comes in addition to everything else they do. As always, I thank Paule Constant for her own work as well as for her interest in mine.

Paule Constant in Context

Claudine Fisher

Biography

Paule Constant was born in Gan (Atlantic Pyrenees, France) on January 25, 1944. The daughter of a military doctor assigned to French colonial troops, Paule, as a child, lived wherever her father was posted: Algeria, Guyana, Cameroon. So it was her mother who taught her to read and directed most of her education, in part at home with correspondence courses, when in remote posts, and in part in local schools.

In the early 1950s, Paule completed the fifth grade (receiving her "entrance-to-sixth-grade diploma" at the end of the school year, a crucial step in the French educational system) at the local school of Batouri, Cameroon, a West-Central African town which serves as model for the colonial-time fictional village of Ouregano in the novel *OUREGANO*.

The following year, she attended the Catholic school of Our Ladies of Saint Maur, in Pau, near the Pyrenees, in Southwest France, where her maternal grandparents lived. She attended this private school, off and on, depending on her parents' assignments. This part of her life would later serve as fictional backdrop for the novel *Propriété privée* (*Private Propery*).

In her adolescence, Paule joined her parents in Djibouti (the Somali Coast) where she attended public school for her ninth grade and received her *Brevet* diploma. Later, the adolescent rejoined her parents in Laos and Cambodia. Eventually, Paule returned to France to Our Ladies of Saint Maur for eleventh and twelfth grades, passing her *Baccalauréat* to enter university.

Constant has a younger sister who lived for a time with their parents in Cayenne. This inspired the writer to present in *The Governor's*

Daughter a fictionalized interpretation of her sister's experiences in French Guyana, through a young girl's personal narrative.

Attending university in the 1960s, Paule Constant first studied political science. She then chose her specialty in comparative (French and American) literatures, during which time she discovered authors such as Hemingway, Dos Passos, Faulkner, and Fitzgerald, and later Flannery O'Connor and Carson McCullers. Her graduate studies took her to Grenoble, Aix-en-Provence, Pau, and Bordeaux. Her English master's thesis was on "Expression and Communication in the Contemporary Autobiographical Novel."

Paule Constant married a medical doctor whose specialty is tropical diseases and teaching. Leaving for Africa again, she brought with her a subject and her research for a doctorate on "New York in the Contemporary French Novel," which she completed in 1974. The couple settled in postcolonial Dakar, Senegal, spending eight years in Abidjan, Ivory Coast. At the University of Abidjan, Paule Constant taught courses on contemporary French literature, African tales, and oral literary tradition. The Ivory Coast experience would later serve as background for the novels *Balta* and *White Spirit*.

With their two children, the couple settled in France, at Aix-en-Provence, in 1975, where she began writing. Constant became Professor of Literature at the French Institute for Foreign Students at the University of Aix-en-Provence, began writing, and published her first novel in 1980. She finished her *Doctorat-ès-Lettres* at Paris-Sorbonne IV in 1987 with "The Education of Young Women of the Aristocracy from Sixteenth to Nineteenth Centuries." It was published in 1987, under the title *Un monde à l'usage des Demoiselles*.

Works

Three of Constant's novels, *OUREGANO* (1980, Prix Valéry Larbaud, 1981), *Balta* (1981), *White Spirit* (1989, Prix François Mauriac, Grand Prix du roman de l'Académie française, 1990) form an African trilogy. Confidence pour confidence (Prix Goncourt, 1998, translated as *Trading Secrets*) and *Sucre et secret* (Prix Amnesty international des droits de l'homme, 2003) take place in the United States. A third "American" novel is in progress. *La fille du Gobernator* (1994, translated as *The Governor's Daughter*, 1998), which takes place in a prison in Cayenne, French Guyana, makes a link between the African tropics and the American continent(s) even as it develops the themes of little girls and their "education," which are also to be found in *Propriété privée* (1981), the sequel to *OUREGANO, Le Grand Ghâpal* (1991), and *Un monde à l'usage des Demoiselles* (1987, Grand Prix de l'essai de l'Académie française). *OUREGANO*, *Propriété privée*, and *Balta* also form a trilogy for the character Tiffany.

Constant has also written two screenplays: *Les périls de la passion*, a modern adaptation of *La Princesse de Clèves* (1987) and *L'Abesse*, the story of an abbess in a seventeenth century French convent (1987).

In 2000, Constant created the *Centre des Ecrivains du Sud - Jean Giono*, of which she is the president, for the promotion of contemporary French literature through interviews, literary events, and conferences.

Paule Constant's novels, published in France by Gallimard, are translated into more than twenty languages. *OUREGANO* was wildly successful as a first novel and brought immediate attention to her promise as an author commenting on contemporary society in an original and disturbing voice.

Fiction and Reality

Paule Constant's life experience and literary interests are, in part, reflected in her *oeuvre* since she interweaves a complex web of autobiographical threads to elaborate her fiction. It would be an error to think that her novels are autobiographical per se, but a certain degree of auto-representation is indirectly mirrored in the text and coexists within the power of the plot and the weight of the existential narratives. *OUREGANO* is the most autorepresentative, but as her work evolves, the biographical allusions become less and less important. For example, as a child and "a military brat," Constant moved continuously between Europe to the African continent. While this movement enlarged her view of the world at a young age, bringing great strength, it also created a lack of belongingness, creating an inner fragility. On the psychological level, the writer has given these gifts and handicaps to her young character, Tiffany, in *OUREGANO*. Tiffany belongs to the whole world and to none of it. The colonial Africa of the 1950s is her adopted homeland although later, in the 1960s/1970s, it holds few illusions for the adults in *Balta* and *White Spirit*. And the France that should be Tiffany's heritage becomes, in part, a land of exile in *Private Property*. The journey of Constant's character can perhaps be compared to the symbolic trajectory of the Wandering Jew, particularly in view of the underlying struggle between despair and hope.

As a young girl, Constant had to deal with the shifting and changing presence of her caregivers: parents, grandparents, teachers, laypersons, and Catholic nuns, as well as her mother as home-teacher. This, again, is visible in the fiction through Tiffany's reaction to her mother and teachers. Closeness and distance, overflow and restraint characterize the relationships, especially the difficult link between mother and daughter, which the writer explores repeatedly in many of her works.

Paule Constant succeeds in transforming her childhood memories and adult philosophical ideas into a fictional world that illustrates the decades from the 1950s all the way to the present. This includes the social and political upheavals as well as the evolution from traditional womanhood to a more liberated era for women. Emotionally, Constant lived first-hand the particularly crucial period between colonialism and postcolonialism. She witnessed the loss of illusion, the destruction of the French military might (her paternal heritage), and the growing awareness of humanistic values that all people should be equal in the totally unequal African and European societies. Ambivalence was the only possible result. Wrenching feelings of love for a land historically conquered, "possessed," and subsequently "dispossessed" bring clarity to the realization that the ex-colonial is left with only a token souvenir of a land that exists only in the heart. In sum, Constant's position can be equated to Camus' philosophical quandary about Algeria.

With this in mind, it will be useful to review the background of the period presented in Constant's novel, which brings into clear focus the subtle nuances of the issues in question.

Within its historical context, *OUREGANO* recalls the last years of French African colonialism from the early 1950s through the memory of Tiffany, the daughter of a colonial military doctor. This was the period when France found itself at a crossroads between its previous colonialist reality and its desire for compromise with the indigenous peoples of the colonies who revolted and aspired to independence. Extricating itself painfully from its war in Indochina after the battle of Dien Bien Phu in 1954, France signed the Geneva agreements, subsequently withdrawing from Vietnam, and leaving North and South Vietnam independent and separated. On the African continent, France faced further independence movements in North Africa (Algeria, Morocco, and Tunisia) and in other colonies in tropical and subtropical Africa: the territories of Senegal, Mauritania, French Sudan, Upper Volta, French Guinea, Niger, Ivory Coast, Dahomey (the former Afrique Occidentale Française, or A.O.F., in English, French West Africa) as well as Gabon, Middle Congo, Oubangui-Chari, Chad (the former Afrique Equatoriale Française, or A.E.F., in English, French Equatorial Africa). The protectorates of Tunisia and Morocco became independent in 1956. Growing pressure on all these fronts had serious repercussions at home and caused the fall of the French Fourth Republic, replaced by the Fifth Republic in 1958 with De Gaulle at the helm. De Gaulle eventually negotiated the independence of the remaining colonies of West and Equatorial Africa from 1958 to 1960. Algeria, in North Africa, was the last to become independent following the war of 1954-1962.

In *OUREGANO*, Constant's African reality springs from this backdrop of uncertainties, shifts of pre-independence days, and the last throes of colonialism. The European characters in the novel have an inkling that they are living the end of an era, but they are unable to change their status or unwilling to give up their privileges. The following discussion offers a number of separate topics, briefly presented, to give readers a variety of ways into *OUREGANO*, as well as the rest of Constant's *oeuvre*, some of which is already translated or is being translated, and all of which chronicles the decline of values inherent in French colonialism and the shift toward other political persuasions including, among others, self-rule for Africa.

Constant's Fictional World

After *OUREGANO*, Constant published *Propriété privée* (*Private Property*) in 1981. The setting is France at the beginning of colonial independence. Tiffany's parents send the distraught little girl to the region where her grandparents live and where she will go to Catholic boarding school. To leave children with relatives in the homeland or in European boarding schools in the 1950s was, in fact, a good alternative for expatriates. They weighed the choices of a better education for the children against the usually less healthy physical or psychological climates of the colonies and war. This second novel focuses on the cherished but elusive grandparents, the home and its private garden near Pau (in the southwest of France), and their love for the child. The positive environment stands in stark contrast with Tiffany's loneliness within the boarding school's "civilized" and orderly framework of the nuns, which in turn clashes with Tiffany's yearning for the warmth of her grandmother and her former and freer African lifestyle. In the end, she experiences yet another abandonment at the death of her beloved grandmother. In *Balta* (1983), Tiffany, now a young woman, comes back to Africa during the "cooperation" era, that is, during the initial years after independence. In the 1960s and early 1970s, some Europeans, mostly civil servants paid by their respective governments, chose a life of adventure in order to help rebuild the new postcolonial Africa. For Tiffany, her return is more bitter than sweet since she feels exiled from both past and present, from the new Africa, and from the memory of her African childhood. As a character, Tiffany has become a minor player[1] alongside a young Frenchman who falls in love with Lola, a brown-skinned prostitute he later marries. The latter has learned to mimic Western mannerisms, whitening her skin to look like a Barbie doll and eventually sealing her sex with tape to reach a sort of virginal rebirth of paradise regained. Finally, *White Spirit* (1989)[2] extends the exploration started in *Balta* and completes the African trilogy. It takes place in the same period of the 1960s-1970s, but focuses

---

1. See Miller, Margot, 2003, 93.
2. Translated by Betsy Wing, University of Nebraska Press, 2005.

more on the indigenous population. This novel is perhaps the cruelest of all Constant's novels in its satire of modern Africa in twentieth-century fiction. According to Constant, industrialized nations use less developed countries as dumping grounds for their damaged goods, objects and humans alike. *La fille du Gobernator* (*The Governor's Daughter*)[3] resembles *OUREGANO* in spirit because the main character is another little girl whose parents leave her free to roam around, but the setting is the penal colony in Cayenne, French Guyana, with the prisoners acting as part-time babysitters. Each of Constant's African or "exotic" novels increases in boldness and in mythical stature, building to a crescendo of almost unbearable pain and cynicism.

In *Confidence pour confidence* (*Trading Secrets*)[4] (1998), the first of Constant's "American" trilogy,[5] the story takes place in the middle of the United States. It underscores the quandary of modern liberated and educated women, from the 1970s generation and from diverse backgrounds, who find themselves as lost as women who had bet on their beauty alone to bring them success. Middle aged now, the women find themselves facing loneliness or despair. In *Sucre et secret*, Constant criticizes the death penalty as practiced in the commonwealth of Virginia, from the point of view of the womenfolk of the accused killer: a mother, a librarian in love with the prisoner, and a journalist. As usual, the author sides neither with the murderer, who, it is implied, may well have been framed (although the reader never knows for sure), nor with the women, portrayed as (sym)pathetic followers. The novel combines a psychological exploration of the evolution of Aurore, a character who reappears from *Confidence pour confidence*, and who is in some sense an adult version of Tiffany and Chrétienne (Miller 2003, 118-126), with an abstract, theoretical plea against capital punishment.

---

3. Translated by Betsy Wing, University of Nebraska Press, 1998.
4. Translated by Betsy Wing, University of Nebraska Press, 2001.
5. The second is *Sucre et secret*, not translated, which found little success in France, and the third is not yet published.

Constant's Irony

The malaise and political unrest of the times in question take on dramatically ironic undercurrents in Paule Constant's African novels, as she depicts, sometimes in subdued tones, at other times with fierce satire or dry wit, the polarizations within the white and black communities. In *OURE-GANO*, the French community, retrenched in its culture, exposes all the flaws of the colonial system while the African villagers symbolize the struggling colonized populations. But the story goes beyond that obvious and facile opposition. To give only one example, Constant is able to illustrate through two characters from the black and white worlds the complex sociological difficulties of the forces at play. A semi-failure in his homeland, the revolutionary French teacher, Albert Refons, who accepts a mediocre teaching job in the village of Ouregano because of his communist past, has his illusions of a new Africa quickly shattered. He hopes to enroll the help of the Senegalese doctor to fight for his ideas and advance the cause of black Africans. Instead, the Frenchman finds himself totally paralyzed by his everyday predicament. His potential ally, the gentle poet Doctor N'Diop, is reluctant to act as a revolutionary black leader. Doctor N'Diop, who, with his medical calling, should be able to offer progress and hope, sadly realizes that he will probably remain transparent for all whites in spite of his European-style training, skill, and higher education. Indeed, he, himself, feels fairly repulsed by some whites, especially by the pregnant Elise Refons, when he examines her before her miscarriage. Moreover, his education has created a wall that separates him from his own people. As a Senegalese, raised in the pleasant breeze-swept coastal town of Saint Louis, the harsher Central African climate does not suit him well. His West African background makes him too different from the less fortunate Central African population. He does not speak their language, forcing him to communicate through an interpreter. N'Diop is alienated by his ideals, his education, his background, and his otherness. His European-based sense and sensibility and his perfect French prevent him from identifying with the sick or the tribal people walking around half naked in Ouregano. They, in turn, call him a "fake" or a "black white man." Doctor N'Diop, who could have been a symbol of a bettering Africa, ends up not *being* at all, and is ultimately destroyed in a most violent death. As a possible positive image for the reader, N'Diop's essence instead conveys sheer hopelessness.

At another level, it is interesting to note that Paule Constant's initials are "P.C." If the readers think they spell "political correctness," they should be forewarned. Indeed, her writings tend to be politically *incor*rect in a world where it is currently better to be correct. Mostly because of this aspect, many readers and critics find her writing troubling or uncomfortable without, at times, being able to identify exactly the origin of this uneasiness within its complexity. Constant constantly walks a fine line between two positions, as if hoping that her readers will hang themselves (figuratively, of course) by revealing their own biases. Constant's writing is nothing if not a pervasive undertow that slowly sweeps the reader away from an easy stand or a pat answer to the problems of the modern world.

Literary Influences

Constant inserts her work into several recognizable literary traditions, both classical and modern. Because she uses a precise and polished French, with little dialogue, often only in the indirect manner of reported speech, the reader can be carried along and carried away by the classical language of the novels. Constant's craft takes its inspiration from the first French psychological novel, *La Princesse de Clèves* (1678), by Madame de La Fayette. As in this novel, points of view shift from one voice to another, then to authorial commentaries, without the reader immediately noticing the difference in perspective. The moderate mood and "sweetness" of tone belie the harsh realities of the themes laid bare in the story. Constant's motifs are intimately connected to such classic French literary themes as exoticism, the cult of nature, philosophy of the eighteenth century, children, negritude, a feminist right to speech, cruelty, and transgression.

Chief among these in the fine arts and literature is France's long tradition of *exoticisme*, fascination for African and other faraway lands. In eighteenth- and nineteenth-century fiction, it presents a glorious, idealized, unrealistic vision of peoples living in contact with nature, as Euro-

peans traveled in and often settled on the American and African conti-
nents where they expressed their colonial, patriarchal, and ultimately
positivist views of the world. The "good savage" was the yardstick
measuring the deeds and moral standards of many generations. Constant's philosophy is based on crucial eighteenth-century theories: she
alludes to Diderot, Rousseau, and the explorer Bougainville (through
Diderot's 1772 satire in his *Supplement to the Voyage of Bougainville*) to
present both sides of the (still) ongoing debate over the good and evil
nature of humanity and of nature versus culture oppositions. Specifically,
she pokes fun at Rousseau's ideas through the character of the Judge,
Bonenfant, who claims that the theory of the good savage is "the biggest
lie ever told in the name of philosophy" (58). The narrator adds sarcasti-
cally that, "Ouregano was exotic all right, enough to go 'round" (58).
Constant underscores life's incoherence when adults behave ferociously
with one another even as she questions the idea of free will and relentlessly demands freedom of thought.

The cult of nature is directly derived from the theme of exoticism,
and Constant follows in her predecessors' footsteps here as well. This
tradition, at least as old as the Greeks and Romans, continues to flourish
in rustic literature even in our time, equating nature with human nature.
Latin writers, such as Virgil, describe the beauty of earth and the joys of
agriculture. Many French writers followed that vein in nineteenth and
twentieth centuries, including George Sand, with her proud peasants, and
the somewhat later Provençal group of Daudet, Mistral, Giono, Pagnol,
and Bosco. For Constant, nature has a good side. Tiffany and Moses enter in communion with their surroundings, with animals, the forest, and
the water. Constant nevertheless emphasizes the relentless decay of natural life in its cycle of birth, death, and rebirth.

Constant is a master at portraying the intricacies of a little girl's psy-
che. It was the nineteenth century that first saw the depiction of children
as worthy of interest, as seen in English literature beginning with Dick-
ens. In France, George Sand, with her *Francois the Champi* (1847), was
the first to present children as protagonists, followed in 1876 by Daudet,
Jack, and in 1894, Jules Renard came out with *Carrot Top*. Most of those
characters are unhappy children for reasons of birth, difficult living conditions, social milieu, and a bad mother or father. *Carrot Top* was con-

sidered innovative since it painted a "normal," middle-class family with a resentful mother. Hervé Bazin and Mauriac followed Renard in the twentieth century by attacking this matriarchal nest of "viper-mothers." Paule Constant can be seen as inheritor of this tradition. In *OUREGANO*, the adults are all oppressors. They crush everyone beneath them: the Africans, the weak, the silent, the sick, the children, and, at the very bottom of the heap, the animals. The book is in fact a full study of the unconscious or deliberate misuse of adult power, a vampirism of the strong sucking on the weak.

With the emergence in the late twentieth and early twenty-first centuries' Francophone literature of the ex-colonized, both the "negritude" movement and "PanAfricanism" underscore solidarity and self-awareness. Writers and poets such as Leopold Sedar Senghor and Aimé Césaire (among scores of others) express a personalized vision, which values the past and expresses hope for the future. Their view of Africa springs from a direct experience of their land from "within" as a rediscovery of identity added to a reconstruction of a modern African conscience. Constant, though white and "colonial," because she lived so much of her life in Africa, also lays claim (although some prickly critics might object) to this heritage.

French exoticism and negritude are easily recognizable and correspond to a fairly clear and specific Manichean ideology. What can be disturbing in Paule Constant's fiction is that none of these opposing views is really depicted as such. In *OUREGANO*, of course, most white characters are villains. Alexandrou, for example, stands as a glaring caricature of human exploitation of others, black as well as white, but all the rest are equally implicated. In *White Spirit*, it is the Africans who exploit and destroy one another, forming a kind of anti-mirror for the villains and victims in *OUREGANO*. So Constant's writing does not fall specifically or only in the category of anti-colonial literature, but it can be seen as anti-everyone and anti-everything, except for the very weak and the innocent. By way of underscoring this distinction, Constant puts Tiffany on the same level as her black counterpart, Moses; they both appreciate the beauty of the land, the pleasure of muddy water after the rain, and the joy of playing with animals. The little girl's viewpoint is a marginalized view from "within" as much as that of Moses.

Because of her generation, Constant lived the evolution of women's rights. The French feminist movement started at the time of the May 1968 demonstrations and developed fully in the 1970s, as in the United States. A tremendous energy existed in France among intellectuals, students, and workers alike. After existentialism and with literary forms like the new novel (circa 1957), structuralism, and deconstruction, great innovations surfaced linking literature to many other disciplines. As for women, they gained practical ground by having more political representation, the right to abortion, the pill reimbursed totally by their medical insurance (French social security), etc. Women intellectuals, such as Hélène Cixoux claimed "the right to difference," i.e., the right to be equal but the right also to be different from men. This "right to difference" was not seen in quite the same way by American feminists, who were striving for total equality. The Americans succeeded in making more practical strides than their French counterparts, but perhaps fewer advances on the theoretical writing level. The French feminist movement gave women, *en masse*, access to the pen (metaphorically linked to the power of the penis), and women's voices, French and Francophone alike, began to be heard fairly loudly in France. When *OUREGANO* came out in 1980, it became part of this new generation of women whose perspectives were different, vocal, and at last published. Interestingly, with *Trading Secrets*, certain readers may feel that, in middle age, Paule Constant chose to remain too non-committal on feminism.

Like Antonin Artaud, the avant-garde French writer who marked the first half of the twentieth-century stage, Constant seems to be a proponent of the theater of cruelty. Like Artaud, Constant's world dwells in transgression, violence, abjection, and death. Tiffany, a transgressive presence in the group, is not a protagonist but an antagonist who seems to attract the forces of evil upon her head. For example, the teacher, Elise Refons, concentrates all her hatred towards children on Tiffany. The girl does not seem to be in defiance of the natural order of nature, but she is in defiance of the order of the family, of patriarchal society, of colonized rules and organizations. Tiffany enters in constant conflict with "otherness," both in herself and in others. The most effective proof is her love/hatred for her mother that reaches obsessional proportions. In the first half of the novel, Tiffany spies on her mother, ghostlike: she observes her, follows her, watches her take a shower or make love. At the end of the novel, after she runs away, Tiffany hates her mother, avoiding her at all costs. There is an extraordinary sense of abandonment in this little girl, an acute psychological distress. Life in the village is like a battlefield where evil forces have claimed victory, as in the religious obsessions of Matilde and Elise Refons, and in the figure of darkness embodied in Alexandrou, the obese hulk sitting in his horned chair, with his right hand, Louis Beretti, the killer and rapist, like a pair of dark Saints Peter holding the keys to paradise-hell.

Themes and Motifs

Numerous motifs can be analyzed in Paule Constant's novels. Points of exile and despair are balanced against points of hope and survival of the spirit. The hypocrisy of the Catholic Church and the horror of "cults" or religious fervor (*White Spirit*) are balanced against traditional Christian and humanistic values. In Constant's work there exist correspondences between the physical and the metaphysical, the psychic and the somatic, the real and the symbolic. A simple way to illustrate this point can be seen in the mirroring of names and proper names. While there is a significant amount of discussion of the meaning of the names of characters and places in *OUREGANO* and in Constant's other novels to be found in Miller's *In Search of Shelter* as well as in her preface to, and in certain notes of, the present translation, it is useful to add, for the non-French reader, several key remarks.

Alexandrou's abandoned truckstop restaurant is called the MIAM-MIAM-GLOUGLOU; literally "YUMYUM-GLUGGLUG." The satire is obvious. In French it is an allusion to baby talk, or to the language used by foreigners not knowing any French, or worse, a language used in jokes about whites trying to communicate with natives, or else of cannibals rejoicing around the caldron before a good meal of explorers. Likewise, with her initials, M.M., Matilde Murano becomes a linguistically truncated Maman (Mommy); and Michel Murano, also M.M., is no Saint Michael (Michel in French), the archangel, though he pretends to an heroic exterior. In spite of the fact that, as a medical doctor, he distributes three white pills, aspirin, penicillin, and quinine, he always falls short when confronted with the African diseases and the lack of supplies. He is a fallen medical hero, the invisible and absent father without the benevolent masculine presence of a "Papa."

No explanation is given for Tiffany's name, either in *OUREGANO* or the other novels in which Tiffany appears. Her name is truly un-French and totally incongruous as well as anachronistic. Constant may have made this choice in order to evoke a reference for the reader to the wide-eyed character played by Audrey Hepburn in the 1961 film, *Breakfast at Tiffany's*, who pretends to be someone other than who she is, an association that has meaning for the novel in spite of the ten-year gap between the times in which the novel and the film are set. Tiffany, however, is unkempt, with dirty hands and messy hair. In French slang, *tiffe* means hair, specifically neglected and rough-looking hair, which is exactly how Tiffany's hair is described. Her character also evokes Little Orphan Annie (Tiffe + Annie = Tiffany). This dual-name interpretation does not seem far-fetched since Paule Constant did a comprehensive study at university on New York in modern French fiction. When she departs for France at the end of *OUREGANO*, Tiffany is thrilled to be labeled by a cardboard sign hung around her neck as "Marie-Françoise," which is her real name, and she thinks to herself, "Tiffany didn't mean anything. Tiffany was nothing. She had been called that because she didn't exist or to make her not exist. It was pleasant to get out of her thing-name" (194). She is nevertheless called Tiffany in all three of the novels and thus remains, even though rejected and exiled, imprisoned within the childlike object status of non-existence.

Elise and Albert Refons' last name signifies "redone" or "made again." In spite of their hopes to rebuild their lives and reconstruct an Africa true to their standards, Africa is going to undo their lives. Nature in Africa is cruel and Darwinian. So the future birth of their child will be transformed into a miscarriage and a male corpse.

The animals that do not deserve to be animals in Tiffany's eyes have names of people. Brigitte is a useless and overprotected poodle, referring, undoubtedly, to the famous actress of the late 1950s and 1960s, Brigitte Bardot, who is still famous today for her great love of animals and her efforts to protect their rights, almost to the point of being ridiculous. As for the chimp, Gaston, the name has to refer to the often given first name of a well-styled servant, in the British manner. This is a monkey mimicking a monkey. The animals that have names are "civilized" but do not appeal to Tiffany. Her favorite animals come from the wild and have no names. They are called the "animal" or the "beastie" and that is enough to identify them in all their glory since they concentrate in all their power what is warm and lovable. Unfortunately, they are also fated to die, like the sheep that will be slaughtered and eaten, the little doe that is sickly, the little crocodile, and the jerboa that is going to be crushed like a ping-pong ball.[6] By showing the fate of these animals, Paule Constant makes her plea for all living creatures.

A lucid and thoughtful writer, Constant is one of the best living representatives of what contemporary French literature has to offer the world. Her work illustrates a certain exile in all of us, yet it begs us to find within "the milk of human kindness."

In closing, I would like to commend Margot Miller and Lexington Books for choosing OUREGANO to present to an English-speaking audience. This translation is intended for various uses and is designed to serve readers new to Constant as well as scholars. It is crucial to Constant's production and path as a writer because, ultimately, all of Constant's other novels find their source in Tiffany's psychological development and initial vision. It is now a fine novel in English because of this sensitive and moving translation, wholly faithful to the original in its specific flavor and idiosyncrasies, which will bring thoughtful English readers to Constant's *oeuvre*. The text will be useful to students of French, Francophone, colonial, English, and comparative literatures, as well as literature in translation, women's studies, international and European studies, and political science. It is the hope of this volume to foster interest, develop further research, and promote additional translations of Paule Constant as well as of other French-language writers.

---

6. There is some additional material on the role of animals in Miller's book (2003).

OUREGANO

for A. B.

Part One

I

In the middle of the summer of 195–, at the end of the prescribed holidays, Captain Murano went to the Ministry to see what was brewing. If they put me in charge of a unit again, I'll quit on the spot. If you assign me another unit, I am warning you, I'll quit. Calm down, Murano, calm down. You've had nothing to complain about up to now, a doctor-colonel replied in a conciliatory manner. This was all that Michel Murano needed to pour out his bitterness. Nothing to complain about! Indochina! Marseilles! And Bordeaux! I'd really like to know how many men of my rank and class have been stuck with posts like that. Yes, how many? The colonel waited a moment. Indochina, okay. But Marseilles wasn't bad and Bordeaux, perfect. What do you have against Bordeaux? Michel exploded. It's a unit! And I, Colonel, I am a doctor, a warrior! I am willing to cure the sick, carry the wounded, operate on the battlefield, but I do not want, ever again, to wait on all these stay-at-home cowards. His eyes shone; his voice was hoarse. That was all it took for the Commanding Medical Officer to make his diagnosis. Well, Murano, I have just what you need. An exceptional post. It's very simple; whoever has it is bound to get promoted. Obviously, everyone's going to want it. Get in line right away, if you've made up your mind. If necessary, give up the rest of your leave. Don't wait. What a job! Chief Medical Officer at the Hospital at OUREGANO, Central Africa.

Well, what is it? asked Matilde Murano, all excited. There was a glint in her husband's dark eyes. He'd definitely gotten the best of them. What worked best with the yellow bellies at the Ministry was the fist on the table. What is it? insisted Matilde. It's OUREGANO: Chief Medical Officer of the hospital at OUREGANO. What's that? Matilde's parents asked their daughter. It's OUREGANO, Matilde said triumphantly. OUREGANO? Yes, OUREGANO. Michel didn't want another unit. After his war, impossible! A collective So it's OUREGANO? greeted Michel's arrival. That's right, he barked sharply. The whole family consulted the encyclocyclopedia: Our, Oural, Ouranos, Ourcq, Ouro Preto, city in Brazil, pop. 8,800. There was no OUREGANO. They would look in Tiffany's atlas.

Elise and Albert Refons, appointed respectively Director of the School for Girls School and Director of the School for Boys at OUREGANO, had to be on the job before the beginning of the school year. The former director, gone home at Easter, had left the post vacant. What was worse, the White Fathers of the Dutch Mission were picking up more and more students. It had to stop. Refons was named to the post in spite of his political past... Let's not go back to that, but signing a petition against the war in Indochina was certainly no guarantee of promotion. It was OUREGANO or nothing. My wife is pregnant, objected Albert Refons, sending a chain of laughter all over the appointment office. So what? There is a doctor at OUREGANO, a hospital, a maternity ward; they have babies in OUREGANO. Elise and Albert opened the atlas and found Central Africa: it was purple, it was big, and it was far away. On another map they located the capital and then searched a little higher up, a little farther, a lot higher, a lot lower, to the left, and there, to the right, OUREGANO. The baby will be born in OUREGANO, said Elise joylessly.

At Niamkey, East Africa, it is noon.* Louis Beretti bustles about in his garage. It's time to close. Where's Mamadou? He's gone. And why has he gone? I don't know. You don't know? You jackass! And you don't know it's time to close up? Lousy country! Scram, you little shit. Mamadou's profile appears in the doorway, a shadow stretches on the floor of the garage, and a shoulder leans against the door, a drunken smile. No excuse to the boss, a sudden idea, no "Sorry, Boss" just to see what would happen. Hey, there! Whaddayou take me for? You know what time it is? Where the hell you been, you bastard? Say: Sorry, Boss, Mamadou. Boss, I'm sorry. That's right, I'm sorry, Boss. That's better. Mamadou opens his mouth, looks Beretti straight in the face. Beretti grabs a wrench, the biggest, and Mamadou gets whacked on the temple. He falls down, dead. Not supposed to happen. Stupid. The sun passes over, his shadow erased with one blow. In the corner, the little helper is trembling. You, you keep your little trap shut! screams Beretti, in a panic. Have to close up the garage, for good. This kind of thing doesn't

---

* Niamkey is a fictional city, probably not Niamey, the capital of Niger.

go over well here. Have to clear off, disappear. Only one name comes to Beretti's mind: OUREGANO. Far, so far, no one would look for him there.

*

The Administrator's Residence at OUREGANO stood high on a hill. This vast dwelling supported by columns on the north side spread out over a slight incline looking south. The Administrator was taking his tea on the terrace. He was looking out of the corner of his eye at the Judge's smaller house. He could have, if he had wanted to, waved hello. But they were in the habit of not greeting each other officially until later, on the premises of the Administrative Services and the Courthouse, identified separately by the men who directed them but confused by the Institutions and by those who used their services. A laborer raked the fine red dust of the driveway. The water carriers appeared below, at the first turn. It would take them a quarter of an hour to reach the house. The light was rising, taking from the night the last moments of calm and emptiness. This was not quite a life but a sort of placid beneficial nothingness that the Administrator could not do without because he had made it the entire meaning of his existence. He wanted to lose himself, past and present, from the least of memories to the slightest sensation, in this afterwards that was already an afterlife.

In his office, the Chief Medical Officer, who had heard from higher up that he would soon be the Commanding Medical Officer, was writing a letter for Murano. PRINCIPAL OBJECTIVE: to get him there, and quickly. ARGUMENT: the appeal and diversity of field medicine. A maternity ward, an operating room, a leper house; it sounds promising. Skip over the stomatology; it might scare him off. Insist on the breadth of power. Your role will not be limited to the hospital, by the way. You will supervise an entire region and different medical posts run by experienced nurses, all perfectly up to date. School medicine, prison medicine, workplace medicine. Skip the inspection of meat butchering and the big endemics. You will be assisted by an entire medical team, perfectly broken

in. You will be able to rely on Doctor N'Diop (African). SECOND ARGU-
MENT: the ease of life. Madame Murano will find here all the essentials
and much more. The doctor's house is one of the most beautiful in
OUREGANO, tennis courts, servant's quarters, stable, orange grove,
kitchen garden. He reread his letter and put in an *s* to make it kitchen
garden*s*. For your personal use, you may drive the ambulance, a Renault*
in very good condition. Sufficient gas is stocked in jerry cans I have had
stored near the tennis courts. Upon reflection, he would not say that.
Driving an ambulance for pleasure and filling the tank oneself from
jerry-cans was something to be taken for granted only after a few months
in-country. Okay, that's enough; now, for the MOST IMPORTANT POINT. I
do not know if I will have the pleasure of welcoming you to OUREGANO,
General Mangin is leaving on the fifth and I will try to take advantage of
this opportunity to get back to France where my wife and children have
been awaiting me for three months. That's it. New line. Sincerely, etc.
Stamp. No stamp. What the hell have they done with my stamp! I wish
him all the luck, this fellow.

Mr. Alexandrou was taking inventory in his store, the only store in
OUREGANO. Sacks of rice, sacks of noodles, sugar, oil in large cans, condensed milk, storm lamps, bolts of fabric. The assistants were busy, moving boxes and cases, unveiling the disaster of a ruined shipment: a length
of cloth, soiled; several cans, swollen. Slumped behind his counter and
looking as if he were asleep, Alexandrou welcomed the damaged goods
in silence. Without moving but motioning with his chin, he had the ruined merchandise placed on the counter. He waited. A client entered
wanting milk, cloth, soap. Alexandrou pointed with his finger at the pile
of refuse. An anxious hand delved lightly into the contents of a carton,
came out a little damp; a thumb pressed discreetly on a can that did not
hide its condition; splatch, the can gave way. The client inquired, were
there any others? Alexandrou indicated once again the garbage. The hand
rummaged about in a bit of a loincloth, a crumpled bill, Bank of Central
Africa. An assistant hurriedly took it to Alexandrou. Alexandrou accepted it. The client waited for change but since he knew neither how

---

* In the original, this is *une tonne Renault*—a small van that has been transformed to function as an ambulance.

much the merchandise cost, nor how much his bill was worth, he turned
to go. Alexandrou never gave change to the natives. A little girl of
twelve brought him a glass of whiskey; he opened a bottle of Perrier
from the display and watered the alcohol. The cap fell on the ground
where there were others, crusted into the beaten dirt floor. They were
there all around his chair. Alexandrou wasn't given to moving.

*

Crossing the border, Louis Beretti was not looking for adventure; he
was going to OUREGANO to Alexandrou's. When he arrived one evening
at the store, a *boy*[*] let him into the rooms of the rear courtyard. He recognized Alexandrou in an armchair whose legs, back, and armrests were
made of zebu horns and the seat was covered in velvet. The picture of the
obese man in his monstrous throne was so impressive that Beretti didn't
notice until later that all the furniture was made of horns; a three-seat
sofa had horns coming out on either side of it with two racks of antlers
joined in an arch marking the center of its back while a low table perched
on pointed feet. He sat down when bidden to and could tell the chairs
were very comfortable: already his forearm rested in the turn of the antler; already his fingers caressed the slender tip.

He said nothing, but his arrival without baggage, at the wheel of a
van red with mud, was sufficiently eloquent. Perhaps even, Alexandrou
imagined, Beretti had done worse than murder an African. Alexandrou
had drinks brought and, as he swallowed the first whiskey he had had in
four days, Beretti knew he had been granted asylum. He did not ask himself why Alexandrou, at the risk of his own security, received him so easily. He did not guess that Alexandrou was sufficiently well placed not to
worry about what the Administrator and the Judge would think in the

---

[*] African male servant of any age working for Europeans. The English word
"boy" is used in French, while English-speaking colonialists used "houseboy."
In translating the text, I have followed the French usage but put it in italics to
indicate that it refers to servants.

event that Beretti's story came to their ears. Perhaps Alexandrou needed him, and it was this idea that attracted Beretti. That's it, Alexandrou needed someone like him. His hands were golden; he knew how to do everything, everything. Repair engines, solder, install electric wiring, repair a kerosene refrigerator, drive, of course, supervise, and looking at his huge hands, he grunted with pride. Start over from scratch, why not? He still had his hands.

He was the first white to penetrate the relatively obscure life of Alexandrou. Why? Alexandrou never quite knew. Certainly Beretti, whom he knew by reputation in his milieu, would be useful to him in business. Alexandrou controlled not only all the food supplies for the Administration but also all the mechanical supplies, gasoline, pharmaceutical orders, school supplies, not to mention the small store he had started with and preferred to all the rest. This Beretti could be useful and would not try to supplant him; he had of his own accord submitted to Alexandrou and Alexandrou had him for sure. Above all, Alexandrou was alone and his solitude, which he filled with drink, weighed more heavily than he realized. In the end Beretti was white, a *petit blanc,** but white all the same, and he wanted to command a white man, yell at him, scream at him, to erase all the "Yes, Sir, Monsieur Administrators," the "Of course, Madame Comandants." He wanted to see how fast a white man would move when he yelled. And also he wanted to like a white man, to be kind to him; he wanted to be in league with someone of his own race.

At the dining table, they spoke of an enterprise that Alexandrou had started in a large native-style shack a few kilometers from OUREGANO on the foresters' road: the MIAMMIAM-GLOUGLOU, its meaning was clear enough that the big trucks would stop there. You could eat chicken grilled with pepper sauce, have a beer or a whiskey; it had worked in its time, and then the forest had receded and the trucks passed farther to the north now. He didn't know what to do with the building. Beretti listened, delighted that action was so close, in this truck stop that they would put

---

* *Petits blancs:* poor whites, often of working-class origin, in the colonies because they cannot find work in the Metropole. The term is not as pejorative as "white trash." I have left it untranslated to give the unfamiliar reader a bit of the flavor of the colonial experience.

back on the map. He agreed vigorously, yes, they couldn't let the MI-AMMIAM-GLOUGLOU disappear; his hands were golden, I tell you, golden.

Their dishes arrived all covered in white linen. As they sat down, they removed napkins from atop the plates and glasses. Alexandrou wanted everything protected. And the young girls who waited on them covered, uncovered, served, and immediately recovered the dishes under napkins. They wiped Beretti's glass, his fork, his knife, and returned them to him respectfully. These strange little girls who put so much zeal into hiding the food came and went almost naked, a slip of fabric passed for a loincloth tied at their narrow backs with two rows of multicolored beads. In the midst of all this whiteness, Beretti looked at the small smooth bodies, brown more than black, where miniscule breasts were just emerging. Half-breeds, said Alexandrou thus presenting his children. The half-breed children did not occupy a privileged place in the household; they were servants. Through the years Alexandrou had surrounded himself with half-breed children. In his warehouse, among the sacks of rice, there was a boy whose clear eyes were those of Alexandrou.

*

Matilde, her forehead poised against the plane window, looked down at the immense rolling green forest. Whenever she raised her eyes, the bluish streaks of the propellers cast a veil over the sky. The airplane, unlike a boat, did not give her the impression that she was traveling. It was a moment, very short and yet too long, that made her languish between the excitement of the departure, the last looks, the words of affection that turn into sermons of love...and the preparations for arrival. She felt no satisfaction since she could not make a single head turn, time wasted. Next to her, Tiffany slept. The child was no longer chubby enough to take in her arms, no longer enough of a baby to require the caresses that Matilde had never given her, but which it would not have displeased her to improvise just now. Tiffany's thinness, her pallor de-

fied the pretty gestures that she would have made. Tiffany wasn't old
enough that by flattering her she could flatter herself a little. Matilde's
gaze went from the disheveled braids to the chewed fingernails, from the
wrinkled Carabi* dress to the thick eyebrows, to the round nose, to the
dusty feet. She wondered how to fix all that. She sighed, there was too
much that needed attention. An unrewarding age. Tiffany was seven.

Michel felt the anxiety that had come over him at the first change in
the sound of the plane descending toward the green earth again, when the
sun disappeared into the gray sky. The oppression he felt was the same,
exactly the same as what he had felt a few years earlier when the Fokker
had dropped him with his squadron in *la Plaine des Joncs*.† It was
strange that he savored this sensation so close to fear, like an intoxicating
pleasure, a kind of desire that made him crazy with impatience. Happiness was there somewhere, imprecise but accessible, suddenly close, after all these lifeless years, this sleepy boredom, this dead time, as old as
Tiffany in fact. He knew that down there, under the foliage, beneath the
trees, time would speed up. He would find his rhythm again, brusque and
quick with its somersaults of terror, its deadly stops, without rest, without
respite, with its zigzags that would only be tactical, pauses that would
keep watch, withdrawals that would take the enemy by surprise.

Madame Dubois' anxiety redoubled the despondency the Administrator felt at the idea of going to welcome the new doctor. Two important
events within three months' time! More than in the two or three years
previous, the departure of the Chief Medical Officer, the arrival of Murano. It was too much—the airport at eleven o'clock, the second-best
ceremonial suit, the first handshake, and, above all, this unknown face he
would have to get used to. How many weeks before the fellow would
find his place and grow silent, swallowed up in the harmony of the days?

---

* "Carabi" was the brand name of a line of fairly expensive, somewhat tai-
lored, colorful dresses that existed until as late as the 1970s. The name probably
comes from the refrain of a children's song, "Compère Guilleri," the story of a
man who climbed up a tree to hunt, fell down, broke his arm, was taken care of
by *les dames de l'hôpital*, whom he thanked with kisses, or perhaps from the
"Marquis de Carabas," a fictional identity created by the cat for his master in
"Puss in Boots."
† A famous battle site in Indochina.

The Administrator knew from experience that it would be around him that the stranger would buzz, against him that the doctor would butt heads with all the force of his harsh, awkward, or desperate moves. He felt a deadly fatigue at the prospect of introducing the newcomer, of explaining things to him, of restarting the machine of silence, acceptance, and nothingness. He couldn't even prepare himself for the onslaught. Madame Dubois was coming after him in his last refuge. Would Bonenfant* go to the airfield? Would they go in the same car? In that case, would they invite the Muranos? So then it would be Bonenfant up front with the driver. Murano on his left, yes. Or Murano in front with him; he would drive and Bonenfant would ride behind with the chauffeur. In any case, Murano's advantage would be noted at the outset. It was impossible to know how this fellow would turn out. Was it a good idea to acknowledge the preeminence of Murano over Bonenfant? Medicine over the Law? Wouldn't it, in a way, diminish the reach of the Administration, thus weaken the power of the Administrator?

The Judge rang for the orderly and asked if the Administrator had finally arrived. Not here, replied the orderly. I will not leave this office before he tells me, by phone, or in writing, until he signals to me that I am to go to the airport or not. And this will be the last straw. I will—not —leave—this—office. Besides, whatever he decides, it'll be for the worst. But I will go in MY car and I will say to Murano: Beware of Dubois. He rang and asked the orderly if the Administrator had arrived. He's here, replied the orderly. Very good, you will have to decide, my friend. He cocked his ear and heard Monsieur Dubois' bell. He waited a moment and then rang himself. What did he ask? He asked if you were here. And you told him? I told him you were here. Very good, very good. You did the right thing. If he were going, he would have to tell Marie so she could get dressed. He could send her the car and tell her to meet him at the office. They would go together. It was only natural for Marie to welcome Madame Murano. And if old lady Dubois didn't come, too bad for her; they'd think she was full of herself, that's all. So much the better.

---

* This name is ironic. *Bon enfant* means a good child, an uncomplicated person.

He would get close to the Muranos through his wife. And then their child, boy or girl? No matter. Whatever it was would play with Jean-Louis and Jean-Marc. It was through the children that he'd beseige the Muranos.

*

The airplane window framed a patch of beaten earth that passed from Matilde's side to Michel's, a tiny bit of laterite that turned crazily in the sky and became stable only when the plane headed straight for it. Tiffany woke up with a hiccup, her head hitting the armrest. As the plane bounced, the hangar, the cars, and the people sped by. The plane came to a stop in a cloud of dust. Michel stood up, brushed the wrinkles out of his white cotton tunic; his hand ran along his collar, lightly touching the red caduceus, the copper buttons. He straightened his epaulettes and picked up his velvet képi.

At the top of the gangway stairs, Matilde held herself back, her gaze averted from the bamboo shack as she pretended not to hear the last pro-peller spluttering, as though it would never finish landing or was ready to take off again, still warmed up. What Matilde was contemplating was her own image projected onto the photograph she had seen a few weeks ear-lier in *Vues et Images:** Queen Elizabeth and Prince Philip visiting the New Hebrides. The queen went forward smiling against the background of the Super Constellation with her gloved hand extended toward a chief, dressed elaborately in his best ceremonial costume, who bowed before her. Behind, Philip stood stiffly...

In front, Michel rather stiffly shook the hand of a short pudgy man. Who was that? Matilde couldn't hear anything and tried to distinguish through Michel's demeanor an indication of the highest deference. The Regional Administrator, perhaps? There was no telling. Michel's back was particularly inexpressive. Toward each person he greeted, he

---

* A cheap magazine similar to *People*.

adopted the same inclination of the shoulders, the same nod of the head, the same sharp little gesture of the elbow against his waist for the handshake. Just as Matilde was about to despair, the fat little man pushed a beanpole of undetermined age toward her. Madame Murano, allow me to introduce Madame Bonenfant. Matilde flashed a brilliant smile at them and took the first hand extended toward her with more energy than she meant to. Her smile faded abruptly when she realized that Michel was greeting Madame Dubois a little farther away. The wife of the Administrator. So these people, who were they? She stepped quickly toward Michel, the Bonenfants latched onto Tiffany. And how old are you? And what grade are you in? She wasn't the same age as Jean-Louis, but would do for Jean-Marc. In any case, the daughter appeared to be as devilish as the mother.

Matilde put that much more effort into greeting Madame Dubois as she suspected she had made a faux pas by responding immediately to the welcoming overtures of the Bonenfants, who seemed, now that she found herself face-to-face with the First Lady of OUREGANO, a little too eager. Madame Dubois turned ostentatiously toward Michel and confided in him the miseries of her three months without a doctor. Brigitte had chosen this time for a sudden hair loss. A hair loss? Goodness! exclaimed Matilde, shaking her magnificent blonde cloud of hair. Lost her hair! But that is awful! Yes, explained Madame Dubois, unmoved by Matilde's efforts. Her back was in such a state! All over the lower back and the beginning of the tail, all pink and crusty. I applied permanganic acid and gave her penicillin. I don't think you can go wrong with penicillin, can you, Doctor?

Matilde didn't understand, Brigitte, bald, the back, the tail.... The Bonenfants, who had taken Tiffany by the hand, were returning to the fray. You must be very tired. We thought you'd like to come and have lunch at our house, our sons.... Oh my God, Matilde groaned, and Michel, listening to the crazy woman. She sent a blind smile toward the Bonenfants, lips tight, a vague, fuzzy look. At the same time an "I didn't understand at all," a "Pardon me?" a "But of course, we'd love to!" an "I am so sorry." Michel turned around and came over to her, declaring: Madame Dubois has offered to put us up at the Residence for several days. Matilde didn't have the courage to announce, in turn, that the Bonenfants had invited them. She grabbed Tiffany, tearing her with the same tentative smile from the clutches of Madame Bonenfant, but this time it meant, Excuse us. You see, we are being kidnapped. We are so popular. One does not turn down an invitation to the Residence. What a snub, what a snub, moaned Madame Bonenfant, climbing back into her car. And Bonenfant slapped Jean-Marc, who had not wanted to get out of the car.

*

The Administrator stuck his neck out the car door and asked, Shall I go first? He nodded, made a gesture of resolve with his left hand, and put the car in gear. The Ford Prairie was very high, wide, and deep; it pitched forward along the road without Monsieur Dubois paying attention. Deaf to the machine's complaints, he kept on accelerating. The small wagon stabilized itself, and the hollow sound and the sudden jerks in the trembling shell disappeared. The Administrator turned toward Michel and explained, If you go sixty* on the washboard, you're screwed.

In the third row of seats, far behind her father, far behind her mother and Madame Dubois, alone on the bench seat that stretched across the entire car, Tiffany moved closer to the window to look at the undulating surface of the roadway. There was nothing but red dust floating there, thick up to the car doors and spreading over the reeds that grew along the narrow road, lining it with a barrier of mud. All there was for a horizon was a uniform crust, as tall as a man. Tiffany looked in front of her at the cloud of her mother's hair, shining, pale and golden, then at the small tight chignon and the neck of the Administrator's wife. Matilde's neck was round, neatly defined in the collar of her white dress; Madame Dubois' gray neck plunged too far down, in a colorless dress that had not been zipped all the way up. This negligence was more a sign of solitude

---

* Sixty kilometers per hour is about thirty-seven miles per hour.

than of haste. No one had repaired the small omission; there had been no light touch of a hand passing there to close the zipper, no small gesture that lingers in a caress on the back of the neck with a gentle word, as Tiffany had seen Michel do.

Tiffany turned toward the back of the car and there, huddled in the middle of the luggage, which he held tightly in his arms, she saw her first black man. So that's how they were, black, with thin legs and long bare feet. Black, with knees pointing to either side of the head, knees bent up to the ears, and outstretched arms, taut like rope that separated under the legs and held the suitcases so they did not bump each other. Did they have faces? Eyes? A nose, a mouth? The black man's head was down. Curled up in the immense effort, he let Tiffany see only the regularity of his head, the soft dustiness of his hair. It was a kind of whipped cream that made the little girl's fingers tremble and ignited an irrepressible desire to touch, partly from curiosity but also from a need to calm herself, to find once again on the choppy roadway and in the sightless ship the warmth of life without the intervention of what is called love, tenderness, with nothing masking the presence, the warm presence of life. That was all. Tiffany extended her hand, first in a faint caress that told her through the barest touch of her hand how thick and dry the hair was, a little prickly, and which made her understand that what she was looking for was buried deep in the cloud of curls. Tiffany sank her hand into the black man's hair; he did not raise his head. She felt a shiver of pleasure along her arm, and she fell asleep.

The Administrator stopped in front of the steps of the Residence. Madame Dubois reached in front and honked several times. The *boys* came running out before the dust had had time to catch up to the car. Brigitte hurled forward too, responding to the beeping horn with her yappy, irritated bark and wagging her tuft of a tail as a sign of satisfaction. In front of the door she began to dance on her hind legs. Madame Dubois, while patting her, ordered the black man who was handling the luggage: Put the car away. Be careful. No bumps, you hear! Tiffany looked at the dog who was dancing about, here and there, its body tense, its mouth open, barking on and on. She wanted to touch her, pick her up. Be careful, said Madame Dubois. She doesn't like children.

For Tiffany, these were terrible words. There were animals that liked children, hunting dogs, outdoor dogs, dogs that slept in the doghouse, nothing dogs, dogs that were made for that, and then there were dogs that didn't like them, indoor dogs, small dogs, sweet little dogs, fragile little dogs. Afraid, jealous, they never wanted patting between the ears. Be careful of the ears! They didn't want you to touch their tails. Watch out for the tail! You mustn't carry them that way. You're going to strangle it. They had their beds, their biscuits, their rugs, their leashes. You couldn't hold the leash or pull on it. These dogs carried their own leashes, all rolled up in their mouths; they walked themselves. They didn't need anyone. Tiffany was on the brink of despair, in this country where animals had the reputation of being wild, cruel, and carnivorous; it seemed that to protect herself from so many threats, she would need at least the intercession of a pet, this little white poodle. Tiffany peered at Brigitte from afar, on whose back the recent baldness left a pink stain, like the map on which they had found OUREGANO.

*

The bedroom was high and green; on the large windows hung linen curtains. The weave let in the glint of changing daylight, making a green shadow in the middle of the room and in its corners. In spite of the impressive size of the room, it was suffocating here. Tiffany felt something crazy, something disintegrating, agitating within her, an animal trapped in the desert of enemy territory. The bedroom offered no help with its two single beds in dark wood frames separated by a massive night table, a celluloid lamp without any decoration, rough green quilts, a bare floor that slipped dizzily toward the bathroom where her mother was showering.

Matilde was naked under the shower, very pale, almost blue, the mark from the previous summer on her buttocks, her breasts resting in her cupped hands. Tiffany shivered, not knowing if she would have preferred to be the hands supporting the heavy softness of the breasts or the breasts that received the caress of the hands. What exquisite pleasure in this gesture, what intimate tenderness, what complicity between them and her, what a precious statement of warmth and closeness. Matilde had lovely, heavy breasts, and they needed, under the pelting of the shower, all the help her hands offered as they supported, caressed, pressed, as they made the firm flesh protrude in a movement of recognition, of knowing, the affirmation of a perfect acceptance of the body. The knowledge she had of her body was so intimate that she combined sensuality and precision with the most banal gestures of hygiene. The hand left the breast and went skillfully down to the dark tuft between her legs, which it separated with a finger, washing there as well, quite simply.

Tiffany looked at her mother, the curve of the body, straining to protect her hair. She marveled at the precise rhythm and the efficiency of the gestures. It was a body-song, accompanied by the water that the hand splashed regularly, always the same hand, by the forearm that supported the breasts, by the soap, the towels, the perfume. A strong body, combative, animal in a way, hard from exercise, surrounding the fragile, heavy breasts. Tiffany loved the muscles that stood out throughout the dance under the shower, the quick rupture from one movement to another, the implacable organization of her mother's bath.

Matilde wrapped herself in a bathrobe and became once again white and blonde, thin and golden, small, without breasts and the dark tuft of hair. The tiniest of empty faces, without eyes because she did not have any eyelashes, without eyebrows because she plucked them, without a mouth because she drew it on, without a nose, of which she was proud, without ears because she hid them. Tiffany melted with tenderness for this emptiness that was bareness itself, a bird without feathers, a kitten with its eyes still closed, a foal that has not found its feet, a cocoon, a baby rat, a bat in the morning, all soft at the end of its tail. Tiffany alone saw this face. The mirror reflected for Matilde only the progression of her insect gestures, little jerky to-ings and fro-ings with tweezers, brushes, and colors. Finally, Matilde opened the tube of lipstick, a strident electric orange-red that was neither the color of her skin nor her lips, not even of flowers, and her face became animated with such violence that it terrified the little girl. Matilde no longer looked like anything but herself, and this mouth wounded Tiffany, the mouth of orders and threats, the mouth of indifference, the abstract mouth without kisses.

Tiffany had to understand: she would not eat lunch with the grown-ups in the dining room, but here, in the bedroom. Her tray would be brought to her. No point in talking about the menu, she would eat what she was served. And NO SCENES. No scenes! No tears. She was big enough to stay alone. She had to understand that adults wanted nothing to do with children. Here, there were no children. Brigitte? Out of the question to try to find her. No, she didn't know if the dog would eat in the dining room. Besides, it was not she who had said it, but Madame Dubois: Brigitte didn't like children. And that was enough. It was the same story every time she had to go out, Tiffany clinging to her, a real leech. And today, honestly, it was sheer perversion since she was dining two or three rooms away. She always played the victim, the abandoned child. No, obviously, she could not go out; she would wait until someone came to get her. If she got bored, she could sleep.

Tiffany heard Matilde's footsteps in the hall, the noise of the high wooded heels, a quick clop-clop at first, then as she entered the living room, more muted. Brigitte's yapping greeted her arrival. The sound of the chairs mixed with the clink of the glasses and the voices with that of the spoons. Tiffany curled up on one of the beds and pressed her hands into her eyes to make red and black landscapes in the golden light.

*

Madame Dubois drove Matilde into town to show her the local resources. The whites did not live in the village of OUREGANO, but in houses spread out on the hills, here and there, surrounded by large plantations, and the huts of the blacks, hidden behind walls of dried mud, gathered in the flat area, as if guarded on each of the corners of the horizon by the stone houses rising around them. The center, where no one lived, was limited to a marketplace for the blacks. They could have had their own commercial center inside their encampment but, on the advice of Alexandrou, the Administrator had settled them here in order to keep tabs on them for sanitary and fiscal reasons. On the little square an enormous flamboyant tree* bloomed, also carefully guarded by the Western enterprises, Alexandrou's and other shops, ochre-colored buildings with long tin roofs supported by wooden stakes covering a gallery that transformed the gray glare of the sun into a stifling heat.

Ladies never went to the open food market; what would they have found there? Misery made all the decay from the belly of the earth rise up: heads of dirty lettuce, a clump of herbs, a squashed chick, a dead bird half devoured by ants, a blue mass of sheep eyes, pig tails resembling gray twine, wasps strung like a necklace on a piece of thread, and then nothing, greenish powders, white powders, balls of clay, a spoonful of black grease. Five francs for a green bean! Twenty francs for a tomato. Decay is expensive. There were also white sheets of manioc pounded thin, so thin, that the whole thing would have stood in the palm of your hand.†

Ladies went to Monsieur Alexandrou's shop. As soon as they entered, a *boy* brought chairs. They sat, elbows on the chair arms, legs discreetly turned toward the exterior. Alexandrou had Perrier served and the *boy* hurried, vigorously wiping the thick glasses, removing the bottle caps with a rough gesture. They rolled away on the floor where a hand promptly collected them. Then the ladies ordered. Ten kilos of rice, five bags of flour, the best, for pastries. Potatoes, have you any? Are they good? Well then, a sack, yes, that'll do. Sugar? But of course! Oil, one can. He had received a delivery of butter and Camembert. Would Madame Commandant like to take advantage of this? But of course! What a joker, Monsieur Alexandrou was. And what about some jam? No. No, she'd gotten everything. Thinking back, her eyes went to a cupboard where she remembered seeing foodstuffs carefully arranged back to the store where she saw nothing, but her squinting eyelids calculated what was behind the doors. No, oil, rice, potatoes…she'd gotten everything. If she had forgotten something, he would send Monsieur Beretti. Agreed, Monsieur Alexandrou? Agreed, Madame Commandant.

He called her back. What about the Administrator's brains? Turning,

---

* royal poinciana (*Delonix regia*).
† Manioc is like cassava, a starchy tuber.

he opened the door of a large refrigerator that rumbled behind him, took out a packet wrapped in brown paper and untied it. The iridescent white brains stuck to the edge of the paper. He held it up to Madame Dubois, who had hurried forward. She nodded, closing her eyes with delight and her eyes excited. She asked, Do you have anything for Brigitte? Ah, I'll have a look, Madame Commandant. He reopened the refrigerator, made a quick tour, grabbed a packet, squeezed it in his fist, took out a bit of newspaper from below the counter, rolled it up, tucked in the edges, and handed it to Madame Dubois. Thank you, Monsieur Alexandrou. Good-bye, Madame Commandant, and turning to Matilde, whom he had not yet acknowledged, Good-bye, Madame Doctor.

The Ford Prairie had stopped in front of the door of the store and passersby saw it loaded with the rice, oil, flour, and sugar that the *boys* carried in their arms, on bent knees, in a jerky race. On the shoulder, the body thrust forward; on the head, eyes fixed straight ahead. The driver waited impassively at the wheel. He watched the *boys* struggle with the doors he had carefully locked. Getting up crossly, he went around the car, pushed them away with a gesture, and opened the lock of the rear doors with such agility that they would not learn how to open it today either. He acquired slowly over the course of time a sort of magical prestige that elevated him to a position of superiority in the eyes of the others.

Brigitte, agitated by such bustle, ran excitedly in circles inside the huge automobile, dashing from one window to the other, jumping on the backs of the seats, carrying on in high style without noticing Tiffany, who at the other end watched this dog that didn't like children. Back and forth, when Brigitte passed over her, it seemed to Tiffany that the dog had not the slightest aggressive intent. Tiffany looked through the window into the faces of all the black people who passed along the car. Like Brigitte, they paid no attention to her. She was an invisible little girl and the market went on as it always did, spread out in a grand confusion of green and black beneath the flamboyant tree with its spears of red flames.

*

Meat in OUREGANO was butchered in Alexandrou's courtyard. Once a week, they would drive into the yard, prodded by sticks, a long skinny zebu, high on its legs, the hump of its back sticking up, the head so fine and so narrow that it seemed sculpted in a light frothy or ivory material that contrasted with the heavy lyre-shaped horns. Tiffany had seen the animal thrown to the ground; it tried to get up, slipping on its hooves, its neck straining, its head too heavy, its eyes terrified. But they kept it down by tying the feet. The huge body would shudder, shake with deep waves that resembled nothing so much as what the little girl had seen when an animal sends a quick and graceful shiver all through its skin to chase off the flies. Terror would rise up along the back of the zebu. The men held its head by the horns—it took four, five, six to twist its neck—while others climbed on its back. And when it was beaten, the butcher came to make his quick cut. Then it would struggle upward, and the enormous effort that Tiffany sensed in the body of the animal that still wanted against everything to get up, this leap expelled its life and the severed neck vomited blood.

The black men brought pans and the butchering began. The taut belly opened under the knife, bluish at first, then red. Intestines were torn, ribs broken, the skull shattered, the tongue cut out, and the testicles sliced off. Bits scattered about, dripped on the ground. Red mud soiled the hide where the face sunk into the earth.

After the zebu parts had been distributed into the pans, Michel did the meat inspection. He walked among the remains of the animal and with a finger indicated the pan where the liver lay. A man hurried forward, and with a sharp knife he opened it, cleaving it into identical lips. If the liver was dark, almost brown, violet, Michel approved it, but occasionally there were large worms, flat and white—liver fluke—and Michel had the meat buried immediately so that it could not be consumed, and then he departed through the hot and stale odor.

Now it was Alexandrou's turn; it was he who divided the meat: the Administrator's filet, the Judge's filet, the steak that he put in the refrigerator, the share for the Mission, for the hospital, and for the prison.

Clear intestines, pink lungs, dark heart, and bones bundled up for the lepers. One bull was not enough for all of OUREGANO, the members of the French colony, the two thousand inhabitants of the village, the three hundred lepers, the one hundred and fifty prisoners.... According to the weight of the zebu, Alexandrou added one or two sheep, and, the dividing continued: a leg for the Administrator, a leg for the Judge... and when he had picked the sheep clean, there was nothing left but the empty skull, which he put on top of the pile for the lepers.

Louis Beretti finished the ceremony, driving off with two orderlies and all the pans in back of the van. He went up to the Residence and carried in Madame Dubois' share himself, protected with a sackcloth, which he opened so she could contemplate the long muscle and bone of the leg of mutton. She poked it with her index finger, surprised at the resistance; he poked it in turn to persuade her that the animal was not as tough as she said. She patted it with her whole hand to show him; he socked it, took the piece up, squeezed it in his fist; she massaged it in turn, their fingers meeting in the still warm meat. In fingering the meat they agreed: two sheets of papaya bark, one on top and one below, would tenderize it, digest it. They exchanged recipes. He addressed her with Dear Madams; she gave him Monsieur Berettis.

At the Bonenfants', Louis Beretti went in through the kitchen. The Judge's function made him nervous. Better not to tempt Providence by being too forward. He worried, against all likelihood, that Bonenfant would appear. His only encounter, and he knew it, would be with Madame Bonenfant, who barely looked at him, eager as she was to examine what Alexandrou had given her for the week. She always found the piece too small; she suspected Madame Dubois had taken a larger portion. Without thinking that the filets or the legs of mutton coming from the same animal ought to be about the same size, she saw monstrous animals on the run, a sheep with one enormous thigh, a zebu fat with all the meat on the Dubois' filets.

At the prison and the hospital, Beretti didn't get out of the truck; the orderlies had to manage on their own with the cooks. But at the leper colony on the other side of the fence of palm trees that marked the border, he had a bit of fun with them. He said to the *boys*, Go on. Carry. Give it to them. Go on. There, that fellow over there will help you, the one with no hand. Off you go. The *boys*, who were frightened, giggled nervously, and, since Beretti was in a hurry, they dumped the contents of the pans on the ground and quickly shut the doors. Beretti gunned the motor and they trembled in fear of being left behind.

II

When Albert and Elise Refons arrived that September morning on the weekly flight, no one came to meet them. They were the only passengers. With their suitcases assembled under the straw awning, they carefully searched the horizon. No bus, no taxi, nothing but an old gray van and some black men bustling around it. All the cargo of the plane went into Beretti's vehicle. The pilot took out a packet of letters for the Administrator and handed it to Beretti, who also served as diplomatic courier. Albert made his way toward them. I can drive you if you like, Beretti offered. They were thrilled. They squeezed into the front of the van, which Beretti catapulted full speed down the road. He nearly ran over a woman who was walking with a calabash full of water on her head. Beretti did not swerve so much as an inch; the woman dove into the ditch, sending the calabash and its contents plummeting. Elise leaned toward the dashboard to see how fast they were going, but the speedometer—which had been broken for a long time—read unabashedly twenty kilometers per hour.

On a hill where a red cross fluttered, Beretti pointed out the hospital. The *toubib** had just arrived, a first-class fighter to be sure, and none too soon. They had been three months with only a joke of a nigger who pretended to be a doctor. Beretti showed them the round huts of the African village sheltered by its mud wall. As they drove through the center, he gestured grandly toward the market under the flamboyant tree, pointed out Alexandrou's boutique, and gallantly, turning toward Elise, he said, Madame, for your shopping. They went along a little farther and caught sight of the Residence. They continued down a slope, coming out in front of some barracks built around a pole where a flag still flapped gently. Your grounds, Monsieur Director. And here, he said backing into an overgrown garden, is your home.

---

* North African Arabic slang for "doctor."

It was a yellowish shack partly swallowed up by a purple bougainvillea. Elise's gaze held on to the vine with all the force of her despair. At least they would have a bougainvillea. Later, she realized that the house was just one of the school buildings: the same proportions, the same porch, the same tobacconists' windows propped open with a stick. Beretti honked several times. A black man, naked to the waist and wearing only shorts, came out of the bushes. Here you go. These are your bosses, Chief! Well, Sir and Madame, welcome. I'm off. Good luck settling in. The *boy* was nervous. With the key in his hand he did his best to open a door swollen with the humidity, then dashed over to open the windows, running from room to room. There was nothing inside—no table, no chair, no sideboard, no oven—as they'd been promised. Nothing was left except a stained straw mattress sagging in the middle of a steel frame with its springs hanging out.

Elise lay down on the dusty fabric. She cried for a long time, tears of anguish and fatigue, disillusionment and weakness. She cried over the indifferent Africans at the airport, over the Administrator who did not come to meet them. She cried over the African doctor she would have to consult and over the furniture that had evaporated. She cried over a country where there was too much earth, too much dust, too much green, and too much black. She cried over her belly that was not yet round, over the coming pains, over her abandonment. Albert questioned the *boy*. He knew nothing; he had not been paid in five months. The boss had left and the new one had just arrived; that made four months. Five months, insisted the *boy*, repeating it over and over, waving his hand, the fingers spread out in front of Refons, five months, five...

The situation had to be dealt with immediately. Albert left on foot with the *boy* for Alexandrou's shop. It was noon. The sun was suffocating in the gray haze. Albert had refused on principle to wear the traditional colonial pith helmet; he went bareheaded, perspiring, all the way up to the Residence, down into the center of town, and all along the flat road. He went to the counter and, like the poor, he ordered a can of condensed milk, a can of sardines, a hurricane lamp, a liter of kerosene. As he did for the poor natives, Alexandrou measured the kerosene exactly and refused to sell the oil except by the keg. Albert saw the Perrier water and suddenly his thirst was intolerable. He asked the price of a bottle; it was too expensive and he went without. When would they be paid? They had nothing here.

On the way back, he let the *boy* carry the packet on his head. He would not have been capable of lifting anything in any case. He trailed far behind the *boy*, exhaustion making him stumble, the heat attacking him in the thorax, the nose, the head, everywhere. When they got back, he looked for water. In the bathroom the faucets made a hollow sound. The *boy* showed him the outdoor cistern where there festered a small amount of red water. Five months, the *boy* said, five months since they last brought water. The *boy* boiled a pot of water, and Albert, his eyes popping out of his head, waited for it to boil, then to cool, then for the mud to separate. Finally he drank tepid water, through clenched teeth to keep from swallowing the earthy residue. That evening they ate directly from the iron pot, white rice and the can of sardines; barely moving in their exhaustion they stretched towels out on the bed. They didn't say anything to each other.

*

Beretti sold them an enormous kerosene refrigerator on credit swearing they would find nothing better and no better price. He also offered to fix them up with a small van, which sat perched wheel-less on two saw-horses. He would repair it and of course find tires. He opened the door to show them the cab. The waxed fabric that covered the bench seat was in tatters. For gasoline, they didn't have to worry; Monsieur Alexandrou would put them on the list of those who were entitled to it, no problem. All that came to a lot of money, but not to worry, he wasn't in a hurry. He trusted them; the government paid them, you know, not to mention the extra. What extra? Why, the hardship pay, for being far from home, the *Lamine Gueye*,[*] you lucky dogs.

---

[*] Lamine Gueye was an African member of the French government from Senegal who proposed a bill to compensate French colonial civil servants stationed in French colonies before independence. This rather substantial supple-

The *boy* raked up the coals and rekindled a brick oven, declaring himself a cook. He brought in a laundry man. Elise halted this invasion by refusing a small child, a kitchen boy. The water came back. Elise was so happy to see it pour into the reservoir she didn't notice that it was coming out of a huge barrel suspended on a length of bamboo carried by two men, two almost naked men dripping with sweat, two prisoners who performed the same chore every day. They went to get the water from the river and delivered it in this way, they and many others like them, to the Administration and to the various houses of the other white people. The Refons were entitled to two barrels a day. And the arrival of the porters, morning and evening—for it took them all day to carry the empty barrel to the river, fill it, and haul it back step by step—marked Elise's days, Sundays and holidays included, with a rhythm as immutable as the rising and setting of the sun, which also happened every day at the same time.

Elise accepted a whole series of compromises because she had no choice. She didn't cook because only a black man could stand the burning heat of the open-fire oven stoked chock full of wood, and besides, she didn't know how to make bread. She didn't do laundry—that happened at the river's edge, far from the house—and for the ironing the laundry *boy* used either little irons of cast-iron that he heated up on the firebox or a huge one resembling an orthopedic shoe. It had a cavity that he filled with hot coals. Both the insides and the outsides had to be ironed, the elastic waists and the folds, to kill the fly larva. She didn't do the cleaning because being pregnant made her tired. It was a huge undertaking that required a brush, water, and soap. The house smelled of bleach and disinfectant. Elise liked to find the mosquito net carefully tucked around a well-made bed. She especially liked the shower of tepid water that the *boy* installed for her in her bathroom. He suspended a bucket on a hook that she tipped by pulling on a cord causing a delightful downpour. The money she would earn, with their two director's salaries, gave her a feeling of independence, the impression of power. She was rich and they were poor; she could buy them.

She had bedsteads made that would also serve as sofas. She didn't

---

ment was paid upon arrival in-country and was referred to as *toucher la Lamine Gueye.*

want anything special, white wood.... The cabinetmaker had only mahogany. He was sorry; here, it was the most common wood. One day, two enormous, very heavy frames were delivered to her. A man carried them on his head. The dark pink of the prestigious wood moved her to tears: mahogany! So she ordered a table and chairs—she would take them back to France—and the same man carried the table on his head as well as the four chairs. She wanted a bookcase, not just anything, but something with glass doors. She got her bookcase but the cabinetmaker apologized for not having put in the "windows"; there was no glass to be had. The doors would remain open and the books would mildew. She dreamed of a cradle for the baby that she would trim in English embroidery. The cabinetmaker delivered a crib with heavy bars; he had artistically mixed the everyday mahogany with more exotic ebony.

OUREGANO was less good to Albert. Starting with the official visits, it stripped him of happiness, hope, and dignity. The Administrator defined his role in no uncertain terms. He had only to continue the work at hand, to restart the heavy machinery and keep it going without thinking about all the ins and outs. The rest was up to the officials, he said, stroking his cheek. As for Refons, at his level, he was a worker, a simple worker who carried out orders. The school's funds, books, notebooks, even the ink, were all dispensed by the Administration. So? Did he see any solution other than submission? Let's be friends, Refons, and I promise to help you...as far as I am able. Otherwise it's war, and there, believe me, I'll break your back. He was dismissed: For day-to-day things, see Monsieur Alexandrou. This brusque use of authority was not normal for Monsieur Dubois, more inclined to indifference than anger. But the arrival of Refons had triggered the mechanism of fear. He knew this sort of fellow well; he had seen them before. They sowed strife just for the fun of it, rebelled on principle, stirred up everything with their dissatisfaction. They were nothing but trouble.

The Judge's welcome was no warmer. He also intended to have orders followed; he too had his weapons, a file full of the political activities of the Refons couple. OUREGANO was a trap; two reprehensible men guarded the door. Because his youth was now long gone, he felt abandoned by Elise, who was wrapped up in her pregnancy. He needed a rest, a little peace to get his ideas into some kind of order.

He realized that he had been a revolutionary more out of momentum than principle. He fed his revolt with violence and passion, not shoring it up, not organizing it, not tempering it. Is faith reasonable? And here, isolated, his ears still heard the sound and the fury of his earlier days, and in his heart he felt that he hated these men, hated this flag flying unfairly over this miserable country. He hated them as much on his own behalf as on behalf of Africa. His humiliated youth told the story of the humiliated country...inspecting inspectors...self-important secondary school teachers...stuffy college professors.... Those were the men who had nearly flunked him out, made him drop out, a failure, a mediocre person (here he was too hard on himself and didn't really believe it). It was they who had turned him into Elise's happy husband.

Retreat rang its panicked alarm; his whole being seemed in headlong flight. To make sense of it, Refons imagined Salvation in the form of N'Diop. Yes, there was still N'Diop. But he resisted going to find him, resisted taking his fear, his anger, and his shame to the African to start another revolt. If N'Diop as a free and determined African existed only in his mind, he would not be able to stand it.

*

Doctor N'Diop had been there for six months. For three months, he had worked relentlessly by the side of the then Chief Medical Officer, in order to learn the essential duties of his new function: surgery, gynecology-obstetrics, radiology. He was so preoccupied by the extent of his responsibilities that he had not even thought about what had inspired the colonial authorities to exile him in OUREGANO. The Chief Medical Officer had buried his energy alive in a succession of acts that were breaking his spirit. Each morning brought its heap of problems; he often felt he would not be able to manage. It was by observing the Chief Medical Officer, who worked unperturbed, that he regained his confidence. He appreciated the white man, for he loaded him up with work and thus treated him as an equal.

The Chief Medical Officer had not noticed N'Diop's arrival, had acted as if he had always been there, and did not say good-bye. One morning, N'Diop was just alone. Instead of exulting in his solitude as liberation, he felt crushed. Because of his other duties the aspects of the hospital's functions that he now had to assume had remained hidden from him. Finding medicines, maintaining the equipment, feeding the sick, organizing the nursing services, vaccinations.... So the Chief Medical Officer did all that as well. He remembered him nostalgically and for the first time asked himself if the other had liked him. He imagined a friendship that had not existed and suffered deeply from the departure of this man whom he respected.

The management of the hospital was not good. Objects and people began to disappear: the only blood pressure machine, thermometers, syringes, ice packs, even the naked beds. The nurse, the orderly, the matron were not to be found. N'Diop insisted on reports, proper uniforms, order, punctuality. He distributed demands for explanation in writing. No one answered. He was hated.

What did he want, this Negro? Where did he come from really, this tall, skinny, pitch-black black man? He bothered everyone and everything, this black monkey of white men. He was not at home here and he was made to know it. The image of a united and indivisible Africa melted in his mind. He couldn't see the Africa of Dakar, of Saint Louis and this place on the same plane. The deserts that disappeared into the sea had a different kind of nobility, different from this prickly savanna drowning in the forest. Could one compare the women in tall turbans who danced like giant elegant butterflies with these shriveled black women who went half naked, breasts hanging, their sex protected by leaves? What did these beings worn down by hunger have in common with the passionate intellectuals among whom he had held his head high? He hated them for displaying before the Chief Medical Officer, day after day, the image of an Africa that was not right. He was afraid that the silent Chief Medical Officer had confused him with all these people, especially with the short-legged male nurses who ordered golden pens without nibs from a catalogue (to display in their breast pockets), unwearable English suits, fake glasses, and watches with fixed hands. He was not one of those. Had the Chief Medical Officer understood? He was humiliated by the thoughts he ascribed to the companion who had never spoken to him and who perhaps had not even looked at him.

He stood shaking with shame and his first revolt brought bitterness to his mouth and his heart. A brilliant student at William Ponty,[*] he had organized their first strike. It had turned out badly. Ever since, the whites were always there to tell him he would be subdued, demoted, broken. But he laughed at their ugly faces twisted in hate and stupidity. The Chief Medical Officer was like the others, like Administrator Dubois, like Judge Bonenfant. He had believed, naively, in a sort of reconciliation. It was destroying him; that was all there was to it. He would never again let himself be taken in.

The whites though, he saw them. Within three months he had received a visit from Madame Bonenfant, who wanted him to pull a tooth for her cook. He sat the poor man in a chair, and with the wife of the Judge looking on, he proceeded with an extraction that gushed blood and screams. Madame Bonenfant declared it a veritable butchery. Madame Dubois brought him Brigitte, demanding penicillin. She didn't ask for a diagnosis; she insisted on shots and that he be gentle. He injected the dog with the last doses in the pharmacy.

*

When he was called to the Refons' house, N'Diop gathered about himself what was left of his submission and silence. He headed for Elise's bedroom, eyes lowered, and it was with his eyes averted that he looked at her. She was lying down, her head in the darkness. He pulled off the white sheet and hesitated as he pulled up the nightgown. The pubis appeared, bushy, spreading over the barely rounded abdomen, pale with blue veins. So this was a white woman, this soft belly, this immense sex. He palpated to find the uterus, a light contraction tightened her ab-

---

[*] William Ponty School, Senegal, where many African leaders have been educated.

domen, and N'Diop saw the space filled by the fetus, the size of a large grapefruit, very low, almost swallowed up in the pubic hair. Elise groaned, You see, Doctor, it does that all the time. She cried. Is it serious, Doctor. Is it serious?

He could not speak to this woman; he was used to precise and silent gestures. What could he say? Albert stood near the door, rigid with anxiety. The silence of the doctor fed the fears Elise had been pounding him with since their arrival, something truly serious and real. N'Diop, seated on the bed, began to examine the young woman internally. She did not have to be asked to slide to the edge of the mattress or to open her legs. Albert saw the deep pink of the vagina, a black hand penetrating, searching, another on the pubis, pressing. Elise, whose abdomen contracted again, moaned quietly. You see, Doctor, you see...? N'Diop held this woman by the insides, and the mucus that soaked his ungloved hand (where would he have found gloves?) disgusted him. He hurried, looking away so that his fingers would find what they sought by themselves.

He did not look at Elise until after washing his hands. She had a thin face, with brown, slightly drooping eyes, the look of a little girl, nothing that indicated the flabby belly and the obscene sex. Tearing the words from her mouth she asked him, Is the baby dead? The cervix is closed. In the hall, Albert was back in charge. What should we do? N'Diop shrugged his shoulders. She must rest. They were annoying him with this white fetus. If it lives or dies, what difference did it make? The anxiety of these people seemed out of proportion. In addition to their *boys* and their dogs, he was presented with their fetuses.... Decidedly, the whites were determined to make him walk in their shit! Albert found N'Diop's advice reassuring. It wasn't serious since all that was needed was rest, and besides, N'Diop had said it for something to say because, in the end, Elise was just imagining things.

Albert was in a hurry to forget Elise, her belly, and the bedroom. He wanted to talk of other things; he just wanted to talk. He dragged N'Diop into the living room, made him sit on one of the mahogany sofas behind the coffee table across from the bookcase. He offered him a drink. A Pernod? Some whiskey. I don't drink alcohol. You're Muslim? asked Albert, interestedly. N'Diop didn't want to talk. He looked at the furniture, the arrangement of the house and compared it to the room he occupied at the hospital. Never had he given a thought to these domestic questions; his room, with its fan, its table, a chair, shelves, had seemed, until then, luxurious. You're Senegalese, aren't you? insisted Albert, who didn't wait for a response. Ah, Senghor...the black pearl....*Ethiopiques*....

N'Diop got up. I have to go operate. Albert let him go with regret. The poem continued to run on in his head. He remained seated in the dark as night fell. He told himself stories as he would have told them to N'Diop. He loved Africa, the Africa of maps and books; he loved the blacks and the legends and the poems, and suddenly, because he had so much love to share, N'Diop's absence was painful to him. He blamed it on Elise and the baby. The poem of friendship could not come to life between those open thighs.

*

Hunger and fear wipe out those they get hold of. He who dies of hunger collapses inwardly as if he were going inside for a last communion; he who is fearful obscures himself; his gray features disappear. The hostile beggar who holds out an insistent bowl, the disfigured cripple who offends with his stump and his wooden leg: Look, there is nothing there. Fear goes unheard when the screams are silenced. Hunger makes no impression when the poor little man lies on the ground, shriveled up.

The whites of OUREGANO did not see the blacks of OUREGANO. They saw their *boys* stealing from them, the water-carriers who emphasized each step as they labored under the weight, an orderly here and there, a woman at the river, a loiterer passing the time under a frangipani tree, a driver, a gardener. They saw all those who were still standing, eating—too much—thanks to themselves. They noticed the noisy edges and, in the distance, a woman who carried a handsome baby. My wife, said the *boy*; my son, said the loiterer. They presented their bowl. Thank you, said the woman, thank you, said the *boy*, and the baby said nothing at all. The whites had their own blacks. These were saved; they lived close to the master's house, in *boyeries*.[*] They didn't mix with the others and even forbade the others access to the house from which all was distributed.

The whites of OUREGANO did not see the blacks dying. There were those who "did nothing," those who "didn't know how to feed themselves," those who "no longer knew how to hunt," those who "didn't want to fish." The bush, it can be cleared; it can be farmed! They didn't clear the land. They waited at the edge of town for something to come that never arrived. There had been a time when the village was on the edge of the forest and the men went hunting. The forest had receded. They had stayed there in the curious earthen enclave that kept them prisoner instead of protecting them. They no longer hunted. They had even lost the frenzy of flight, the push to escape the swamp, to get out. Since childhood they had been enclosed in mud, held back, bearing their loss at the very limits of their strength. The tsetse fly was a big part of it and the malnourished and dopey village waited to pass from one kind of sleep to another. Babies sucked at the dried up breasts of grandmothers.

In the immense monotonous landscape covered in a green stupor, the red village covered in brown straw was striking on first sight. They had all noticed it; Monsieur Dubois, Madame Dubois, Monsieur Bonenfant, Madame Bonenfant, Doctor Murano, Madame Murano, Monsieur Refons, and Madame Refons, coming in from the airport, and then they had forgotten it. They confused the village with the landscape from which it had absorbed the earth, the branches, and the grasses. The village of silence! Nothing moved inside; nothing drifted in the air; nothing could be seen from the road. In there another story was told, a story of gasping, suffocating life but life that goes on with its births and deaths all the same, with its own language and screams of pain. A drumbeat at the end of the earth, a sound that drugs the listener because it goes on and on until you don't hear it anymore, a fatal moaning.

N'Diop had come into this place and had found nothing. Even though all the things of his childhood were there, the pestle and the black calabash, the pierced pipe, the smell and the sound were missing. They had noticed and did not recognize him. One woman and then another had

---

[*] Huts in the courtyard of colonial houses where the *boys* (servants) live.

disappeared. The sleepy loiterer in front of a hut, his head on his shoulder, didn't see him. The children watched. He wanted to call to them, which he did in his language, but it was not theirs. He greeted them in French, but they didn't respond. He walked in the rutted pathways, leaned into the door of a house. At night he felt that something was moving. He fled. He couldn't care for these people; he couldn't even talk to them. N'Diop never came back to the village. On the map of endemic diseases, Murano had pinned the flag of trypanosomiasis* there.

*

OUREGANO didn't need an Administrator. Emptiness cannot be administered, nor death, nor hunger. All that takes care of itself according to an infernal cycle men have nothing to do with. Hunger begets illness—illness, hunger, and death. Treating illness, feeding the hungry, hauling off the dead, these are not the chores of an Administrator. Besides, Monsieur Dubois administered an entire region, and OUREGANO served only as the seat of operations. It was reassuring when one saw the other villages, one after another; the power of Monsieur Dubois was always felt elsewhere. He was the man of "farther on" and "later."

Aside from the office, Monsieur Dubois' functions included the official visits around the region. He went out in a car loaded with mosquito nets, camp beds, toilet and shower buckets, hurricane lamps, cases of food, a cook, and a *boy*, thank you very much. He crossed the river, and on the other side went off into the bush, the forest of rust and green when the sky was gray, black when the sky was black. A flock of guinea fowl. A woman alone near a river crossing. A long time later, a man on foot going who knows where, coming from who knew where, and who disappeared into the dust. Finally a village, an OUREGANO without a name, without a doctor, without an administrator, without Alexandrou, without a school, but with a small official place to spend the night.

---

* Constant has deliberately chosen the medical term for what is otherwise known as "sleeping sickness."

In these villages that was all Dubois knew. The bed in a corner, the colonial sitting room with armchairs covered in canvas. You had to chase away the cockroaches; boy, was it dirty! Time to take a good shower, the room was ready, and the whiskey served fresh. On the table, across from the bed, the cook laid the tablecloth and folded the napkins into cornets. He ate the same dishes as at OUREGANO. Aside from the bed, in which he could not sleep—I prefer a bed with a webbed support—the night passed as at OUREGANO. Madame Dubois, when she accompanied him, always found it hotter or colder, but with the same noises and the same screams. They felt alone.

Day cream for the face and a bathrobe crossed at the chest for Madame Dubois, who was getting bored sipping her lemon tea. Bush costume, pith helmet and khaki shorts, for the Administrator, who was doing his difficult duties. They visited the chief, one sleepy fellow among the others who had kept a bottle of whiskey on hand. So as not to insult him—it was part of the Administrator's psychology—Dubois swallowed the first glass. Where did he get the idea that he had to toss it back all at once, draining it to the last drop? The sleepy chief refilled the glass until the bottle was empty. Everything was fine, said the sleepy chief, who had forgotten all of it. So much the better, replied Dubois, who was tired. It took the translator a century to report to their mutual satisfaction. Dubois got up tipsy and the sleepy chief collapsed on his bench.

The noise of the car going out tore the sleepy chief from his slumber and oblivion. He ran after the Ford, carrying two chickens, a "fresh" squealing pig, and begged. We're hungry. We need medicines. Too late. The cook snatched the chickens and hit the pig over the head to keep it quiet. Too late, old man. You'll tell him the next time. Later, later. The Administrator was in a hurry; they were waiting for him farther on. These fellows were amazing the way they were always the same!

Madame Dubois had stopped accompanying her husband. What would she have done? Dubois planned no more visits. What would he have done? They said one thing while asking you another. Always the same refrain: food, medicine. He wasn't God, after all. He liked to repeat to himself the Chinese proverb: If you give a man a fish, you feed him for a day; if you teach him to fish, you feed him for life. He didn't teach them anything but consoled himself for not having given them anything either.

*

The Administrator was not a cynic, but a philosopher. Death being always in the offing makes one wise. It breaks all strides, undercuts all ambitions, destroys all follies. Monsieur Dubois looked death in the face with stoic wisdom. No scenes, just the slow and obsessive contemplation of the thing growing. No incidents in his life, no incidents in the life of the country. Calm, it was only death after all, nothing more. His time at OUREGANO was only a period of waiting like any other. He had been forgotten; he made so little noise, Administrator Dubois, in his sleepy country, so little noise that it would have been a shame to wake all that up.

On the terrace, in the evening between five and six, at the hour in Africa when everything quickens in the setting sun's embrace, Monsieur Dubois looked at the slow apparition of death, a shadow in the distance that advanced imperceptibly. He watched closely to see it move. He couldn't see anything but it leapt, as in the game with the sun: *Un, deux, trois, soleil!** behind his back. He knew it and was not surprised. But he was happy to know where it was and to stare toward the west. An irrepressible anxiety clenched at the base of his heart and lifted him towards the west. The light fused red and orange; the whole landscape came alive in the shadow and the light. He had already had two whiskies, and the frenzied race to the end of the day calmed down in his heart. Now was the real moment of contemplation. His head empty, his limbs heavy, he gave himself up to the lightness of dusk. All the noises resonated in his chest, occupying deserted places. A rooster call instead of Love, a drumbeat instead of Tolerance, running water for Charity, wood breaking in the guise of Hope. He no longer existed and the Africa that washed over him brought him to tears.

---

* Literally "One, Two, Three, Sun!" a children's game similar to Red Light, Green Light.

Death on those evenings had the open smell of four o'clocks, the irresistible scent of the frangipanis, sweet and soft, the acrid odor of the cut grass, and the warmth of the glass in which he buried his nose. This was good. He was grateful to it for coming to him softly from the depths of the forest, for coming on so many sounds and so many smells, for getting him used to it without surprising him, for flooding and penetrating him tenderly. It seemed to him, when the light flickered, that he was already dead and he felt immense gratitude for the whiskey that gave him the strength of daily gestures: speaking, eating, paying a compliment. He heard himself speak, as from a distance. He saw his swollen hand, striated with purple veins, on the knife and the face of Matilde, so made up, so perfect that he amused himself imagining a meal where they would all be like him, absent.

He understood irony, the Administrator did; nothing really touched him. He knew how to laugh at everything, nothing really belonged to him. He had never fathered anything resembling life, not a child, not a law, not a decision. Nothing. Absolutely nothing. He had a quiet conscience; he had not deviated so much as an inch from his path, from death. He didn't remember ever having felt any other feeling than that of complete and consenting death, the darling. Not so much as a body between himself and death. He didn't know what it felt like to be alive.

He was getting angry again, it was true, but it was the fault of the days, the work, of all the hours that took up his time until evening. He had to put up with this idiotic diversion. He had a headache. It would have been worse in this hole if there had not been Alexandrou, who had relieved him of the difficulties of ordering food and supplies, relieved him of all the calls for orders and the market demands, relieved him of the hundreds of reports and the troublesome middlemen. He still had a few letters to send to the General Administration; it was enough to do. Each day, he found himself before the same sheet of paper until it was time for the mail to go out. Beretti arrived. It wasn't ready. Too bad. No news is good news. *Monsieur Commandant* would get it done for the next mail. Useless, these daily reports; there was plenty of time. Another three days until the next plane. They drank a whiskey together to celebrate the decision. Dubois felt freed, until the evening, until the next day when it would all start over again. It was awful being ruled by the daily report. He was impatient with what kept him, in spite of himself, at his post. For years, Administrator Dubois had kept himself just above the well of oblivion with a single sheet of paper.

III

Matilde was delighted; they were busy morning, noon, and night. There was a luncheon at the Bonenfants to which the Dubois, had also been invited. There had been a dinner at the Dubois which the Bonenfants attended. Matilde rushed to show herself their equal, inviting the Dubois and the Bonenfants to dinner. She asked their forgiveness: the cook was new; they made do with what they could throw together. Who is your cook? asked Madame Bonenfant. Oh, an Ibrahim something-or-other. A little hunchback? the Judge persisted. Why? cried Matilde panicked. Do you know him? Is he a thief? No, no, the Judge reassured her. He was your predecessor's cook. Keep an eye on him. He's a lazy one.

The cycle started over. The Bonenfants waited for the Dubois to return the invitation to the Muranos before inviting them again themselves. The Muranos closed the circle. Mmm! Mmm! The Judge groaned in pleasure eating a leg of lamb with lima beans. He's making progress, the rascal. Matilde was too new to have absorbed all the nuances of social protocol. Out of turn, she surprised them all by organizing two dinners in a row. She invited the Dubois and the Bonenfants only two days after having had them all to dinner on the pretext that she had been given an antelope and that they couldn't possibly eat it themselves. The Bonenfants and the Dubois each wondered what was going on. What could it mean that the rhythm was broken? Madame Bonenfant was beside herself. Arriving at the Muranos', she let out a sigh of relief. The Dubois were there. All excited, Matilde exclaimed that they were going to have antelope! She had been given a young one, a real massacre. Ibrahim had prepared it with a *grand veneur* sauce.* The meat was dry and the canned

---

* *Sauce grand veneur* appears on many menus. It is also known as Royal Hunting Sauce in England. It consists of another sauce, *Poivrade* (carrots, onions, shallots, bouquet garni, oil, white wine, vinegar, veal bouillon, black pepper, flour, butter, and Cayenne), and red currants.

gooseberry sauce bought at an exorbitant price from Alexandrou smelled of apples. Bonenfant had the cook called to the table and, poking the meat with his fork, demanded: Did you rub it with oil before cooking it? The cook made multiple confused remarks from which it was possible to make out that it was very difficult to cook an antelope in Royal Hunting Sauce. That's not what I asked you, cut in the Judge. Did you rub it with oil? Did you tenderize it? Yes or no? The cook stood there with his mouth open, looking frightened. It's simple, said the Judge pushing his interrogation, answer me yes or no. Yes or No? Ibrahim shook his head negatively. A-ha! triumphed Bonenfant. You did not tenderize it. You did not follow my advice and now the meat is inedible. And to punctuate his remarks he pushed a large portion of meat to the edge of his plate. It's true, he explained to Matilde, who was slightly dumbstruck, I've been telling him for years but he refuses to listen.

When it was the Dubois' turn, Madame Dubois agonized over how to seat her small world at the table. If I put Doctor Murano on my right and Madame Murano on your left, the Muranos will be next to each other, and we can't have that. But if I put the Muranos on the left and the Bonenfants on the right or the Muranos on the right and the Bonenfants on the left, it sets an uncomfortable precedent any way you look at it. Madame Dubois set the place-cards, on which she had carefully written the names of her guests in elegant calligraphy, on the table in front of the glasses. There. Tonight we'll do it like that. That's done. And when she heard the sound of a motor, choosing at random, she exchanged two cards. She waited with bated breath to see what chance had ordained.

Madame Bonenfant arrived all flustered. Where had Madame Dubois placed her? Jean, because of his function as Judge, deserved to be on the right; they wouldn't demote him, surely. It would be she and only she who would suffer the acrimony of the Administrator's wife. In the wagon that brought them to the Residence, she worked out the possibilities. Absolutely, I must be on the right; I am the Judge's wife and I am the oldest. During the cocktails her worries gnawed at her; she tried to estimate her chances. She looked at the charming Matilde. Naturally the old dog Dubois would prefer to have her next to him. She was eating herself alive without thinking that whether Matilde sat on the right or the left, she would be next to one of the Dubois, who would look at no one in any case. She looked Murano over, and what if Madame Dubois had put him on her right? She was ready to collapse.

Madame is served, announced a butler belted in green, the color of the Residence. Why don't we go in to dinner? proposed Madame Dubois. Madame Bonenfant couldn't walk; it was as a victim that she approached the table where she would be burned at the stake. To learn the worst she glanced at the card to the right of the Head of the House and melted into her seat. Without knowing it was chance that had seated her, she spent the entire meal pulling herself together; her fear had cut off her appetite. The hors d'oeuvres were passed, the leg of lamb went around, and she still sat there, incapable of savoring her fragile victory. If Madame Dubois' last minute exchange had demoted her, the world would have collapsed. Her rancor remained, like a small island, an impermeable fortress. She knew her husband would agree with her on at least one thing: it was astonishing how bad the cooking was at the Dubois'!

*

But Jean, you cannot possibly know! sobbed Madame Bonenfant, succumbing to her despair. You cannot imagine. Of course, you are always on the right! Come on, come on. That's not true, you know it, replied the Judge. The last time, at the Muranos', I was on the left. Did I make a scene? Of course you were on the left because Dubois was there. You can't get ahead of the Administrator! She calmed down. This woman hated her; she wanted her death. Jean had to understand. It wasn't for her sake that she insisted, but for his. By treating her badly, they insulted him. If he didn't defend her, if he didn't hold up the standards, he would see what happened. They'd be dragged in the mud, in the mud.... Pronouncing this word her tears make a sobbing noise in her throat.

Matilde began to be discouraged. She had already worn her yellow dress, the strapless white one, the violet one with the large tulips, the black skirt with the low-cut top, and now she had to choose what to wear for a second time to go to the Bonenfants'. To go to the Judge's she dressed a little less elegantly than to go to the Administrator's. She tried to remember what she had worn to the various dinners, but everything ran together. Strangely, it seemed to her she had been here for years. She put on the black dress that made her look so thin, long gloves, and a ribbon in her uplifted hair. She liked the way she looked. She would have liked to see a glint in Michel's eye that said he had noticed her. He was driving too fast. She held herself stiffly in the car, supporting herself with a hand on the dashboard; the tips of her black-gloved fingers were covered in dust. She would have liked to see Bonenfant stop short when he saw her enter, struck by so much grace. She would have liked Dubois to kiss her hand saying, Ravishing, as always. The others had already had quite a bit to drink when they arrived, late as usual. The Administrator seemed more numb than he was normally; the Judge chewed on his index finger, a sign of irritation. Madame Bonenfant got up to give orders in the kitchen. Only Madame Dubois looked unrelentingly at the dirty tips of Matilde's gloves.

Madame Dubois dreamed of gatherings without protocol, simply done, without fuss, just "Come and have a bite with us!" Impossible at the Residence, and her eyes went lovingly over the large room, the twelve armchairs, the three tables. Yes, she lived in the House of France! The fourteenth of July, the eleventh of November, the eighteenth of June,* Christmas, Easter. A certain standard had to be met. You couldn't mix apples and oranges. The solemn feasts and the little get-togethers.... The official functions could not be avoided; it was the ransom of glory. It was hard sometimes, being First Lady. Madame Dubois sighed, but all these reasons, far from weakening her, bolstered her courage. She thought herself heroic, a role model of sorts.

To make herself seem important, she confessed her troubled state to Dubois: she had regrets. What? She longed for mundane pleasures while they were devoting themselves to such a noble and exalted task! From his wife's long lament the Administrator saw only a situation in which

---

* Bastille Day (beginning of the French Revolution), Armistice Day (end of World War I), and Charles de Gaulle's call to resistance in 1940, after Maréchal Pétain was named head of the French government.

they would meet each other even more, where they would be even more bored than they already were. She tried hard to convince him. It wasn't such a bad idea, even for the Administration. In their official dinners who did they see? The Bonenfants, the Muranos; in short, the elite. But the others, the police, the teachers, the African doctor, they never saw them. France shouldn't be so divided in two. Since Dubois claimed that the prospect of spending an evening with a communist, an alcoholic, or a Negro did not enchant him and that he wouldn't get dressed up for it, his wife encouraged him to look beyond his personal pleasure. With the whole community together they could keep an eye on everyone. You'll see. The communist won't try anything with everyone on his tail.

Do you play sports, Bonenfant? The Administrator asked the Judge for the first time ever a non-business question. I say, replied the Judge, I play a little tennis. Why do you ask? Monsieur Administrator? Well, we should take each other's measure some time, Bonenfant. Whenever you like, Monsieur Administrator. Hold on! Hold on! Not so fast. We'll play in the English style, at a club. A club, Monsieur Administrator? Yes, at a club, our club, on our own courts. I have an idea working in my head. Come and see me in my office.

A club, Jean? You don't say! What a wonderful idea! I'm only telling you what Dubois told me this morning. And he told her about the encounter with Dubois: I was in the hall, on my way to see what the orderly was up to when Dubois comes out of his office and approaches me, all relaxed, affable, respectful even. He says to me: Your Honor, I want you to give me your opinion. I wasn't going to refuse, but I'm telling you, Dubois was as excited as a child. I couldn't say no.

*

The salvation of OUREGANO depended on a tennis court because it seemed to them that the sport would bring together the cultural community. They would play tennis to be together. They played badly. They had never practiced? No matter! It was better to be ridiculous two or four at a

time than to be ridiculous alone. This was what they were reduced to because they had disdained the country they were colonizing. Not once had
they envisioned its existence positively. They had not noticed the natural
surroundings, which they could have discovered simply by looking at
them or by hunting in them. They were not interested in its people,
whom they might have noticed out of pity or curiosity. They took no notice of its culture, whose knowledge and magic they could have appreciated. Which of them had troubled to watch the frenetic Poro dances under the wings of a giant wooden bird? Who among them looked at the
red masks, the kaolin[*] paintings? All this was just so much primitiveness.
Primitive nature, primitive people, primitive culture.

It was nevertheless curious that the rejection of this new world was
not modeled on the criteria of their own world; it did not demand a wor-
ship of the past. It seemed only right that having rejected this culture they
should retrench themselves in their own culture with faith and passion.
After all, if they were looking for isolation, it could only be to commune
with their origins. They had all played the desert-island game. If you
asked them, each one had a sure answer: Proust and Balzac.... The *Iliad*
and the *Odyssey*.

They had never opened any of these books because acquired learning
carries more weight than culture. They knew that CULTURE existed; they
no longer knew very well how or why. It was a bit like the way you recognize someone by his name. Balzac? I know Balzac. And knowing neither where culture comes from nor what it does, it is easy to say: I know
that very well. Proust and Balzac, deluxe editions with leather bindings
and fine endpapers, had stayed in France, too precious for OUREGANO.

Without electricity, they didn't listen to music. They had however
rushed to purchase what Alexandrou proposed: the Teppaz, a portable,
battery-powered record player, brand new with belt drive and speaker
included, the last word in technology. They had bought the electronic
Teppaz machines and enthroned them in the living rooms, a green one at
the Dubois', a brown one at the Bonenfants'. Music was the silent Teppaz. The presence of the beautiful instrument confirmed that they loved
music. They said over and over: Ah! The Brandenburgs! The Branden-

---

[*] Kaolin clay.

burgs—especially the second!

Yes, for these people culture was read on book bindings and heard on record players hauled around with shoulder straps. They assured themselves that these appealing national and Western images were in the family albums, put away from life, protected, classified, and filed, like any other object, like Tiffany's Sunday dress: Don't muss it! Which meant, don't use it, and don't take any but an absurd and limited pleasure in it. File, file, tuck away. Keep in reserve. Desire no longer existed. The possession of a culture, or at least the idea that it belonged to them prevented them from valuing other things. At OUREGANO, a book was bought because Madame Dubois had recommended it, had found it "very good," or because Monsieur Bonenfant spoke about it saying it was "well written." Books were never bought for pleasure.

The only form of culture that was practiced at OUREGANO was religion. They abandoned themselves to it without thinking. They accepted the Catholic, apostolic, and Roman harmony as music from the past that had accompanied their childhood, their youth, their lives.... Religion was a ready-made culture of which they were the beneficiaries without risk and without spending a penny. Religion had its own literature, its music, its philosophy, a world unto itself in fact. In practice, each one made himself or herself master of this world, of the Bible as well as the writings of Saint Augustine and the poetry of Claudel. They had never read them? No matter, it didn't take anything away from them since they were free. It was not recommended to go looking too closely at all that; faith could not be made to account for itself. Better to remain simple, unspoiled like the child who recites the Our Father....

*

On a hill by itself, the Dutch Mission also existed on the margins of OUREGANO. It existed from another life, for another life, which was perhaps the life of God. It sheltered the tall red-haired priests in cassocks so immaculate that it was a surprise to see the red earth stain the hem of such whiteness. They were not of this world. Sturdy house, chapel filled with music, flower gardens in bloom, exquisite leeks, tender carrots. Active nuns on the path of the Lord. On either side of the altar ceramic pots overflowed with flamboyant flowers. English embroidery, sheaves of wheat stitched in gold, a silver chalice, and a monstrance of brass. It all shined brilliantly with the innocence of genuine respectability. Nothing supernatural there, but it smelled of a goodly measure of ammonia, a generous use of bleach, disinfectant poured everywhere, and beautiful outstretched forearms.

Africa participated little in this life, just the indispensable, the ground. And even at that, taming it was required; without fertilizer nothing would have come of it. Africa was the subbasement on which developed the perennial mushroom of the Mission from the West that held on, as if by an umbilical cord, to Holland. Milk from Holland, preserves from Holland, glassware from Holland, needles and thread from Holland. And Africa didn't enter into this world except disinfected, bleached, combed, and curried. The only door that was open to the public was that of the chapel and then only on Sundays and Holy Days. The only people who penetrated this fissure were the French of OUREGANO, Monsieur Dubois at the front next to the *prie-dieu* of waxed wood, Madame Dubois wearing a hat. The Bonenfants with their sons and their large missals. Michel and Matilde Murano without Tiffany. What would she have done here? The nuns completed the circle and filled the entire left half of the front part of the chapel. They made a rustle of perfect light movements, of bowed heads, all rising at once, all sitting on the edge of their chairs; they took communion like a shower of birds falling on a handful of seeds. On the sly, Monsieur Dubois maintained a face neither pale nor yellow, but happy and pink.

Communion was Madame Bonenfant's favorite moment because it allowed her to regain the place of which the Sunday Mass deprived her when all OUREGANO was assembled together. She rose, passed in front of Monsieur Bonenfant, who stepped ostentatiously into the aisle to let her by. She advanced toward the altar, waited for quiet to settle once again upon the nuns. Then, alone before the Holy Table, she fully extended her tongue. The assembly waited for her to return from her mysterious journey. The nuns had already regained their calm while Madame Bonenfant remained prostrate in joyful mystery, her face in her hands. The priest respected this sublime prostration; Sunday after Sunday brought these wonderful moments until the polite cough of Monsieur Dubois returned them to order.

Unbelievable! said Madame Dubois to the Administrator. It's turning into Madame Bonenfant's Mass! There were, however, more discreet faiths, which were hinted to be neither weaker nor equal but stronger. References were made to the Pharisees and the Gospel. Certainly, said Monsieur Dubois, who had never in his life hidden behind a pillar. The Mass was criticized. Really, they made no effort to speak French. The Mass had gone from Latin to Dutch. How to find the Gospel in that! Did they have the right to do that? You should look into that, demanded Madame Dubois. We're on French territory, after all! Well, it's not that simple, responded Monsieur Dubois. The Mission didn't depend on him except for a few administrative formalities, and believe me they had reduced that to the bare minimum. As for the Church, they answered to the bishop. We'll see about that, insisted Madame Dubois. It's a political gesture isn't it, the use of a foreign language? It wasn't a good idea for the power to seem divided to the natives, and with (it had to be admitted) an apparently larger share going to the Mission. Oh, you know, the Administrator tried to insinuate, the natives don't understand. What they see is white people.... So Madame Dubois returned to the Mission, but oh, the strapping fellows, the girls with red cheeks, it was disgusting! Did such people pray? They were such materialists, the Dutch! They could make you turn away from religion, whereas an old priest in his tired cassock and with his drawn face, there you had an entirely different picture!

*

Looking at Madame Dubois anyone would think that Madame Bonenfant was compromising France at the Dutch Mission. Madame Bonenfant did not give a sense of national honor to her visits to the altar. She was looking after herself, her soul, her place in the community, and her being, which was already a lot. She had been welcomed warmly on the recommendation of the bishop as the representative of the traditional family, the bourgeoisie, and as a devout Catholic all rolled in one. The nuns loved it because it gave them access to an entire family. They knew the tastes of the Judge in matters of peas, the squabbles of the little boys —they are so adorable! The devotion of Madame—she is so kind! Right in front of them they had the structure of the family they had left so far behind. They taught the career of the father and the abnegation of the mother. They impulsively recalled childhoods with little brothers and told stories of a married sister who had a son and a daughter. And since most of them spoke French badly, they were hard to understand; there was a lot of laughter. It was very cheerful.

Madame Bonenfant tired, however, of her altar visits, which couldn't be observed except inside the chapel and garden. Thankfully, there was a sort-of convent that gave a more official character to her presence. There, the nuns had collected about forty little girls, orphans for the most part, to whom they dispensed lessons in home economics. These girls gave off a proud allure once they were dressed in white and organized in impeccable classes. The nuns cultivated about twenty other students whose parents occupied nursing, prison guard, orderly, and other subaltern positions and who paid for their little girls' education in hopes that it would better their lives.

They were taught to read and to count, numbers and the alphabet, just what was indispensable. On the other hand, they went into a great deal of detail in matters of embroidery: cross-stitch, running stitch, *grand jeté*. There were pretty altar linens with poppies and bluebells nestled in sheaves of wheat. She had some lovely tea towels, Madame Bonenfant did, with large *B*s, nicely rounded in red, blue, and green, very rustic! There were classes in sewing in which the children made undershirts and bloomers with lace at the thighs. The older ones made aprons, simple dresses for the orphan girls and others as well. The dream of the nuns was to dress the entire population of OUREGANO in white. The girls learned cooking, starting with pastry making. They had studied in sequence sponge cake and buttercream, and what can be done with sponge cake and buttercream? Go ahead, you there, the tall one. Answer! A cream cake, whispered the class to the embarrassed student.

There was a class for the smart ones, those who wanted the certificate. A heavy nun was in charge and since she also supervised the garden, she was overburdened. Happily the flower borders and the carrot
beds ran almost under the windows of the classroom, so she could set out
the plants while supervising the lessons from the garden. In fact, there
were not many smart students and they were encouraged as little as possible. If the class was kept on, it was to keep them from going to the public school. For their girls, the nuns preferred a program that prepared
them for their future lives as women, mothers, wives, and why not nuns?

Madame Bonenfant agreed completely: the future was there and, my
God, the present as well. These children were protected. What would
have become of them if.... Better not to think about that. She had
brought the daughters of thieves and criminals here. It wasn't the fault of
these little ones! She had had to scold, threaten, and carry on at length to
make the families give them over; they didn't realize how lucky they
were. The children were there; that was what mattered. Madame Bonenfant even went to Alexandrou to get him to consent to the instruction of
several of his half-breed daughters. There had been a mass baptism,
white dresses and short hair. The priest had bowed their heads one after
the other over the basin. Madame Bonenfant stood nearby with a candle
in her hand. She was the godmother. Since her first name was Marie, it
was easy to name them. They were called Marie-Rose, Marie-Anne,
Marie-Claire, Marie-France, and when there was nothing else classic,
Marie-Augustine, Marie-Honorine, Marie-Charlotte, Marie-Rosalie...

*

It was intolerable that Madame Bonenfant should find the means to
fill her needs away from the group. She had to be brought back, whatever
the cost. The Club would be, for this problem as well, a solution. The
idea had had time to mature and on the eleventh of November the Dubois
announced their project officially to the other members of their faith
gathered in the large living room. Madame Dubois had been the inspira-

tion. The Administrator, for once enthusiastic, did not fail to support her and said: Without her it would not have happened. How did it come about? She didn't know, an inspiration! Imagine that one morning when she was examining her meat delivery with Beretti, she had said to him, Does Monsieur Alexandrou still have his greasy spoon, the Miammiam something-or-other? Did he have it! Indeed he did! And after that it took off by itself—well almost. Madame Dubois turned lovingly toward her husband to give him all the credit. It was the vision of Monsieur Dubois that had made it happen.

Monsieur Dubois made a deal with Monsieur Alexandrou. Monsieur Beretti had conducted the negotiations and it had to be said that he had really devoted himself, gone out of his way, beyond the call of duty, to get the tradesman to agree. The good fellow, patting himself, had said: The community would be the big winners. Here's the thing: They didn't have to buy the Club! Monsieur Dubois defied the group with his amused smile. They would rent it for a ridiculously small sum, to be legal occupants, just to have a contract and all…. Of course the various repairs and improvements would be on the members. That was normal. On the other hand, Alexandrou would furnish drinks, supplies, etc—at a Club price, of course! He must be getting something? Yes, it was the guarantee that the affair would go. He was supplying a manager. He was right there at hand, Monsieur Beretti.

Dubois was applauded warmly. Details were demanded: Would they be able to eat at the Club? Invite guests to dinner? Why not? replied the Administrator. It would add money to the coffers, which were empty at the moment. Did that need repeating? How much would it cost to join? Too soon to tell, it would depend on the price of the rent, which was not fixed yet, and on the work to be done. But it wouldn't be so much. No, it could be arranged. For example, he would bring in the materials, bricks, cement, etc. He had funds for that. Monsieur Bonenfant would send a few prisoners to do the hardest work. And you, Doctor, he turned to Murano, you can have the roof done by your lepers…

They were delighted, ready to help, to go out of their way, to do anything. They had to start immediately, no sense waiting. All their walks took them to the place; they couldn't get enough of it. They didn't see a large isolated hut off in the bush. No, they imagined the kitchens they would put at a distance to keep "the odors" away, the tennis courts that would be built next to the building, the water source that they would divert from a marshy watering hole swarming with mosquitoes and other creatures. Inside, they would install large fans that would be wired to a generator, a bar, bar stools, little tables, and a judo mat.

The dilapidated building was empty. Alexandrou had sold them the tables he had removed before closing the deal. He had the original bar brought in. He would sell the fans and refrigerators at an inflated price— why not make the best deal he could? They would be secondhand. Beretti would know how to make them work. A generator was needed? Alexandrou ordered one and one day Beretti went to get it from the airplane. It was in pieces but Beretti would assemble it as soon as the utility room that would house it was ready.

The prisoners laid Alexandrou's bricks and mortared them with Alexandrou's cement; they covered the roof with Alexandrou's tin. Beretti went to work in shorts and without a shirt, but his feet carefully enclosed in socks and pointed shoes. He twisted wires, put in fuses, adjusted parts covered with grease; he was as happy as he could be. What would we do without you, Beretti? the Judge, who came to the Club every day, said to him. Beretti had enough courage to answer him, You see, Your Honor, my hands are made of gold, of *gold*. And he raised in front of Bonenfant his hands, black with oil sludge and yellow with grease. The Judge nodded. It's true, it's true, he said. So Beretti, full of pride, pushed his point: No offense, Your Honor, but I prefer doing what I do with my hands to what you do with your head. You deal in important ideas, but this! The Judge left puzzled. Was there something in these words that was intended to offend? He didn't know. He only heard the words "important ideas," an image that pleased him. Monsieur Bonenfant didn't doubt that there were superior beings who worked with their heads, as Monsieur Beretti said, and there were the others.

*

If anything got Bonenfant going it was the eighteenth century, Diderot, Rousseau, and all the others.... Man is good! I'll show you good...the biggest lie ever told in the name of philosophy. He just couldn't believe it and went over and over the same examples. Man is good; Nature is good; melons are made to be eaten in the family and the flea on white skin to be squashed. And what about the fleas on the Negroes? They didn't think about that, the ancestors! What he liked in all this gibberish was old man Bougainville, the Noble Savage and all that. One world! He couldn't have seen beyond the feather on his hat, the stooge!

He thought it exceptionally odd that meat rotted in the refrigerators of Paradise on Earth, amazing that pillars grew real branches after a good rain, bizarre that the toadfish in the river carried an electrical discharge, inexplicable that certain herbs were poisonous, astonishing that venomous snakes could camouflage themselves to look like a small pile of leaves. What perfection, ants that could scour a fellow in one night, clean the guy out, pardon the pun. The chigger that gets in your feet, the worms under your skin, first here, then there.* Exotic, OUREGANO was exotic all right, enough to go 'round. To survive you had to fight day to day, check under the bedsheets at night to see if anything was snuggled in at the bottom of the bed.... What they said, it was for the others, fools like Refons and his sort, because as for him, he knew how to manage. The vampire bat replaced the generator nicely and the Judge couldn't sleep until the creature came to hang about the mosquito net lightly agitating its wings.

What was irreplaceable in Africa, at OUREGANO in particular, was the Negroes. It was worth the distance, the length of the tour of duty, and the extension, he guaranteed it. It was worth more to see them than to hear about them, it was worth all the rest. You died laughing morning

---

* This is part of a nursery rime: Il court, il court le furet / Le furet du bois, Mesdames / Il court, il court le furet / Le furet du bois joli / Il est passé par ici / Il repassera par là / Il court, il court le furet / Le furet du bois, Mesdames / Il court, il court le furet/ Le furet du bois joli. [He runs, he runs, the wood ferret does/ The wood ferret, my Ladies/ He runs, he runs/ The wood ferret/ the pretty ferret/ he goes here/ He'll go there/ He runs, he runs, the ferret does, My Ladies/ He runs, he runs, the pretty wood ferret].

and night. Ah! The bastards, the dirty bastards. They were there with their expressions, their manners, their tricks; who did they think they were kidding? There were the ones who walked around very sure of themselves: they were not guilty; they had not stolen, they had not killed. And they wanted to talk, and they talked about proof, and they said it was important. Give 'em an inch and they take a mile. Not with me, my friend, oh no! No way. Stop right there. The Judge knows everything; he knows what you are going to say next: Not'in' to eat, no med'cine. So, you won't say it? I'll say it for you. It'll go faster that way. What are you saying now? Nothing. That does it. In the clink with you. You'll rot to the bone. Bonenfant sucked the marrow from these bones.

Wonder of wonders, it was the sleeping sickness, they said. Made to measure, that bullshit excuse, but it suited them! It suited perfectly. Organized loafing, the palace of Sleeping Beauty, but there was no waking up, only death. It didn't faze them. I don't know how old I am. I don't know how many children there are and I don't know how he died. And on and on.... The Judge wondered sometimes when faced with a plaintiff or a convict—because they liked justice, the buggers, they hung around to the last word—if he would deign to speak to them. He'd have them on for a minute, get them going, show them he was stronger than they, and if it weren't for his curiosity that won out in the end, he'd have looked them deep in the eyes and he'd have laughed until his sides split. One day a fellow laughed in his court and it displeased him. It was a nervous laugh, a laugh of desperation, a laugh when nothing else comes to mind. The treasonous echo of happiness had outraged him.

*

He didn't trust children at all. Their crafty tricks, their schemes, he sniffed them out instinctively; he was sure that he knew what they were going to do before they did. A kid who was going to do something bad wore it on his face. He had a special look, a certain absence, his thoughts already turned toward the crime he was going to commit. He didn't know what yet, but he knew when something was afoot. He was guilty even before transgressing parental laws because children were born headed for trouble; he could imagine nothing else. You had to see the scared kid on the run in the dark when it had to do with trouble, the softie exerting physical strength to get hold of the forbidden object, the lazybones losing control reading a dirty book, the idiot suddenly becoming clever! And then there were the others, the anorexics who ate on the sly in the pantries, the sweethearts who tortured animals, the neat ones who rolled in the dirt, the honest ones who lied through their teeth inventing stories and excuses...

It was true, in his two sons the Judge had a rich terrain of observation. He had not wanted them, imagine that! But since Jean-Louis and Jean-Marc existed, they delighted their father even to the extent of a tender complicity. The father expected his sons to get into trouble and they knew that they would be pardoned their faults if they recognized their father's superiority: How did you know? You couldn't fool the father who saw everything that was feigned in that false surprise, but he liked them to keep up at least this form of respect. The main thing was to remain in control no matter what the situation: I knew it. That's all. And the sons lowered their eyes in shame, humiliation, and adoration for this divine father. They did it again not so much to surprise their father as so he could be right once again. It was a very successful relationship. Jean-Louis and Jean-Marc wouldn't have been themselves without their father, and without his sons Monsieur Bonenfant would have felt amputated from himself. In a sense it was organized crime, that of evil and its condemnation, far stronger than the pull of paternity and other feelings.

Admission of fault by either party did not exclude punishment. On the contrary, it accompanied it. What would have been the point of admitting to a crime that could not be punished afterward? What would have been the sense of discovering a mistake if it could not be expiated? All the logic of the relationship rested on the existence of punishment; in a way it was the stakes of the game. In order to attenuate the rigors of the punishment, the Bonenfant boys resorted routinely to lying. They didn't do it, however, without weighing the risks beforehand, because lying was itself a crime possibly more serious than the original transgression. With evil, it was lying that the Judge sniffed out first. Everything was lies because everything was dissimulation; it was only a question of degree in the half-truths, and the Honorable Monsieur Bonenfant was the only one clever enough to appreciate it. Jean-Louis and Jean-Marc never knew exactly what the stakes were. The Judge wanted children to be at fault but at the same time naked of blame. He wanted a pure and perfect evil.

When he first looked at Tiffany, Bonenfant had made an immediate diagnosis: devious, the worst of the lot, leaning naturally toward dissimulation. Thoroughly corrupt in sum because, although certainly without vices, neither glutton nor lazy, neither tormented by the flesh nor a thief, she was attracted by everything that brewed on the edges, tasting everything as long as she stayed on the unknowable margin. Glutton because the refrigerator was in the shadow, thief because it would not be known, vicious because it happened under the sheets. In short, hopelessly lazy because these children only acted this way out of arrogance, a monstrous sentiment of superiority that allowed them to take adults for idiots. They looked at you straight in the eyes and saw right through hypocrisy, played with words, and never said anything; just little angels they were. Filth!

IV

It was Tiffany who was the first to join the Administrator in the absurd territory of absence. He held tenaciously to this meaninglessness because, having seen everything, having felt everything, he knew intimately that the place of happiness is nowhere, everywhere, elsewhere. Fear of the Unknown had thrust Tiffany into an absence in the world that is an absence in time. The child, who because of her young age had yet to live, began to die at OUREGANO. Time passed without her recognizing the most obvious signs of its movement. Nothing happened for her. The activities of the adults did not touch her. It was as if they were not there. The events that she did encounter had no relation to time, were outside time itself. She could have lived her story backwards and been none the wiser.

Before OUREGANO, Tiffany's world resembled nothing so much as sensations choked with feeling. The scent of her grandmother in the hollow of a large silver fox filled her with the happiness of loving, or the roughness of the brown, square blanket in which her grandfather wrapped her to cross the icy corridors of fear and which kept her eyelids open, brimming with sleep. A world both full and fine in the tenderness of a cheek, the warm invitation of an old blanket wrapped around her and completed by the strong thighs on which her feet rested. Tastes and smells, not only of the fruits she loved, like wild strawberries collected at dawn in July, but the flavor of unforgettable encounters like the copper handle of the stove; her lips were always ready to sample and suck new objects. She had understood otherness within a world bounded by the curve of HER hips, her grandmother, and by HIM, her grandfather, by the span of an embrace. It was a space she crossed over and over in memory.

At OUREGANO Tiffany found herself cut off from everything. Michel's arms surrounding Matilde's shoulders, his knee lightly slipping between the thighs of the young woman, defined a world closed and complete that had perhaps given her life, but in which she found neither a place nor love. Beyond, there extended a gigantic terrain larger than her father's duties. There was the house, and the huts in which the *boys* lived, the hospital, the leper colony, and the village below that spread out past the park of tennis courts and greenhouses in bloom, to the edges of its walls where it became the Dubois' house, or farther on, to the Bonenfants', but always within the confines of a world that belonged to the people who were white and powerful.

So Tiffany had to invent her own borders or, like a cat, mark her territory. It was in the course of the first months that she unconsciously began to outline the strange terrain that sheltered her both from her parents —therefore as far away from the tennis courts as possible—and from the lepers, who terrified her. Her path went by the *boys'* huts, dove into the gardens, and went past the large rusty water tanks that served as reservoirs for the garden. She stayed close to the first huts of the village, watching the women dressed in leaves standing heavily over long pillars of wood. But the forest, more than anything else, attracted her. Not the forest of Little Red Riding Hood or Snow White, full of traitors and dangerous mushrooms, but the forest of Mowgli or the Lost Paradise, full of warm life dripping through trembling fingers, the softness of a duvet, slippery short-haired fur. The trees always bore fruit, she found bitter oranges and limes that she peeled with her fingernails, and burned her lips on what was left of the skins. She made celebrations of bitterness, of acid, sprinkled salt on the dreadful pulp, and, sitting underneath the lemon tree, sent her mouth into an infernal sensation that brought tears to her eyes. There was no place for sugar in the garden of delights. Tiffany approached the terrible subtleties of unknown herbs that instantly dry the mouth and unripe green mangos that set the teeth on edge.

*

Matilde said to Tiffany, Don't stay HERE. What are you doing HERE? Get out of HERE. HERE was an elastic territory that included the living room, the dining room, Matilde and Michel's bedroom, the bathroom, but which could extend to the lawn in front of the house, to the terrace, the tennis courts, even the kitchen and the *boys'* area; in short, everywhere Matilde could appear. HERE was less a geographic location than a chronological entity. The dining room for the first service was not included in HERE, nor was the living room during the afternoon nap, but they abruptly became so if Tiffany lingered making designs in her mashed potatoes: You're still HERE! Or if Michel cut short his nap by coming into the living room to find a cigarette: You're HERE!

In order to find peace, Tiffany forced herself never to be HERE. There were places where she could not risk going except when her parents were certain to be absent for a long time, the living room and their bedroom. For everything else it was sufficient to be careful and to listen for the sound of Matilde's high heels in order to guess where her mother was going. The clip of the heels could come close and then turn off suddenly; no need to flee, only to stand still and to be absolutely quiet until the noise faded and died. Obviously, it would have been an error to take a sudden silence of the shoes for departure. In the beginning, Tiffany was caught once or twice, one day in the refrigerator, another afternoon in her mother's closet when she had been HERE more than ever. If the threat persisted, it didn't do to panic, to run, or to make noise, but to slip quietly away, slowly, with efficient gestures, without stopping an instant to listen. She had to fold herself up as if she were hunting.

Tiffany wondered if she was the hunter or the prey. In the end she was both because as soon as the quarry was on the run came the quiet certainty of the huntsman. She had perfected a tactic that she had tried out with gazelles: not to move away but to stand in the shadow, even if discovered, perfectly immobile, without breathing. The gazelles always saw her, but it worked with Matilde. With her yellow shoes, her large skirts that swished, and her heavy charm bracelet that clinked, she made a paltry prey. With her eyes that did not see, her ears that did not hear, she could never have held her own alone in the bush.

This idea reassured Tiffany. Instead of retreating in vague anxiety, she decided to go on the attack. In the living room, in the bar, all she had to do was to get there before they came in and to leave just after they left. In the bedroom, by climbing along the high window ledge of the bathroom where Tiffany had seen a place where she could sit tucked in, she could see them. It was the afternoon *sieste*. Michel and Matilde were naked on their bed. Like someone taking possession of an object Tiffany watched Matilde's heavy breasts and Michel's thin body. But when she saw Matilde take Michel's sex in her hand and stroke it until it became long and full, when she heard Michel groan and push Matilde's head toward the enormous sex, when she saw Matilde take it in her mouth, she was terribly afraid, her heart beat fast in her chest, and her hand on the window was cold. Being so high up, she was afraid of falling, of making noise. She didn't want to watch anymore. She didn't want to know if Matilde would lift her head with her mouth full of blood. The hunter's instinct took over. She did not make the mistake of trying to get away. She stayed there numb, her ears ringing. She waited with her eyes averted until her parents finished making love. Then she got down quietly, quickly, without any noise save the sound of bare feet on the floor. Her legs felt like rubber.

She had just seen a terrible thing; it seemed to her at once dirty and natural, cruel and sensual. She was ashamed; she alone was guilty. She was also surprised to discover her parents this way; she had expected them to be as they were in the living room, in the clothes that deformed their bodies, a long-line bra that pushed the breasts forward and strangled the waist, a suffocating necktie and epaulettes that enlarged the back. She expected to hear their voices and high-pitched laughter but not this face-to-face encounter, at once rough and tender, the soft voices groaning with pleasure. Tiffany told herself that, in the end, her parents were large animals, uglier than the others, more vulnerable too (she could have killed them a hundred times with arrows), who took cover in clothes. And she told herself that she had gotten what she deserved. She remained deeply disturbed, not knowing if Michel still had the monstrous sex between his legs or if Matilde had deprived him of it forever.

*

What was good was when the house was empty, or at least empty of Michel and Matilde. It happened a lot at the very beginning, when Michel was busy reorganizing the hospital and when Matilde was helping

Madame Dubois get the Club set up. Tiffany began by paying a visit to the refrigerator. She liked to eat in the cool shadow of the machine, in front of the door opened just enough for her to reach inside. She put a finger in the congealed sauces, a hand into the gelatinous cream pastries; she took a small piece of meat from the leg of lamb; she munched a biscuit, going back and forth between the salted and sugared foods. Finally she camouflaged the damage, the trace of her finger in the sauce, the drips of the creamed pastries, the bone missing its meat. She carefully closed the tin of biscuits, but quickly drained a mouthful of chilled water off the top of a bottle.

She went to play in the garden. Tiffany never went out with a particular game in mind. Ideas came to her little by little as she walked about. From the hibiscus that bordered the lawn she collected an insect that could have been mistaken for a bit of wood. Farther on she harvested acidic Surinam cherries or green guavas. Near the tennis courts she observed the gazelles, but as she tried to get closer, a small head always looked up, jerked back. The animal gave a kick and disappeared. Tiffany came back to the kitchen tearing off the pistil of a flower, the loose fiber of a cocoa nut. She hung around the *boys*, watching them work. A kitchen boy plucked a chicken after plunging it into boiling water, and the skin came off with the feathers. The cook spread out the bread dough with all the strength of his forearms. The dirty dishes from the night before were on the ground; a cat advanced its neck cautiously toward the debris. The laundry *boy* tapped his little irons on the ironing table, kneading the dry clothes, sprinkling them with water. There was nothing more to do here, so she went farther, down toward the *boyerie*. She squatted down near the pillars and watched the many comings and goings from the mass of wood piled up for making fires. The women offered to let her try their sticks but she couldn't lift them. Because she asked, they let her hold a heavy baby. Tiffany didn't like this squirming mass. The infant was not happy either and jerked backward. Tiffany had a hard time not dropping it. The laughing mother took it back.

What Tiffany liked best was hunting termites. It was easy and useful since the women cooked them in sauce. Tiffany would go to the termite hill, extending a long fiber attached to a bamboo shoot into the nest. She immediately pulled out a termite holding on with its pincers. All she had to do was cut off the head between the nails of her thumb and index finger. She put the bodies in the lid of a mason jar and went back to work. The main thing was to do it quickly in order to surprise the termites before they raised the alarm. The last thing you wanted to do was to leave one alive; that would be the end of the hunt!

Tiffany attended all sorts of preparations, culinary and otherwise. The rings of a snake boiling in an old can of powdered baby food revealed, under gray skin, a white meat dense with fibers. A mother, moving quickly and happily, a razor blade in her hand, covered her child with light slashes that bled while another poured citrus juices and red pepper into the cuts. The child cried. It's good for him, said his mother. Tiffany knew that it was GOOD to blow into the nose of a newborn with a cold to clean out the nasal cavity, it was GOOD to coat its head with kaolin to bring down a fever, and she watched impassively as the bleeding child cried with terror.

Adventure awaited her in Michel and Matilde's bedroom. Tiffany stretched out on the bed over which the mosquito net had been drawn up. She took the long pillow in her arms and pulled it on top of her. She looked at the ceiling, the shadow of the mosquito net, the opening of a cupboard. She got up and rummaged in the closet, recognizing by touch the long dresses, the short dresses, the pleated ones, the printed ones, the plain ones; the small bumps of piqué and seersucker felt good. She put her feet into her mother's shoes and walked about the room with her knees bent and her hamstrings tensed. The mirror reflected the image of an incredibly dirty little girl with tangled hair (Tiffany wore all the stigmata of the day, and also of the day before) perched on immensely high heels. What fun it was to profane this sacred place! Tiffany would have paraded around the room until evening, trying on shoes, dresses, and bras. But the noise of the car entering the driveway destroyed her harmony among the things. She had just enough time to repair the disorder and to flee into the bathroom to wash herself a little. Matilde found her daughter standing still in front of the washstand with a tadpole floating in the sink.

*

As soon as Matilde was near a grown-up, or as soon as there was a child in the area, which was the same to her, she said to her daughter: Go. Go and play. Then: Do you mind? Go out and play. And finally: You are going to go out and play, now! Tiffany detached herself with regret from the armchair she occupied and went out to play. No word was more horrible; it was humiliating to be recalled so harshly to one's function as a child. It was annoying to be deprived of what she liked best, adult conversations, their expressions, and their laughter. If there were no children, Tiffany soon slipped back and followed all that was said. If there were children, she had to go out to play.

The children were the perennial Bonenfant boys, and Tiffany knew from experience that no game was possible with those two. They went to hang out in the garden. They climbed a few trees, swinging with their arms. They nosed around here and there. They looked for holes to crawl into, undergrowth to hide in; all their energies went into trying to disappear completely. When they found a good place, they took out cigarettes and matches; they smoked, collected a few branches and set them on fire, panicked immediately, and put the fire out straight away by peeing on it. Then they showed their penises to Tiffany. It was always the same, and Tiffany was completely bored by it. Only once did they show any imagination. It was on a rainy afternoon when they had gone toward the kitchen, and the boys got hold of a liter of kerosene. They showed her an exciting game. You had to douse your hand in kerosene and set it on fire. The hand looked like it was going up in flames, but the victim didn't feel anything except the kerosene burning. You had to plunge your hand immediately under water before it really began to burn. Tiffany found this exciting, sprayed herself abundantly when it was her turn, and since she was no less bright than the Bonenfant boys, she didn't burn herself.

The Bonenfant boys were also interested in anatomy books. They were delighted to come to the Muranos'. They opened a medical book to the illustrations of the genital organs, looked at the cutaway view of the penis, and laughed at the hair with which the artist had decorated his drawing. Tiffany, who did not feel responsible for the excesses of the Bonenfant boys, was nevertheless their accomplice. They had worked it out in advance: If you tell, we'll say you forced us to look. She did not know how to deal with such accusations. She had indeed taken the book on sexual organs from Michel's shelves; she preferred to keep quiet. She kept the rest to herself as well, especially the raid they made on one of the *boys'* huts, kicking over everything (there were only a few dishes, a calabash, and a cooking pot). She had not participated but she had been there and she had even laughed because Jean-Louis, the older boy, was a real clown.

Go and play, recommended Matilde. Take your friends with you, Tiffany! She told her before and after. Before, so that it would be understood that this time, Tiffany would go out by herself after saying hello: I hate to see children hanging on adults. It's not their place. And she told her afterward: Tiffany, it is intolerable! I had to tell you again to go out. The next time, I will not say anything but you will get a real spanking! As soon as a car stopped in front of the house, *pfft*, Tiffany had to disappear, evaporate, no longer exist. Because, when it came down to it, there was really no point in her coming in to say hello; she made such a display that Matilde died of shame. Or she came in without looking at anyone. She was a real sight in her gingham bloomers (it had been a long time since she had worn dresses at home), managing a half curtsy as she had been taught to avoid the awkwardness of shaking hands. It's not important, said Michel. No one notices. Tiffany did not doubt that it was her and not her curtsy that people didn't notice.

Her presence could, however, be negotiated when the parties took place outside, tennis parties and cocktails on the lawn. By going outside, weren't the adults encroaching on the territory of play? They were happy to have her watch them, or that she play or do something else. What was forbidden was to be HERE, period. She had noticed that her presence, unless it was flagrant, was tolerated. Flagrant presence included sitting in a chair, feet in the pathway, eyes turned too directly toward he who was speaking or she who was silent. It included discomfiting questions: Who are you talking about, Mama? Do you mean Madame Bonenfant? Who is a pitiful fellow? She could, for example, after a fairly long absence, return and infiltrate the group by a roundabout approach that took her first through the back of the garden, then into the kitchen with a stop at the refrigerator. All that was needed was a bit of shadow, of a table or a large club chair. She was forgotten. And Matilde, who did not notice Tiffany's haggard look and the dilated pupils that had spent the entire evening in the dark, asked her: Did you have a good time playing, Tiffany?

*

Tiffany was enrolled in the public school for girls. She escaped the Sisters, the prayers, and the pretty white dresses with the matching white pith helmets that the *boy* "made" along with the "tennis" shoes that completed the outfit. Instead, by going to the less prestigious school, Tiffany wore a stock of Carabi dresses Matilde had thought to provide before leaving France. Her head was covered in a khaki colonial cap and her feet in pigskin sandals.

She was going to school for the first time. Her grandparents had taught her to read and to count; she had been doing dictations and arithmetic for a long time, but it was hard to know in which class this little bit of baggage would best fit. So, during an entire term, Tiffany happily descended the rungs of the scholastic ladder, because Matilde's assertions had made them put her in a class too high; then she was slowly bumped back up as her shyness began to fade, worn out by repetitions and threats. She landed between the fourth grade, which did not do geography, and the fifth grade, which did. From there, in one day (was it in fall, winter, or spring?) she jumped to the sixth grade, which was distinguished from the others by Latin and English.

It should be said in Tiffany's defense that the degrees of teaching were not absolute in the School for Girls. Since there were few girls to begin with, Tiffany and the big Yvonne, the daughter of an itinerant military policeman, who was preparing for the Certificate of Primary Studies exam, Elise Refons had thrown them in with—"thrown" is perhaps unjust—combined their class with the white boys from the public school for boys. These included the Bonenfant boys and a young one just learning to write, maybe the son of an airport technician, and to get to the requisite number of ten for such a class, a few little Africans. This class guaranteed instruction from the first through the sixth grades with what was for the daughter of the policeman an intensive preparation for the certificate, an undertaking that seemed to the others fraught with difficulty. From the youngest, whose sleeved hand she guided with its Sergeant-Major[*] fountain pen poised in its wooden holder, to the big Yvonne, whom she drove like a beast of burden, Elise dispensed a bastardized education that consisted of copying for the youngest one and impossibly tricky dictations for the oldest one. At the School for Girls, equality triumphed. Elise made light of the difficulties with a grandiose system of grades. An error committed in the sixth grade counted twice as much as the same error in the fifth and, obviously, four times as much as in fourth grade. Big Yvonne cried over a forgotten accent that had cost her five points at once; at her level, Tiffany could afford to leave several past participles out of agreement with their subjects before getting a zero.

Still, Tiffany collected zeros. Zeros for ten errors in fifth grade, zeros for five errors in the sixth; as she passed from grade to grade, she passed from one zero to another. Elise pointed out her errors, Right there, thoroughly underlined in red. You see? Panicking, she saw only a gaping void from which she could not look away. At the worst moments of the daily dictation and arithmetic lessons, for Yvonne's benefit no doubt, there were fleeting moments of pleasure torn from childhood: languishing over the illustrated border to be made at the bottom of a page, no more than two squares high on the graph paper pages, at the end of each lesson. Elise ordered them to use the geometry of the notebook to make paper shapes, small pyramids, squares, triangles in a cute design and to use the too-pale pencil marks to distinguish one from the other. A visual effect, Elise said.

More than anything else, it was for the compositions that Elise focused on the younger children. Describe the house in which you would like to live. While Yvonne constructed in solid materials and the Africans reproduced in straw and mud the huts of their parents, Tiffany dreamed of a house from the past, more beautiful than the others, that

---

[*] The brand name of a type of fountain pen that had to be dipped into an inkwell.

existed in memories, and brought tears to her eyes. The time of the fox-tails and the seringa, the time of the blue-green linden trees and the pink bedroom. Although she was a little embarrassed at having gone so far into the past in her notebook, she had no idea that in Elise's eyes her awkward words became so many traces of a bourgeois existence. In correcting the mistakes, the schoolteacher corrected an entire childhood that she detested.

Elise was wrong. Tiffany's realm did not extend past the doors of her grandparents' house. If she possessed in her memory a park, an enclosed garden, Tiffany did not possess the world; it was Elise who taught her this. In an atlas she learned that besides the delicate colors of memory, she held all the violet, for a time some of the orange, and, happily, there was no more green. OUREGANO was in the violet space. Tiffany appropriated OUREGANO and so much more.

*

In class they were called th'Africans, and no one spoke to them, even if Elise, occasionally coming to their rescue, demanded that everyone play together. But it was impossible. The little ones couldn't play with the big ones, the boys couldn't play with the girls, and th'Africans couldn't play with white children. Of that Yvonne was sure, case closed. And she knew what she was talking about. Nevertheless, th'Africans managed to integrate the group. The Bonenfant boys opened the doors to them for a game of soccer, of course on the condition that they not touch the ball, or a game of Four Corners, just to have a fifth player. The integration of th'Africans was, it must be said, episodic. Most of the time, nothing was played; everyone sat thirstily and waited on the low wall in the shade under their colonial caps, with the chin straps hanging down. Th'Africans made the most of this by jumping over the wall; they were going to play with th'Africans of the School for Boys. It was forbidden. When one accepts the advantages of a situation, one also accepts the difficulties, intoned Elise. Yvonne told on them.

For Tiffany, outside of school th'Africans had a name. They were called Moses. He was not the tallest in the class; he was even smaller than Tiffany. He didn't know his birth date. He had said to Elise: Around, I'd say about 1946, with a gesture that reinforced the approximation of the words "around" and "about." Tiffany noticed him in the distance near the house. He was watching for her in the stillness. She approached holding her distance. They didn't speak. Then he took an animal out of his too-large khaki shorts' pocket, an animal with beige and black striped fur. From where she stood, Tiffany felt the presence of a rare and marvelous animal. Moses played with it, taking dangerous risks, holding tightly to the leash he had fashioned, and let it run over his arms, catching it again suddenly and making it fall.

The animal, about fifteen centimeters long, with its round head, small ears, and immense protruding eyes that shone like black pearls, squealed. For Tiffany it was too much. She approached, already begging: Lend it to me; let me have it, just to touch it for a minute. She knew that no child in the world would let go of so adorable an animal. But Moses, unexpectedly, handed it to her. She held it close (he would want it back surely) ready to satisfy in a few minutes her love for this creature. Laying it in the crook of her arm, she lifted it to her cheek to feel its softness. She examined it all over, its dark little hands, tiny nails no larger than the *o* in books written for grown-ups, a flat nose, transparent ears, a fluffy tail. Tiffany and the animal looked at each other, sniffed each other, touched each other. Tiffany inhaled the thick down in small respirations, and the animal licked Tiffany's finger with a small raspy tongue. The little girl fell in love with the animal. She couldn't give it back, and when Moses held out his hand, she thought she would faint; panic seized her chest and her knees trembled. You can have it if you want, said Moses, but it's not good to eat.

Pleasure replaced terror. The animal was hers! She cried: What? He would have eaten it! And besides, he had tied the leash too tight and carried it in his pocket where he could have suffocated it, and it hadn't had anything to drink.... Tiffany no longer saw in Moses someone who had made a gesture unheard of in children, but someone who had threatened to harm an animal, an animal that now belonged to her. It was a ceremony of transferred possession for Tiffany. She persuaded herself that, in denying Moses' competence, she would be able to care for and raise the little animal. Moses thought she exaggerated over an animal with a mediocre pelt. If it died, there were plenty of others in the forest. If she hadn't wanted it, he would have let it go and killed it with a slingshot.

He came back every Thursday. He took out of his pockets every kind of wild thing, a small black rat, nice and fat, a female parakeet with its feathers ruffled up, a giant scarab beetle, a yellow toad. Tiffany accepted them with stately detachment. They were just animals and she agreed with Moses: if they died, it would not be important. Her heart was given; on her shoulder the animal nibbled at a crumb of bread she held in her hand while resting close to her neck, and when the child ran, it held onto one of her braids.

*

Tiffany didn't feel any need to name her animals. There had been a rabbit, a small antelope, a parakeet, and now the Animal. The adults who had seen it couldn't identify it for sure. A jerboa? A lemur? A monkey? It contained all the qualities Tiffany required in the animal world. Soft and warm, active yet docile, attractive and funny, it was irrevocably attached to Tiffany. It never strayed. The Animal slept with Tiffany, played with Tiffany, ate with Tiffany. Looking at his daughter one day, Michel noticed the little animal climbing cautiously down her shoulder; it looked at her plate and carefully chose a piece of potato, which it delicately ate without haste. He was disgusted; Tiffany was filthy. Braids undone, greasy hands and half-naked little body, and the animal next to her skin. He tried to get Matilde to notice, but Matilde said it was a bit late to be indignant; she had been like that for weeks.

Madame Dubois happily baptized her companions. Brigitte was the daughter of the house, its little queen. Behind the bars of a cage, pacing back and forth with a rapid and loping gate, was Sylvie, a civet; in the garden, chained to a tree, Gaston, a chimpanzee, a real goon that one! Hector, the rooster, wasn't worth much more. She knew her animals. She knew how to take care of them better than anyone. They came to her sick, and she cured them but then couldn't let them go. Brigitte, for example, had been the smallest of the litter. She would have died without the prodigious care of Madame Dubois. Brigitte couldn't drink milk. She had had to have bouillon in small doses. I'll skip over the enteritis, the decalcification, and, since it's a bit out of the way, her ear infections. Brigitte, she had chronic purulent ear infections. Sylvie? Her masterpiece. She went right over to the cage, opened it and grabbed the animal, turned it over, and showed its missing paw. Yes, she had done surgery on it; the paw was drying, tied to a white string that must have been a tendon. The animal's paws had been tied so tightly by the hunters.... *Oof,* that lot! Hunting should be regulated. Gaston had been found near his dead mother. They kill anything, especially chimpanzees. She had bought Gaston so he would not be eaten. Afterwards he had become a thief, a liar, and had had a difficult puberty. The big monkey looked at them without moving a muscle. He was tied up very short. I don't want him climbing the trees, said Madame Dubois.

Madame Dubois was consulted about the Animal. Well, it's not a jerboa. No, it's not. Look at its four hands, the flat nose. Do you think it's rare? asked Matilde. Even Michel came to see it up close. It's not a monkey; the tail looks a bit like a squirrel. Madame Dubois turned it over, blew on its fur to see the color of its skin. It's light blue, said Tiffany. Gray, pronounced Madame Dubois. She opened the small dark lips to look at the teeth. It's a carnivore. No, it's not, said Tiffany. It eats fruit. Brigitte, who didn't like it that her mistress displayed so much interest in a stranger, began to bark and dance on her hind legs. The Animal took fright at the assembled crowd and the dog's crying. It leapt away. Tiffany looked for it, making a little noise with her mouth, a little promising, soothing noise. She looked first up high, at the level of the table, the chairs, the sideboard, and then down low, near the ground, where she saw the irreparable: in the melee that had ensued after it had leapt away, the animal had been crushed. It lay writhing on the ground, its head bashed in. There was no blood, only a dent on the left side, so clean that you could have punched it back out like a ping-pong ball. But a paw thrashed spasmodically in a movement unrelated to life. Better finish it off, said Madame Dubois. Yes, finish it off, cried Matilde. They stomped on it with their heels. The animal was still moving. Tiffany got up quietly; the animal trembled between the palms of the child's hands.

Tiffany began to tremble. Kill it! Kill it, I say! yelled Michel. The animal fell out of the little girl's hands. It was still moving. Kill it! Kill it, now! screamed her father. Tiffany picked up the little body again and carried it away, holding it against her mouth. She didn't know how to kill. Outside a *boy* took the animal from her and, swinging it by the tail, hit it against the wall. There was blood. They threw it into the bushes.

It was only a jerboa, said Madame Dubois. You'll find others. NO SCENES, groaned Michel. It was disgusting. If it hadn't died I'd have made you let it go. Tiffany, pale, did not cry. There was a pain so strong, so atrocious, that it prevented tears from falling. It was a horror that crushed her.

*

Michel was saying: You are not going to make a SCENE. Making a scene included not only an unbelievable number of words, but also actions and attitudes. It could be a certain reticence of the body that kept her from immediately obeying all sorts of orders, especially the one to leave the room, or to eat or to go to bed. Not liking rice was making a scene. Having a nightmare was making a scene. Tiffany employed a whole series of small actions that Michel instantly deciphered: silent tears rolling down her cheeks, pouting lips, trembling chin, pinched nostrils, hiccups of disgust. He detected even the slightest stiffness in her body.

It had been ages since Tiffany had stopped making scenes with words or phrases. Tiffany had long since set her body so as to express nothing, more absent than transparent. Nothing. Nothing at all. She conscientiously ate rice salad, risotto, and rice pudding at her early dinner, repressing her nausea. She strangled the sobs of her nightmares in her pillow, or, when she was really frightened, under the bed. It was better than making a scene. Making a scene while eating rice was taking small bites with tentative teeth, chewing meticulously every grain while presenting a happy face. Gulps of water to wash it down attracted her parents' attention, and Tiffany felt shivers of revulsion running down her spine as the threats and the horror—the huge spoon full of rice—came at her lips! All that? Yes, all that. Swallow. You will swallow! The plate seemed monstrous. No, it was better to hurry, hide what she was doing, and escape from her parents, who were reassured by the dance of the fork on the plate, to where she could dispose of everything that she had been able to distract them from seeing. With nightmares it was the same; she had to discipline herself. Tiffany remembered the first nightmare at OUREGANO, the one with the lepers who wanted to embrace her. She had gone into her parents' room to find comfort. Half asleep, she had gotten lost in the dark. Her father had yelled at her. Terrified, she had started to scream. Michel kept on yelling. Matilde had not gotten up, and Tiffany went back to bed swearing that she would never get up again.

Making a scene was, in the end, getting in the way of her parents' life. Making a scene was being, liking or hating, taking pleasure or being afraid, showing feelings in front of adults. Tiffany was free to be afraid, to spit in disgust when a stinkbug was found on fruit, to be tired enough to drop in the high grass, to cry her eyes out, to be as happy as the day was long. What was forbidden was to share it, to talk about it. Tiffany quickly understood that her salvation was outside, far from the eyes of Michel and Matilde. Tiffany could have traced the border of this domain to within a centimeter, because even though they had definitively placed the furniture inside the house facing the view, they had limited their field of vision to the garden. It was curious to have so much to see and to see so little. Inside the house, Matilde looked at few places, the backs of the furniture, the feet of the club chairs, and outside her gaze took in the lawn up to the steps that led to the first tennis court. Michel occupied himself with the medical books in the library but did not see anything beyond the hibiscus. By passing behind the hibiscus and carefully going around the first tennis court, ready to bolt if necessary past the second court, Tiffany disappeared.

Tiffany made scenes outside, only two steps from the house that rejected her. She thrashed the hibiscus blooms! And another for the noontime rice, and two more for the evening rice, and three for YOU'RE HERE! She had bitten the heart out of one of them. It had revolted her; the flower was soft and sticky. But the anger of the little girl didn't last long; she turned gently on her heels and, looking into the edge of the sunshine, noticed a column of ants whose parade she quickly went to disrupt. Above, a vulture turned faster and faster; in the distant bush, a flurry of wings. A scream in the forest.

Part Two

I

In the shower Elise felt her womb contract. There was no pain, just the blood coming in long spurts. It trickled down her thighs, slowly at first, then swept quickly, mixing with the water in the shower. She screamed. A scream from deep inside, a scream of horror and sadness. Something irreversible was happening. Albert broke through the door, saw her there, eyes wide open, her thighs clamped together yet powerless to stop the flow, the disgusting trail of blood, life washing away.

While waiting for the doctor, she remained lying down, as if the blood could be fooled this way, kept from finding its way out. Her entire being, stiff with the effort focused on this immense desire. Nothing obeyed inside; the blood escaped, without cramps, without a wound. There was nothing she could do to calm the flow, nothing to stem, nothing to plug up, nothing to tie off; there was nothing that could be stopped. The blood flowed with authority but without violence. Elise hated this sex that stood open and that permitted life to drain out, this sex that did not obey her. She groaned, not from pain but from terror. Does it hurt? asked Albert. Her only response was another groan. Are you bleeding still? asked Albert. She continued to groan. Elise, her womb, her blood, her pain, her child, formed a closed world that excluded him. Under the sheet, under her closed eyelids, something was happening that he could not fathom. Because she felt the moist warmth, only Elise knew that the bleeding continued. Only Elise knew, with all her strength, if the child, her child, what child? still lived.

She screamed. A sudden pain overtook her. She screamed because it meant she was being torn apart; it was the sign of her complete consummation. She was ablaze with terror; the idea was too atrocious. So it was really over. The pain came again and she screamed again. Panicked, Albert went to the bed and lay down next to her, taking her in his arms, pressing his hand over her mouth. She struggled at first but then felt reassured by the soft weight of this shadow that kept the light out of her eyes.

She thought it wonderful that he helped her in this way and she hung on to this large body that rescued her. Albert was afraid. Afraid of the screams he didn't understand, afraid of the body that contracted at regular intervals, expelling hope with each spurt of blood. He was aware of Elise's body with every inch of his own, under his palm the small bony chin, wet with sticky tears, under his arms the trembling shoulders, under his own hips the belly, under his thighs the thighs held tightly closed. He felt an enormous tenderness for what was no longer Elise but a being in peril. He didn't see her; he imagined her and understood her better that way.

When Michel Murano arrived, he found them calmer, still wrapped together. Albert got up heavily; the blood that had soaked through the sheet had left a large red stain on his pants and shirt. Elise was crying. Albert looked at the sheet and his pants as if it were his own blood that had seeped out of a hidden wound. He left the room. Michel did what he had to do, asking Elise questions. She recounted each detail of a pregnancy that was confused with the story of her entire existence. Hadn't she watched this baby long before her belly had begun to swell? DIFFI-CULT CONCEPTION. In the beginning she had been tired and she had lost weight. ANEMIA. She had had strange cramps that had frightened her. CONTRACTIONS. Doctor N'Diop had come. AH? He had reassured her, it was only fatigue. OBVIOUSLY! It had continued. CERTAINLY! She shouldn't have, but he had reassured her, so she had believed.... INDEED! And then today in the shower she had felt her womb contract differently. MISCARRIAGE.

When Michel had finished, Elise did not want to see what he had taken out of her uterus. Still, she did want to know, had the child existed in the midst of all the clots, the bits of placenta, the tissue and blood? Had there been room for it in all that flesh? She felt reassured that it was a real pregnancy; she had seen so much blood that she could not imagine that there had been anything else. Had she conceived something other than this sticky, repulsively colored liquid? It would console her to know this, if there had been a child, a fetus, an embryo, a ball of flesh, a knot of cells, anything that would confirm that she had created more than just blood. She would not have had a child but she would have, at least for a short time, been the source of a bit of life. Once the sheets had been changed, she asked Michel, Was it a boy or a girl?

*

Near the bed the cradle of ebony and mahogany sat waiting, where it had been since the carpenter had made it to order. What to do with it? It was not "dressed" and the rails that protected nothing added to the feeling of emptiness. The women of OUREGANO came to visit. Matilde came first since she was the first to hear, a medical grapevine of sorts. She brought flowers from her garden, flowers of OUREGANO, flowers of Africa, a bouquet of hibiscus, bougainvillea, and frangipani. She was comforting and animated. Elise would recover quickly. After all she had only had a routine miscarriage; Michel said so. They talked about motherhood. It was never to those who desired it that these accidents happened. You could say that again! They remained thoughtful for a moment on either end of the bed. They spoke about school and Tiffany's difficulties. She doesn't pay attention, said the schoolteacher. They were both slightly angry by the end of the visit. No, what had happened to her was not routine; she would never recover! No, Tiffany was not hopeless; you had to know how to handle her!

Madame Dubois and Madame Bonenfant arrived together. Madame Dubois brought juicy slices of lamb: To help you recover. Madame Bonenfant brought fruit. They instinctively lowered their voices as their eyes swept around the room and fell on the cradle, where they remained pointedly. Definitively: nothing there. Madame Dubois, not challenging the superiority of her knowledge in matters of reproduction, let Madame Bonenfant talk. She had never conceived, never, and this left her without pain or regret. Everything seemed strange to her, the pallor of the young woman, the cradle, the sadness of the remarks. That they carried on this way, in the name of something abstract that she could not even imagine, left her speechless, vaguely nauseated. Madame Bonenfant for the first time was ahead of Madame Dubois. She recounted her pregnancies, her deliveries, her milk coming in, and her difficult periods. She didn't stop there. She enlarged upon her own experience with that of her friends and acquaintances, past, present, and future. There had been stillborn children, quite pale, blue ones, red ones, and black ones, all suffocated. There had been monsters, unfinished kittens, without paws, with lizard scales, fish tails, and pig snouts. There had been babies quartered in their mothers' wombs and cesarean sections that had split the child like a melon. Only Jean-Marc and Jean-Louis emerged from this horror as rosy blond babies, so intelligent for their age. Isn't that right, Madame Refons?

Lying in bed, the schoolteacher could not keep up with the mother. It was to her status as a mother that Elise bowed in spite of everything. True, she had conceived with a great deal of difficulty, but at the beginning things had been fine; it was not until she had begun to have contractions (she liked to use this word reserved for deliveries because it brought her closer to motherhood) that she knew it was serious, or at least abnormal, but Doctor N'Diop had reassured her. Say no more! exclaimed Madame Dubois, severed too long from authority. N'Diop reassured you and you believed him! He is a doctor, isn't he? Elise did not defend Doctor N'Diop so much as absolve herself of all responsibility. A doctor! An African doctor, yes, cried Madame Bonenfant. A doctor like me! Madame Dubois jumped back in. Absent gynecological knowledge, she didn't want it forgotten that she knew how to care for animals. Madame Bonenfant returned the ball, a finesse that Madame Commander appreciated: If only he were a doctor like you, that would be perfect! To recall how her cook had suffered from his dental extraction, she felt obliged to start with the story of Brigitte's baldness. She told how Madame Dubois had cared for her dog and just look at the result! Well, I didn't beat around the bush, Madame Dubois started in again. I told him, Penicillin and fast. Do it now. It was all I could do not to speak to him like a child.... Madame Dubois had the floor and she didn't let it go again. Elise and Madame Bonenfant waited patiently for her to stop in order to come back to their own stories.

*

Elise ran out of her bedroom without thinking about being seen by the servants and hurried over to Albert. She was nude from the waist up and in her two hands she held her breasts. Between her fingers her nipples oozed a few drops of cloudy liquid. Milk! I have milk, Albert! There was in her voice a note of satisfaction, almost of joy. She was in the shadow but advanced into the light of the hurricane lamp and for the first time looked upon her breasts with a sort of love, an intimate friendship. Albert, ready to vomit, told her, Wipe that up, but she collected the sap on her index finger and licked it.

She had always more or less nauseated him. He thought it was because of the texture of her body, her soft breasts, her flabby belly, the lightly quivering fat in the hollow of her thighs, nothing really, and the look in her deep brown eyes had overcome it. Since the abortion,[*] he had to admit that he was repulsed by the female body. Since she had been revealed to him, he couldn't forget: in bed, contact with the body packed in cotton, and fear that "it won't stop," gauze coming out of her panties, soiled sanitary napkins in the bathroom wastebasket, the tubes, the antiseptic solutions, and the *boy* who brought the huge pot of boiling water. Albert asked himself with anguish if he would be able to have sex with her again one day, to insert himself into those troubled waters, to part the walls of skin and to go all the way in, to touch the throbbing mass, that trembled, contracted, and that would hold him, maybe even suck him in. He redoubled his attentions, exaggerated the fragility of his wife. She had to rest, be careful. He brought her back to her blood, her milk, and her womb. He cleaned up the bloody pads, folded another hand towel under Elise's buttocks: Don't move. Just rest, Darling!

Elise kept busy; she made large knowing gestures. In the morning her sleepy hand had reached into her panties to collect the night's loss of blood. She knew how to examine it, measure its phlegm content, its texture. She knew without looking if it was fresh red blood or old dried brown-red blood, or black dross. She washed herself, applied antiseptic,

---

[*] The medical term "abortion" is used as frequently in French as the lay term "miscarriage." Although in English "abortion" carries with it a degree of deliberate intention not necessarily there in French, it is possible that in Refons' mind he feels in some way that this loss was intentional since he seems to blame Elise's inadequate body for the loss of the baby.

and changed her dressings. That was what was needed! The same again at noon, at four in the afternoon, and in the evening before going to bed. If she felt sad, she changed herself for no reason. Since her nipples had dripped, she spent a little less time on her womb. In front of the mirror she gently squeezed her breasts and liked to see the milk appear at this simple touch.

The sanitary napkins became spotless and the milk dried up. Elise looked with anger at the body that had cheated her; already it had forgotten. She gently rubbed her breasts, harder now. Nothing. She squeezed them until it hurt. So that was it. The body no longer responded to the call of memory. There was nothing left but words. Had Albert been afraid? Had he thought she would die? Yes, he had been afraid. There had been reason to be afraid! She had bled so much. Elise wanted to talk about it again and again, about the blood, but it had to be taken in order. What had been the scariest were the contractions, you remember? Every ten minutes, then every five. Albert didn't remember her timing them but he let her talk. Everything had been the fault of this N'Diop; he hadn't diagnosed anything at all. He pretended to know what he was doing, the Big Doctor. And her baby had died! Thank God Murano had saved her, her—because with N'Diop it would have been the baby *and* the mother that died. It's my fault, my fault, groaned Albert. We should never have come here. My poor darling, my poor baby, stuttered Elise.

*

When Elise returned to teaching, she no longer felt any pain. She didn't see the children. At fifteen, twelve, ten, eight, or four years old, they didn't belong to the childhood she had envisioned. They were students, hardworking or indolent, one strong in spelling, another weak in math. Entities, finished beings, forever linked to their aptitudes and their insufficiencies, which did not merit her attention. At most her job required her to catch an unsteady hand, to bring just the right word to a line, to mark errors in vast streaks of red ink, to scold, to punish. Elise was right; no one here expected to be hugged, touched, changed. For a long time the schoolchildren had sublimated their energy, washed away their misfortunes, consoled their pain. Yes, they were from the other world, Elise's students were.

Only a baby could have softened her, and at that only a very small one, an absolute newborn with its hair still sticky and its bluish eyes. And yet that still wouldn't have been enough; she wanted her own child. Nothing in the class could bring it back. She was bored doing the same things over and over, tied to the blackboard by the date, the copybooks and grades, tied to the children by "Quiet!" Everything started with the cradle, at home. Albert had wanted to get rid of the cradle but she had refused. Never! She would rather die. Wasn't it enough that the child had died? If she had to let go of the cradle as well! She would take it back to France! LIFE continued between the thighs of the women of OUREGANO, just under the bit of belly pushed out by the too-tight belt. Why had Madame Dubois never had children? Had she lost a baby too? Was it a long time ago? Madame Bonenfant was especially impressive with her two boys, one after the other. They had in common the experience of pain and blood. She couldn't stop asking and Madame Bonenfant couldn't stop answering. Finally, someone had recognized that she belonged here. Madame Bonenfant's gynecological experience came with a quantity of diverse reflections that included charity, religion, justice, etiquette, and meteorology. Everything was filtered through this lens. And it was through this aperture that the world opened to Elise.

Have another child? She didn't think so. Albert agreed. He had been so frightened! The EXPULSION had sent him reeling; the DELIVERY had sent him out of the room. She was still weak. In her heart she knew why now: ultimately no child could replace another. Women who lose a child are looked upon as having had an accident or having been ill. They are expected to conceive again but they remain sad, mute, sterile, in the face of their terrible heartbreak. Elise knew this. She was forever linked to the memory of the poor little dead baby, murdered! Oh, God! She didn't have a grave where she could go and meditate, but no matter; her womb served as both cradle and coffin. She prayed over herself, there, deep inside. She was both mold and memory.

Albert looked at Elise who walked with a new step, a little bent, as if thinking. If it hadn't been for the horror of her body, life would have been almost simple. He was no longer the only thing in Elise's life. Madame Bonenfant stopped by as soon as she had a free moment. It was good for Elise; it distracted her. These outings with the Judge's wife pleased her so much that she neglected her work. Elise could no longer tolerate children. In the evening when she came home, she was right at the end of her tether. But she had to hold on.

*

By taking Elise in hand, Madame Bonenfant killed two birds with one stone. Not only did she imagine putting her to work for the Sisters, which would be good for them, but also she would save the schoolteacher's soul. Nothing proved one's devotion better than bringing a lost lamb back to the fold. She triumphed on all fronts, faith and teaching at the same time. No question about it, someone like Elise—a communist *and* an atheist—she was worth more in the eyes of God than a dozen more baptized Maries. Such a victory for Madame Bonenfant!

Madame Bonenfant cleverly presented Elise to all the Good Sisters. The poor thing was coming out of a great trial; she didn't say what sort of trial. She needed to forget, although it would be difficult. The Sisters understood. It was a child taken away from her too soon. The dear angel! exclaimed the nuns. Was it baptized? Alas! Poor little soul! But Limbo was also a good place. They made Elise visit everything, the kitchen gardens and the chicken house, the point being to bring her to the class of students studying for the certificate, but they lost her in the chapel where Elise came face-to-face with the Virgin Mary, a small statue of golden plaster, with its large rosy face and blue eyes, in its left arm a fat baby with a surprised look. My God, why had she not seen this figurine before? She no longer knew, what memory should she cling to? Which image of lost childhood? Nothing came to her of catechism and white roses. The doors of religion had never opened on the childhood of Elise Refons. So what was happening here in the musty smell of frangipani flowers, in the flat blue eyes of the statue? Elise felt weak and dropped to her knees at the base of the statue of the Virgin, a huge sob full of understanding overtook her; she knew: HER.

This display of piety delighted the Good Sisters and disquieted Marie Bonenfant. Was Elise robbing her of her exclusivity? Things were going just a little too fast. Hold on! First things first! Elise agreed to come to "teach French" three times a week after school; it was only natural. She was taken to meet the students. There were some in the sewing room. Weren't they cute, all these little things! There were more in the kitchen. Didn't that smell good! And in the nursery, a pale-faced doll lay in its cradle, the mechanism of its sleepy eyes was stuck; it looked at Elise with round blue eyes that recalled those of the Virgin a few moments ago.

Everything had worked so well that Madame Bonenfant felt cheated out of her role. She had imagined a difficult struggle, a protracted resistance that she would have overcome after long harangues, almost threats. Her final argument was to have been that the death of the child was God's Will. A pure and good being could not grow in a place where God was hated. Elise had only to look around her. Where were there children? At the Bonenfants', the Muranos' even, to be charitable. But did she see them at the Dubois'? Madame Bonenfant obviously didn't think about the others, the black families overflowing with dozens of children, or the half-breed children always multiplying around Alexandrou. Madame Bonenfant conjured up Elise's revolt. I will crush you, break you. Bend. Bow your head. Lick the floor! God is great! This was too easy. Honestly, anything passed these days, anything at all, and suddenly a bent knee! How to stir up a little anger, make her say, "I do not believe in God" or better yet, "God does not exist." There had to be a rending of the soul! She would have expected it over the existence of God. It cannot be proved. But of course, it is only the Grace of God.... Ah yes, the Grace of God!

*

Elise graciously contributed the lessons. The nuns were thrilled. They liked this young woman, a mere child, so knowledgeable, to whom happiness had been refused. One gets the martyrs one deserves. Madame

Bonenfant surveyed with sadness the progression Elise made in the Sisters' esteem. Using the pretext of driving her to the Mission, Madame Bonenfant accompanied Elise. While the latter taught, she stayed close to the nuns. Where did the time go talking of one thing and another? All conversations led back to Elise. Madame Bonenfant was livid; she couldn't undo her lies, couldn't declare Elise a liar: Pious, her? She's a communist through and through! That would have been taken badly; she would not have been forgiven for introducing a wolf into the flock. A communist! So, to bring Elise back down where she belonged, she went after Albert; the young woman would surely suffer the consequences. Yes, she was married to a bad one. Refons had...opinions.... He was being watched; they had a thick file on him. And an atheist into the bargain! The poor thing, groaned the Sisters, a dead child, an unsavory husband; there was such unimaginable injustice, such hidden sadness. Since Madame Bonenfant had been so good as to let them know, they would not be ungrateful to her.

When Elise came out of class, she was offered a *sirop*, something sweet, cool; she declined. Would she like to go into the chapel? Oh, yes. Night had invaded the altar of the Virgin and the statue emerged from a bouquet of candles that made the gold of her dress vibrate like small trembling breaths. The light bathed the face of sadness and joy; the child slept, its head falling on its shoulder. Elise felt only the wild happiness of inspired discovery and peace, the reassurance of her place. Would you like us to pray for your baby? asked a nun. Yes, please, Sister! begged Elise. Was it a boy or a girl? asked another. Elise looked at her, distressed. She stammered, I don't know, stopped herself. Yes, she did know! A boy.

Praying together became the rule after Elise's class. Madame Bonenfant had to put up with this gathering in the darkness where identities were erased in the shadows. The heavy meditation suffocated her. What should her manner be? What should she say? It was unhealthy, all this. She had other things to do besides praying for Elise, praying for a stillborn child. She had had enough. She told Bonenfant: You see how she manipulates, the little bitch! The Judge burst out laughing in a way that reassured her. She's completely crazy! That's it! Boff! She's mad, of course, nothing more serious than that. They referred to her after that as the Madwoman and when Jean-Marc or Jean-Louis got a zero, they said simply, the Madwoman has gone off again.

Madame Bonenfant hurried to tell Madame Dubois the news so that she could make the most of it. Madame Dubois came several times to see Madame Bonenfant in order to hear the latest. Perhaps I should go with her as well, begged Madame Commander, dying of curiosity. No, no, replied Madame Judge, we must not get involved. We don't want to be held responsible. She'll have to manage the best she can. Doesn't she have a husband? Doesn't she have a car? It's out of our hands now. One morning as they were talking in this way, they ran into Matilde at Alexandrou's. She didn't know? Well, it's like this.... Could she ask the doctor his opinion? Could it be treated? Would she have to be put away? Matilde's reaction surprised them. She didn't agree at all. It was important not to make Cartesian judgments. Faith was inexplicable; you couldn't tell on whom Grace would fall. They noted the animation in her face, her quiet anger. What was happening to this one too?

*

What to do at OUREGANO once the pleasure of the never-ending leg of lamb was exhausted? Matilde discovered with sadness that everything that had ordered her life was absent here. No hairdresser, no beauty parlor, no department stores. Not essential, of course; anyone saying so would have been taken for an idiot, a socialite, but their absence disorganized an existence in which these things counted for a great deal. The airy color of the morning, the pleasure of seeing what would be worn this winter; she had already guessed as much. Decidedly, red-orange was HER color. It was not much but it was happiness. A dressmaker exclaiming over her figure, it was just a small pleasure! What richness, what volume, cried the hairdresser. What size? asked a saleswoman. Try this one; it's made for you. You have a head for hats, said the stylist to whom she had taken her mother, and, laughing, she threw on an impossible hat that looked ravishing on her.

There was nothing at OUREGANO, and Matilde's face bore the stigmata of this absence. It took on a serious hardness, which she had missed as she was so busy smiling at her reflection a hundred times in the mirror. In the hairdresser's mirror: Shall I put a streak just there? Where? Just here. She sucked in her cheeks, opened her eyes wide, to imagine the streak in her hair. Before the dressmaker's looking glass: Shall we take it in a bit more here? Matilde looked at herself on the bias, and her leg stretched out, lengthening the image of her body, indicated that the dress could indeed be taken in more. In the upright mirror of a dress shop, she wore every outfit as if it belonged to her. She played the imp mischievously at the stylist's, putting on a little more violet eye shadow, rejecting a dark hat. Her face lived, as it were, by the subtle intervention of excessive necklaces, evolving, changing, vibrating.... She was not the same person in the yellow dress, or the violet one with the purple tulips, or in the black one. In each one she felt so different!

Alas, worn so often, her dresses began to lose their magic; seen so often they no longer evoked pleasure in company. Looking at her small empty face, Matilde made stereotypic gestures that, not surprisingly, reestablished the mask of the former Matilde. But this was not a face, no matter who inhabited it; it lived but only as an image. Matilde painted on Matilde. And not very well either, because coloring on this mouth required the inflated words that cooed her desire to please; to see the blue of her eyes they needed to be laughing as they received the required compliments; to brush rouge on the cheekbones required a chain of gestures that came from someone noticing them. Who would talk to her? Who would notice her here? How much more difficult it became to draw on the absent face, the mouth, the eyes, the cheeks. She did it with apprehension as if to reassure herself that she still had a face: I have a mouth, I have eyes, and I don't have a nose.

The sessions in front of the nude face, its features pulled up by a towel around the hair, became painful. It was no longer the quick touch here, another there, that had once been a joyful procedure but a long deliberation in which she tried to recall herself. The memories didn't come. Is it possible to recover a single memory among a hundred? Can the furtive caress of a word that brought pleasure be evoked? Somewhere in the past someone had spoken of the fleetingness of beauty that, on this silent evening, ravaged her face. A chance encounter between a word and a moment of loveliness. It wasn't Matilde and it wasn't anyone else. Matilde tried the incantations of imagination and, just as Tiffany consoled her terrors with overheard words and phrases, Matilde bandaged hers with the compliments of the past dredged up from the void. They used to say that she was pretty. She was the hostess at fantastic balls. She was beautiful and seductive. Who went to these parties? Who did she charm? She didn't know and the words that flattered always came back in the same way to consecrate a beauty that no longer existed.

If the voice dancing its white waltz spoke to her of gold in her hair, of the perfect curve of her mouth, or of any other detail of which she was proud, it spoke of what was no more. Gone was the cloud of golden locks: there was no peroxide here. Absent the full taut arch of the lips, the mouth was small and flat, and the rest was fading as well. In the requiem for lost beauty a troubled veil hung between the two faces, both nude. The Matilde of today looked at herself in the mirror trying desperately to find the image of the Matilde from before.

*

And everyone saw this young woman, not more than thirty at most, who hung desperately to a face that fashion, had she stayed in France, would have erased at least ten times already. If fashion had demanded flat hair, how she would have longed for it now. If a makeup craze suddenly called for clean faces like hers, she would not have been alone; she would have overcome this change with enthusiasm, the enthusiasm that greets all fads. The radio, the newspapers, and films reproducing her image millions of times would have made it commonplace. She would have seen herself elsewhere before seeing herself in the mirror. And if that had not been enough, she would have been told repeatedly that it was so much better this way, so much more natural, so much more real. The descriptions would have been "childlike," "sporty," and "a real young lady." The models would have been decked out in leather caps and scarves; they would have been dressed in riding breeches; they would have worn golf shoes. And Matilde, seeing thousands of duplications, would have said, Of course!

At OUREGANO, she was alone. No one encouraged her, not even her husband, who by a trick of logic distanced himself from her. What Michel liked in his wife, wasn't it the image of himself that she reflected back to him? Invisible for others, it was normal that Matilde no longer existed for him. But Matilde's body, their coordinated gestures, what was left there? Did Matilde's body live in her face? Wasn't this a totality? And love, was it simply the fortuitous conjunction of pleasure that didn't really engage either of them? Matilde felt herself losing her footing. Incapable of remembering who she was, she could not invent herself, for imagination is an art, and perhaps what a woman can be most objective about is to consider herself as another, to choose herself as an other. Matilde was incapable of accepting herself because she did not exist. Who was she? If only she knew, she who had not wanted children but who had accepted motherhood, she who had married because it was to a doctor. Who was this woman who liked to eat with moderation, to drink, to make love, who felt—in moderation—pity, joy, sadness. Did she have any passions? No, not really, but...a GOOD book, a GOOD play, a GOOD film with GOOD actors. Did she believe in God? Yes, of course, well, as a matter of habit.

In the end it was all absurd. Matilde wasn't sorry for anything real like lost youth or a destroyed or mutilated face. It wouldn't have taken much to repair the charming mask; a little color was all that was missing and could have been acquired in time. Yet nothing could have shored up her fears. The wrinkles were not yet permanent and her face was still attractive in its almost neutral perfection. Indeed, that was what tortured her. She was at the peak of her beauty, at the peak of her life. Makeup had made it visible, revealed it, and had created this fragility. Out of the question now to get ready for an evening out, a party, or to try out a new fashion. Time was too short, the interval of a charade that had the duration of truth.

Matilde acknowledged that she was beautiful with her makeup, but refused to see herself as still beautiful without anything. She wanted to please and not to be. She had tried every kind of metamorphosis, hoping to wake up each day more beautiful, and, in a sense, she was, because the style she perfected coincided with the taste of the day at the point where it met her true personality. She had come to the moment in the life of a woman's beauty when she refuses all the tomorrows imagined too well under the makeup that arranges and substitutes, remedial makeup, not toy makeup. It was moving to know she was at this point in her life. Had she been so impatient to grow up and to grow old? Now, it was a matter of holding on. Matilde didn't believe in the beauty of maturity, in "intelligent" faces, in features full of character. In the tones of fashion magazines, she condemned the wrinkle that turned the mouth bitter, the bags that sadden the eyes, the anxious line on the forehead, and the fibrous constellation of wrinkles that come from expressing emotion.

The most painful part was to have come to this almost by surprise, hidden from colors and scents. The most anguishing of all was that it had happened here, where the memory of her beauty would be lost, where no one would look at her. She could not bear that the face to which she had dedicated her life be exposed because it had given her an intuition of what she was really. She refused to look, refused to exist in the name of another principle that would have given her, if not eternity, at least a future. The solution was everywhere and she was nowhere. The solution could have been Tiffany, if Matilde had known how to bind together their sadness and at the same time their happiness. Matilde would have sensed the little girl's life and would have found warmth. She could even, all else failing and because it was impossible that she conceive for herself an individual destiny, have found a place with Madame Dubois and Madame Bonenfant. All she would have had to do was to roll her hair up into a French twist, to put on a flowered dress, and join them in their discussions of bargains and good works, respectable activities. Who was she to disdain all this? For Matilde, salvation came from outside; it had the face of a priest.

*

Four men who were closemouthed about where they had come from had brought Father John in a month before on a stretcher. This was what came of giving one's self and one's life to a solitary mission somewhere in the bush. Father John was dying of a terrible viral hepatitis. Michel took him in, gave him a bed. Matilde lent a set of her very own sheets and they forgot about him, so quiet was the life, waxing and waning there in the suffocating room behind the X-ray machine. One day the priest raised his head, Michel spoke to him, and Matilde sent in three boiled potatoes. The Father didn't eat them, having forgotten the simplest response to food, but he looked at them, moved by this charitable attention that, for once, was addressed to him.

When he could get around a bit without his head spinning, without being seized with the monstrous cramp of nausea, it was toward Matilde that he moved, less to thank her than to discover, like water running downstream, a giving person. And the young woman whose face was smoothed in its simplicity by makeup and whom he met on the terrace that morning, became for him charity itself because it was the only thing he saw or recognized. He spoke the only language he knew, that of the poor and the sick, that of all "poor souls." Matilde listened to this plaintive music, nostalgic and strong as the autumn rain on the acacia trees still in leaf, the soft fall of damp leaves, like pieces of unleavened Holy Bread. She was sure she recognized the melody, although here it was strangely painful, like this monk. Matilde clung to whatever could be separated from OUREGANO.

How could anyone be so unaware of oneself? Ignoring hands and feet to the extent of such suffering? If the body was failing (sometimes it teetered and fell), the priest remained on this side, his soul elsewhere. What did the last jerking movements of a being he had so long ago abandoned matter to him? Matilde watched this man, so unaware of himself, with respect. By what was not so much force of character as divine provenance he had been able to live beyond the limits of his face, his body, of life. They had begun to take short walks, once around the lawn, to the end of the driveway, walks imprinted with the motion of meditation. Father John saw nothing, not the delicate flowers of the morning and not the little girl, Tiffany, playing nearby. And since he didn't see them, Matilde no longer saw them either, shamed by the thought of being seduced by what was beautiful or innocent, distractions that lead away from God.

Illness had ravaged the priest's bony face, his bristling beard, his cloudy eyes that no longer saw; bilious color, yellow, brown of the skin smoothed because sunken in at the mouth. The emaciated body under the brown cassock, two ankles with bulging black veins, and the feet hard with corns in sandals made of recycled tire treads. He was shocking to look upon; his poverty sliced the eye compared to that of others because it was an active and chosen poverty, inhabited, lived, miserable certainly, but decent. This humble man was right to extend his hand to those poorer still, to those more ill than he, even though he was dying and others had time to recover. The poverty and illness from which the people of OUREGANO suffered and which spoiled their bodies were their only possessions; Father John had God and saw only Him.

The force of his vision was such, and the weakness of Matilde so remarkable, that the young woman no longer saw the world except through the priest's eyes, walking in time with the sound of his voice toward "the poor souls." She was completely outside herself, suddenly relieved to no longer be. Something inside her, something essential, was in charge. Finally, she was at rest after the long period of disarray in which she had been unable to invent herself. It was strange to find this serenity in other peoples' pain, but it was toward this pain that the priest conducted her irresistibly.

*

Little by little the monk revealed to Matilde a new part of the world. The world around her opened onto a deeper reality. The sick, Father John's greatest interest, finally came within Matilde's field of vision. She had up until then lived surrounded by patients; the park around the house joined the hospital grounds; and it was not unusual to see a patient straying beyond the authorized territory. It was even common to have certain disagreeable labors performed by the lepers, such as chopping wood, clearing brush, tamping the tennis courts, and so on.... But these patients, she had never really seen them. These were Michel's patients. The more there were, the better for his professional prestige, for his reputation as a man devoted, burdened, a man who "killed himself over his work." The patients were a cause of fatigue, an element of evil and a source of glory. His standing was measured by the number of filled beds, elements of good. For Matilde they had never been sick people.

With Father John, she learned that the sick were suffering. She saw the emaciated bodies no longer marked by the regularity of rhythmic respiration where, on the contrary, tortured and panicked breathlessness is lost and found, as in a long and terrifying race. She saw little redheaded children with their heads hanging limply and the efforts of the mothers to cheat death by holding the necks up. She saw the blue and black colors of gangrene, the buckets of blood near the morgue. She heard the groans and the death rattles, the screams and the tears, the wailing and the fitful sobs of the patients and the healthy family members unified in their discordant but continuous chants where SILENCE written on the message board no longer forbade anything. Father John saw the misery of Man. Matilde saw the poverty of people. And the patients became for her, after being Michel's people, God's people.

The patients went effortlessly from the state of being objects to manifestations of the divine. These people were no longer people in the simplest sense of the term because Matilde, who associated them with her husband's military and medical career, no longer separated them from the Will of God. She was not troubled that God could have chosen to express himself on earth through so many broken bodies, so many sighs, so much hoarseness, and so many coughs. She did not rail against the injustice; she thought it appropriate that the voices of these "poor souls" were no longer human but instead divine. She easily accepted their cries just as she accepted the crucifixion of Christ because she had seen it so often on so many crosses. At OUREGANO the death of God made no more noise in Matilde's heart than the suffering of these people.

They visited the lepers, the poorest of the poor. She expected a mass grave full of them; she saw a village living its life within leprosy. There were whole families of lepers, a father, a mother, a grandmother, cousins. There were leper weddings, leper lovers, leper adulterers, leper crimes of passion, the dramas of jealousy. There were chiefs, criminals, thieves. There were scoundrels and victims. There were even children, newborns on the backs of their mothers without hands, small boys who built toy automobiles out of metal wires, little girls carrying jugs to the water hole.

Children of lepers who were not yet lepers themselves. These "poor souls" spoke with words that went beyond suffering; they asked for food above all, as if the mutilated bodies needed more nourishment in order to forget their wounds. With lepers, God expressed himself differently; he demanded meat and manioc, just enough food to stop the stomach from growling.

At Father John's side, Matilde prayed as if in a dream; far from un-hinging her, these images engraved her soul with conviction. God did exist; if it were not so, there would not have been these signs of distress beyond human bearing. Man could never have introduced into the world so much suffering by himself; God's hand had to be in it. God touched the people with his power. He didn't humiliate them; he didn't renew endlessly, minute by minute for centuries on end, the suffering of his only Son. He was saving his people. Matilde's faith was restored. As long as desolation existed, man would not be abandoned.

On one peaceful morning such as there are often in Africa, before the heat introduces its violently mixed colors and its insistent sounds, Father John celebrated Mass on the Muranos' terrace. He wanted to thank his hosts, take leave of them in the name of God before disappearing once more into the bush, which would not give him up again. Matilde invited the Dubois, the Bonenfants, and the Refons, the essential corps of the neighborhood Christian community, the first families of OUREGANO. They came with the feeling of faith that touches anyone who approaches the unusual. Going to Mass on Sunday was to mark a ritual associated with the ordinary. Going to Mass at the Muranos', as they called it, was a mark of faith.

The place, the priest's personality, even the fact that the Mass was read on the margins of the usual representations of God, gave to the ceremony both an archaic character, more honest perhaps, and something of the schismatic that each participant felt in his or her own way. This faith, displayed for no reason, was it totally pure? Wasn't doing what was right without obligation walking along the border of evil pride? One had to be wary of the unmotivated; nothing is without significance. But the personalities of OUREGANO did not lack for resources to quiet their doubts. No, curiosity was an excellent alibi, closely followed by analysis, because throughout the Mass they analyzed the quality of the prayers, of

Matilde's faith, of Michel's medical expertise, and what the chances were of the priest collapsing! Indeed, they assisted at a social gathering like any other, and imagining divine sacrifice from this angle reassured them immensely.

The dining table pulled out onto the terrace was covered simply with a white sheet. There was a saucer with a piece of bread, a glass with a little wine, and the brown monk turned his back to the group settled on the chairs that had been placed by the *boys* on the gravel driveway. Off to the side, Tiffany stood watching with the families of the servants, with her hands on her hips. Everyone meditated on the center of the dining table with its utensils, so banal that they appeared vulgar, foodstuffs so ordinary that they seemed meager. Everything was happening at the center of the inanimate objects into which the priest breathed life with all his mystical strength. Heaven had nothing to do with this scene, nothing to do with the tall green mango trees high above the roof of the house, nothing to do with the bougainvillea that made a purple screen for the altar, nothing to do with the zinnias in the borders that surrounded the terrace with their red-hot and hard-orange splash. God was at the center of this pallor; his back was turned on Man.

Then Father John took the bread in his two hands and raised it above his head; only the participants in the front row bowed their heads. The spectators at the back and Tiffany, who had never seen anything like it, watched as best they could while the emaciated arms, looking like knotty vines in the forest, rose upward to present the bread. Their eyes followed the wine, carefully examining the face of the priest, who in his gesture of adoration saw only God. They heard him speak of the "poor souls" and this image was as abstract to them as that of the bread, the wine, and God. The poor people too were foreign, sacred characters, respectable, God's heroes. They saw nothing of the sort around themselves. Their poverty was not worthy, their misery not honorable. Their hunger was not ascetic and death did not bring glory.

With heads bowed, the good society of OUREGANO did not witness the bread transform itself into flesh, nor the wine into blood. These minds did not imagine the faces of poor people. The faces of the poor were neither the water carrier tottering at noon under the bamboo pole, nor the child alone on the road walking for hours before reaching school.

Not the woman, who was sent away from the morgue in the early morning with empty arms.... Not even their *boys*, whom they abused for no reason at all and whom they had permitted this morning to attend the Mass. The poor were elsewhere, far away, not here. And if pushed to name someone, they once again designated themselves. They were, according to the rhythm of the prayers and the parables, pure as the driven snow, innocent as children, sad in order to be consoled, simple in order to know the light. They always wanted more from God and never gave up the hope that after death they would be just as they had been in life, as if by magic everything would be taken care of, something would be arranged, they would be in good standing with God. On the Muranos' driveway advance reservations were made in Heaven.

Father John had before him those responsible for the evil forces that subjugated the poor people: the Administrator who administered nothingness, the Judge without charity, the schoolteacher without courage, the wife without love, the doctor without medicine. All the biggest charlatans who subjugated the people without giving them anything. And he said nothing. On this morning, God was praised by those who fought Him the hardest, and he who loved God spoke not a word. Charity was trampled at every turn by these people because even their breath was unjust and the priest did not see it. All was well in the end: the people didn't see God, the priest didn't see the people, and God was looking elsewhere.

II

Michel Murano noticed with irritation that the walls around the flag platform had not been whitewashed for a long time and that the grass at the base of the pole had not been cut either. For Heaven's sake! Keeping up appearances was not that difficult! As for the bush hospital, nothing more and nothing less, with its little brick buildings and wooden signs above the doors: RADIOLOGY, MATERNITY, MEN, WOMEN, CONSULTATIONS, SURGERY, PEDIATRICS, ENDEMIC DISEASES, CHIEF MEDICAL OFFICER.

A male nurse, seated at a table barring the entrance of each building, performed the triage examination by looking at the patient. Most of the time he did not touch the patient and, without getting up, sent him home with the definitive verdict: Not sick. But the practice had hardened the sick as well as their suffering, even as it took their arms and legs. They stayed, blocking the line, moaning loudly, except for a few who were too weak. For them their families performed the necessary sound effects. The nurse waited for this signal before digging into an old Guigoz milk box to find a small handful of chalky white tablets that he poured into a bit of paper. While he twisted the ends, he explained, gesturing with his fingers that there were enough for three days, twice a day. The patient looked avidly at the auspicious packet and paid no attention to the digital gymnastics of the nurse.

The gate opened, however, for emergency cases evaluated by the nurse with a certainty acquired from experience: relatives he brought himself to the doctor and paying clients, the poor man who had folded thirty francs into his health record to attract the kind complicity of Cerberus. He was not without feelings, that one. He first looked absently at the health record ignoring the bill. What if it weren't enough? A hostile glare pretended to return the booklet: No need of that here. The patient would leave without medication, too ashamed to ask for the white pills when, with a small gesture, the nurse pushed him behind into the line of "sick" patients while handing over the health record, this time for real. Carefully, when he judged the line behind him to be sufficiently long, the survivor opened his booklet to the place where the bill had been. Gone. Relieved, he could concentrate on his illness.

There were no fixed office hours for consulting the doctors, and the patients knew this. They might come that day or the next, depending on other business, operations, the myriad duties of Doctors. There were bad signs: a nurse who came into the office and left with the Chief Medical Officer on his heels, an African who came in with a note in his hand, a government worker with a voucher signed by the Administrator, a white person who brought in a black one. They all went to the head of the line, and once inside the office they stayed, and they stayed until the white Doctor accompanied the white person and the black one to the car. Patients who leaned in at the door could see the Doctor speaking to the white person, shaking the hand of the white person while the black one, the lucky dog who had climbed under the sheet, waited for his boss to step on the gas. They had seen it happen with Madame Bonenfant and her cook and with Madame Dubois and her dog. Such excitement!

The long wait was a gamble; you could get the black Doctor or the white Doctor. For the latter there was no possibility of a thirty-franc bribe. At this level it would cost five hundred or a thousand francs and best not even to think about it because everyone thought it was only a question of money, being seen by the white Doctor, the Chief Medical Officer—a real Doctor, he was good. The black wasn't the same; he looked like a nurse except that he wasn't even of the same ethnicity. For N'Diop, as for the Chief Medical Officer, you had to have an interpreter. With Murano, the patients explained at length and sometimes inserted a bit of French to show that they were trying. They nodded vigorously when the interpreter described their symptoms to the Doctor, illustrating his words by designating the site of the pain. With N'Diop, they spoke to the interpreter but avoided eye contact with the suspicious Doctor; they joked in their own language about the black white man, the "fake," and the interpreter laughed out loud.

*

This organization was as good as another and, because it was based on the military system, it suited the Chief Medical Officer—Captain Murano. There was little to be changed: slightly reorder the waiting procedures, repaint the departmental signs, wash the nurses' shirts. Upon arriving at the hospital, Michel Murano had not been surprised; it was what he had expected, that is to say, what he had experienced, the army, and even better—the army at war. He drew from the attitude of the patients an atmosphere of urgency, as if it were necessary to take death on quickly. This had not been his impression with the successive unit commands; here there were treatment units spread about, in the bush torn out of the jungle, with the dying, the wounded carried in on shoulders. To act, that was what he was there for, to act right up to the limits of his strength, always harried, taking both pleasure and rest in the blood and the pain of others, but taking them nevertheless in the name of the fierce virility of war, in the name of immeasurable fatigue, in the name of the dedication he had made once and for all to the uniform of his life and of his knowledge. An act of love, even if spoiled like an ugly woman, was worthy of life, well at least of suffering, at worst of waiting. Michel knew all this and his existence, in all its ordinariness, was crowned by the most extreme worthiness. He could not forget the time when he had been God.

The hospital at OUREGANO had only the appearance of this haunted past. Behind the whitewashed walls, the flag in tatters, the stretcher standing by the door, the fleeting apparition of a white coat, it was all crumbling. The QUIET-HOSPITAL sign was the only reality of OUREGANO's health unit. Gulping all at once the week's supply of analgesic tablets, the real sick of OUREGANO made the only healthy gesture at the hospital. Even with the thirty francs needed to buy the sentry at the door, once inside the hospital, the patients found only the emptiness of assumptions, of promises, of treatments unperformed. At OUREGANO treatment had always been based on "if." Diagnosis was provisional upon the confirmation of laboratory tests that did not exist; the patient with his presumed illness entered into the world of conditional treatment.

He didn't know of course that his cure would depend on the stock of penicillin. He waited outside the building for his assumed illness to disappear by itself without the help of the medicines that would have been appropriate.

It is surprising that given these conditions the hospital at OUREGANO still had patients and doctors. What were they looking for behind the façade, in the rooms where the dying lay next to their pallets of straw, in the unused microscope, in the kidney-shaped bowls full of stained syringes and dull needles? Africa palliated the insufficiencies of civilization and hid the failure of science in its hallowed beliefs. The blood pressure machine was gone? The X-ray reader didn't work? No more thermometers? Not even a probe? No matter, there was still the patient and the doctor, a magical association, because that was where everything happened, in the relationship between the doctor who didn't understand and the patient who didn't know how to speak. They both knew the limitless power of the only thing that linked them, THE MEDICINE. The doctor gave it, the patient received it, the junction was made, and illness was cheated. At OUREGANO there were no medicines for specific illnesses but there was MEDICINE for ILLNESS.

Death was no more frequent at OUREGANO than elsewhere, neither was it any less so. It was just "luck." You had to wait for death to decide. It was neither up to the doctor, nor the patient, but destiny. Did it matter what the filter was made of? The patient waited for the medicine to act and he wouldn't know until the end. The doctor watched the patient fight with only the help of what he had dug out of a bottle not yet dried up. Colors were not a problem in the pharmacy although quantities were. When one drug ran out, it was considered strong and another was put in its bottle. Often it was the same thing, quinine or aspirin, at any rate white, nothing at all.

*

For those with a taste for heroism OUREGANO was quickly disappointing. All the more so since it was easy to be taken in for a time by the lure of suffering and death. These were dispensed largely by the gods on the red earth beyond the green hills, in every thing, in every place, day and night, as much as you could stand, and then more. Michel exalted in this "more." He wanted to gather it all to himself, embrace it in the terrible battle that he would wage over time, over space, in the shadow and in the light. He wanted to cover himself, disgustingly, in the blood he would have torn from pain, splattered from the death he would have beaten. He took it all on because he was a hero and because heroes no longer simply stand in the light.

But when suffering blends into sleep, when death slips quietly in and relaxes the fingers, when what runs out of the patient's stomach in huge quantities is not blood, when the dying man loses his life vomiting, when what crawls on the living child's cheek are the worms of death, when flesh rots without a wound, what do the strong arms and the proud hearts of heroes do? This was a long way from the glorious story of war with its slashing swords, its sharp bayonets, its polished bullets, its exploded bombs, its red grenades. Here, death came in the head and in the heart, in the stomach, or the arms, and blood washed everything in a huge heroic wave. At OUREGANO rot gnawed at life: the story of man and earth, a primitive story in which man must conquer the earth before conquering himself. At OUREGANO, war was still centuries in the future.

Heroism is the color of what it fights. At OUREGANO it could only sense the tones of decomposition. Michel stumbled in front of the mass grave the hospital opened up for him. No longer able to make the gestures of the hero, he wanted to create those of the Chief Medical Officer. He demanded funds, medicines, going to see the Administrator, trembling as he placed his request on the desk and with it the meaning of his existence and the lives of thousands. It was for these others that he spoke. Monsieur Dubois listened and then told him what he had told every other doctor who had arrived in OUREGANO. This was Africa. Death, and therefore illness and suffering, did not carry the same weight as elsewhere. You couldn't worry about the way things were. In the end, it was much simpler that way. There was no scandal here because everything belonged to an imminent order that hid its mysteries. Nothing was logical but everything had to accept and was accepted in turn. Wasn't this the point of logic? He was to keep watch but to upset nothing. He liked this role of quiet witness, complacent and fatalistic. And since Michel didn't seem to understand, he sent him to Alexandrou, who was the purchasing agent for all medical and pharmaceutical supplies. He could check with him to see if there were any unused funds.

Alexandrou told Michel that not only was the budget for this year exhausted but the next year's was as well. He showed him the statements, the bill for the penicillin. He showed him the complete inventory of what the hospital owed. Forgetting that he was talking to Alexandrou, Michel spoke of quitting, of failure, of being trapped. His mouth filled with all sorts of energetic words that he would never again pronounce. He blamed N'Diop, the doctor who had preceded him, for managing the transition so badly. He cursed the authorities that had abandoned him thus. There was despair in this defeat, shame and the horror of losing his reputation, which was the terror of not living his dream. There was nothing, nothing more at all. There was only the wait until Michel would come to acknowledge this emptiness.

On the way out, Beretti tried to calm him. He had called him "Captain, Sir" with an unmistakable tone. He too had been in Indochina. In the name of the fraternity of war, he proposed his services; a trifle, to move money for food into the columns for medicines, for example. It would never be noticed because the Negroes didn't get any food at the hospital; their families brought everything they needed. Michel was as reassured by the promised solution as by Beretti himself, who brought him back to the past. They didn't talk about the present and they avoided speaking about themselves with the modesty that, by talking of others, always brings attention to one's self.

Albert Refons' van also came in due course to the market square. He came to ask what could be done for the school, following the same path as Michel Murano, Dubois first, Alexandrou second. There was no more money for the school than for the hospital. And what did he want, Refons? Chalk, a blackboard, desks and benches, Alexandrou had everything, didn't he? What would it be?

Albert didn't know what he wanted because he wanted it all and the enjoyment of working as a bonus. He wanted teachers, assistants, notebooks, and books. He wanted everything and at the same time he didn't want it because, in his dream, teaching excluded it all. Yet with Alexandrou he asked that his funds be accounted for under the old system, more power for the colonial school! What did the authorities expect from such an education? That all the children have it; that this education should initiate them unfailingly in the French language, the only language they would speak, the only language they would read. Their only means of communicating ultimately, the final triumph: You see, it's true, to speak and to speak about yourself, you must use French! Your independence, you say? What a laugh.

How is it possible to like one's job when all one does is perpetuate the unjust power that one hates? How not to hate oneself when every word forces the fresh mind to serve rules and laws that seem, here more than anywhere, unnatural? Most annoying was this force, coming from the children themselves, pushing him every day down this shameful path. They demanded the French language, the medium of reading and writing. And such faith they had in it! It was, atrociously, their only hope of a life, to get out of the mud where no one could read or write and into the ranks of administration, even if it meant at the prison, reserved for the initiated. French. It meant a little less hunger and perhaps better health. At best, Albert could have presented French as a tool, the way English was taught to the children of France, not for its beauty but because it was a "commercial" language. But French in OUREGANO was dishonest in other ways. You couldn't limit them to the social "Please pass the bread." That just muddied everything; it was the only route to anywhere. In History, Africa's past was excluded; it was a vast sleepy continent until the colonizer came to wake it up just to pacify it. In Geography, maps of Africa were color-washed in bright marshmallow pink, candy colors far showier than lemon yellow or almond green: the French pink went against nature.

For the children of OUREGANO the French language carried with it the absolute power of the written word over the spoken word. Albert found himself in a frustrating double bind, caught between the children and the Administration. The Administration knew it and expected it at the end of the year from the innovative schoolteachers, those who would not even bother to present a plan for the next year and those who would stubbornly defend plans: All very well and good, that, but there is no money. Yes, very nice, but have you considered what it would cost, in teachers alone? It was good for the teachers to "plan" in this way, nothing too dangerous there. By "planning" they kept themselves busy, and besides, their political evolution was visible in their successive years' plans. As for the rest of their time, well, the students kept them on their toes.

It was humiliating to have to ask for funding, for money, from Alexandrou, slumped into his horned armchair. But this didn't stop Albert. Everything was for sale in this world of intolerable solitude. Just to be able to speak was invaluable, for beneath his silence Alexandrou seemed to be listening. Apart from this disgusting ape, who would pay attention to him? Elise was interested only in her womb. Dubois interrupted him and sent him to Alexandrou. The students chanted their lessons. No one else saw him, save N'Diop who avoided him like the plague and whom he no longer tried to see because of Elise. It was pleasant to talk here. Every word was worth its weight in silver pieces; each idea was carefully evaluated with an eye to possible funding. Albert would have liked to dedicate his life to the principles of Freedom and Justice, but he settled in the name of the C.F.A. franc.*

What was humiliating for Albert was not so much having to speak to Alexandrou; he accepted this much without difficulty, as accepting his own deepest feelings, the lack of nobility, the selfishness that slipped into his projects. What was really important in what he proposed to Alexandrou, the children's well-being or his own? The tradesman's silence let him know that it was himself that his plans were about, himself above all. His voice cracked. He had at his disposal neither violence, nor anger: these were the weapons of fairness. When one begs for oneself, there are only supplication and tears. And, since he was asking for money, his pitiful request had the fetid odor of alms and charity. He did not feel shame in coming before Alexandrou in this way because he had already sunk beneath the level of self-respect. If he felt anything other than his own distress, it was revolt that seized him and from which there was no release, except into despair. As it was for the Administration, France was cruel to individuals. No way to know who was to blame. There was no speaking in the name of France without being suspected, tarred mon-

---

* Colonies Françaises d'Afrique. This franc was pegged to the French franc at a fixed rate.

strously with the brush of self-interest. Albert, in order to speak about himself, spoke of the children of OUREGANO.

He realized when he noticed that Alexandrou's attitude was hardening imperceptibly, that he was distressed, beside himself. He said something about the children, or the money, which came to the same thing as far as the fat man was concerned, pushing him into a defensive attitude. His dreams took over. In France, he had more or less accepted the compromises of teaching, because there had to be another place, where everything was possible. He was in this other place and he could not get out. Alexandrou understood him; Albert was not naïve. He didn't want to remake the world. He knew that was impossible. He asked only that the illusion of existing, of acting, of influencing the course of events, be preserved. Could he live if everything that mattered to him turned out to be as empty as the desert? Could he stand it if he managed to do nothing at the school, nothing in this country, nothing in his own family where the illusion was fading, the illusion of a love that had never been?

*

It was pleasant to see the handsome masks falling into ruin in the horned sitting room. Those who had worn them were somewhere else, out of time and space. Alexandrou knew that his silence weighed heavily. It made him inaccessible: he did not see; he listened. The speakers were others whose words exposed their very souls. Alexandrou's eyes mirrored the exterior; the plaintiffs saw in those eyes nothing but themselves. Up against this garbage heap invested with discretionary powers, they did not even imagine how wide their shot in the dark was. Alexandrou rejoiced in the privilege that put him in this position of power. Only the Administrator was capable of trumping the tradesman. But Alexandrou knew he would never do it; it would take too much effort. He had not gotten into this situation without Dubois' consent, without Dubois day after day delegating to him even the most trifling affairs in return for quietude, for silence, for mental vacancy. With Alexandrou there were no scenes.

In the horned sitting room, he had seen the Chief Medical Officer's great war machine disintegrate; he had seen the schoolmaster Refons' political certainties reduced to nothing. He had not said so much as a word. He had not lifted a finger to push them to despair. He had done nothing; heroes destroyed themselves. Alexandrou thought about all the weaknesses that heroism and passion covered. He knew the vulnerability of the big ideas behind which hid all the fragilities of the world. He was already convinced that violent destinies camouflaged individual disabilities and he was happy to have seen this confirmed twice within a few minutes by men as different as Murano and Refons. He loved above all the pathetic moment when a man bowed his head before the truth.

In the store, it was different with the women. Among the noodles, he was all-powerful, and since he guarded the huge refrigerator, the women, who would never have looked at him in the street, smiled at him graciously with their sweet, mincing mouths. They wanted a food-favor, to which their financial power entitled them, but they pretended to be coy. He wondered if they behaved like that at night with their husbands. The Murano woman, flashing her fiery eyes like a cornered doe.* Old lady Bonenfant, who pouted with her entire large mouth to reduce the size of her pitiful face. The second-rate schoolteacher…. Each one revealed her true self, the innate female self of compromise, always given to avoid being taken. On the days when deliveries were made, he felt like he was sleeping with each of them. It was ecstasy over two packets of butter, delirium for a pot of heavy cream, groans of pleasure for an extra Camembert. And yet these women were not hungry. They were far less hungry than the black people who also shopped, but in whom submission was not synonymous with loss of dignity.

Not content to be his prisoners in everyday life, incredibly, the colonizers named him the master of their pleasures. Under his roof at the MI-AMMIAM-GLOUGLOU, the idiots bought his whiskey at twice the cost and they thanked him happily. Even better, they had made him an honorary member, with no obligations, the only honorary member of the Club. And when the women came into the shop, they simpered: But why don't you come join us at the Club? Come on, come! We're going to throw a party. There'll be dancing…. Alexandrou demurred. Too much work. The

---

* See discussion in translator's preface.

women were stunned. Imagine! Someone who worked in OUREGANO!

*

All of OUREGANO's social life happened at the Club, called the SPORTS CLUB because of the tennis courts. At six o'clock the huge salons of the Residence were no longer lit up for cocktails, happy hours, or aperitifs. Darkness invaded the houses of the notables. The *boys* took the hurricane lamps from the dining room. They lit the covered areas that served as kitchens, and this squalid place took on an eerie aspect from the violet and blue lights. Every detail was unfailingly emphasized, the filth, the spiderweb, the cockroach running back and forth, the tears in the paint. The *boys*, without the white people, took refuge in the protective light. Huddled together they talked but never quarreled.

At the Club, the parents and the children gathered for an evening also conceived for the pleasure of being together in the light, the social light. The unknown was unwelcome. From the entrance, the carefully parked cars and vans revealed the presence of their owners. The latest arrival could greet them even before seeing the Muranos, the Dubois, or the Refons: Hmph, they're already here! A *poof* of impatience. If the motor stalled at the turn, the wife, thus detained, could open her window, panting to rejoin her counterparts. The children knew this well and they clamored to call the names of their friends whom they had only just left at the end of the school day. Don't think for a moment that the creation of the SPORTS CLUB had reconciled the inhabitants of OUREGANO and that their manifestations of impatience were signs of affection. Far from it; everything had remained in its original state but with a slightly exaggerated desire to rub shoulders, to dull the petty hatreds and the sufferings. Evening after evening Madame Bonenfant arrived cheerily to assure herself of what crucified her with anguish, the ascendancy of Madame Dubois. A pathological need sent Matilde hurtling toward the lights that no longer illuminated her well-worn outfits, toward the eyes that did not look at her.

When they understood that the Club was finished, that is, there was nothing left to invent, the members recognized the end of the chaotic amusement of all beginnings and gave themselves over to rules and governance. There had to be a president, a treasurer, someone in charge of sports, someone in charge of organizing parties. They voted. Dubois was elected president unanimously; the Bonenfants didn't even have the courage to vote for themselves. Dubois was thereafter called Monsieur President. Madame Dubois became Madame President. Since she was dynamic, she was also named chair of entertainments. Bonenfant was the treasurer. Murano, the former soldier, was in charge of sports. The results of these elections surprised no one because there was no other imaginable reality than the one they lived; they were delighted or wounded just as they would have been in public life. The Bonenfants ruminated with bitterness over the whole thing. They had wanted to be the Presidents. It tortured them yet at the same time they wouldn't have imagined that they could be in first place.

They were all satisfied to find themselves together and to study one another, as a lesson. Upon arrival at the Club, they knew right down to the ground the essence of their relationships, the obligations that allowed them to survive, the conditions of their participation. During the day they lived a kind of truncated existence at home or at the office; at the Club in the evening it was life in its entirety. Being together, being a group, submissive to the Dubois but lording it over the Refons.... This transformation was facilitated by quantities of alcohol, by the cleavage of the women. Yet the hours spent here only let off steam. They obeyed the laws of life. The group pretended to be alive.

*

Madame Dubois was a past master of parlor games. She mined her memory for ideas, organizing an evening of METRO STATIONS in which each person had to wear something that would evoke the name of a subway station. It was out of the question for just anyone to decode just anything. They drew lots to see who would go first and the person whose image had been guessed went next, and so forth; otherwise it would have been too confusing and the game wouldn't have lasted a minute. Madame Bonenfant, who arrived carrying a small knitted gold purse, was decrypted immediately. She would certainly have been disappointed with this failure if her husband had not himself been a great success.

He sniggered with delight. No one had figured it out. There he was, standing as tall as his short stature permitted, extending a curved leg to the anxious group. The audience saw nothing and began to get agitated, wanting above all to guess correctly. Monsieur Bonenfant didn't want to give any clues, but around him hundreds of itineraries had been humbled. African Parisians and Parisian provincials had crossed the capital in the same way. In the end they all came to this place, shifted about in the same way that bound them together today. Only Bonenfant had detoured from this trajectory; his professional journey was not limited to the Ministry of France Overseas. He held a secret, perhaps the secret of pleasure, a secret that would allow him to occupy for once the place that Dubois routinely stole from him. He wasn't going to let it go easily. He derided the group for their difficulty in guessing by climbing on a table to give them a better look. They were exasperated now; he lifted his pants leg and they saw that he wore ugly little shoes. What could be said of a man wearing a clog fashioned out of aluminum foil, the kind you put chocolates in at Christmas with lots of straw and decorate with a huge bow stiffened with wire? Disappointed, the members of the club turned their attention to other things.*

This triumph gave the Judge a prestige he would never have found in his daily chores. He knew things; he had lived; he had read. Madame Dubois asked him to organize a literary evening in which, like the METRO STATIONS game, the participants would wear a clue to the title of a novel. It was not easy. Put on the spot like that, the members of the Club could not name a single one. Thinking about it though, they came up with many, although they could not all be used. If *The Red and the Black* (one red sleeve and one black sleeve) was too obvious, what could be done with more contemporary titles.... It smacked of heresy, that did,

---

* Constant seems to wish to leave her readers as much perplexed as the members of the Club, for it is impossible to guess what Metro station is intended here. Madame Bonenfant's gold purse is understood by French readers as La Bourse, the Metro stop on Line Three nearest the Paris Stock Exchange.

and it led down a dangerous path. For Refons, there was only one novel worth reading, *The Human Condition,* and his heart was so committed to its contents that he could not imagine any other. Matilde wore a rose pinned on the strap of her white dress. She didn't doubt that literature had used bundles of this flower. She was this flower;she was all of them.

What was remarkable in all these games that animated the life of the Club was the frenzy the Bonenfants demonstrated to participate, a mad pleasure that erased their secondary status. At the Club they no longer held back. They wanted to laugh, to play, to have a good time, each time better than the last. Bonenfant even had a special vocabulary for talking about it. The man who weighed his words now spoke of A NIGHT OUT, HAVING A WILD TIME, GOING ALL OUT, REALLY COOKIN.' In short it was PARTY TIME.... The Club arena became a miserable retreat in which despite their efforts they encountered the sad regrets of their previous PARTIES. Thus, in at least one of France's provinces, the name OUREGANO became synonymous with pleasure. The French in France who went to the theater, to the movies, to restaurants, balls, and concerts would have envied the Bonenfants who had known how to UNWIND.

*

For Christmas, Madame Dubois got the children involved. She wanted to put on a Nativity pageant. They had to recruit outside the ranks of the Club. Yvonne was the Holy Virgin, the oldest of the Bonenfants was Joseph, and the smallest of the babies at the Dutch Mission was the Baby Jesus. The others gathered as the Three Kings or as Angels, a category suited for eternal extension, very useful for all the unclassable elements, indistinguishable as to height, sex, or color. Moses was Balthazar. Tiffany, with her braids undone, was Melchior; it was not a great role for a little girl. They had to sing: *We Three Kings of Orient aaaare; Bearing gifts, we traverse afaaa....* The curtain opened on Christmas in Provence: In a cardboard box slept the little crèche figures, the shepherd, the blacksmith, and Jesus the Redeemer.... Not only did Madame Dubois turn the children into divine or historical characters, but she transformed them into statuettes. She was all-powerful.

Big Yvonne stood so still under her blue veil that she trembled. The Bonenfant boy, skinny as a rail, standing next to her couldn't hold his expression of adoration very well looking at the pallid, screaming child whose stiff little arms reached for the sky. Moses made a rather bony Balthazar and Tiffany was monstrous as a little girl in a beard. Moses carried a tray of fruit from the Dubois garden on which the mangoes had already begun to rot giving off an odor of acetone. Tiffany held in her clenched fingers Madame Bonenfant's jewelry box, a black box on top of which two entwined dancers twirled. It made an odd picture to offer to the infant Son of God, this little man in a shiny tuxedo and this little woman in her skirt of pink tulle. The decorations were perfect; Madame Dubois had not skimped on the cotton batting or the construction paper. She had suspended a number of "ornaments" from the branches of a guava tree—Father Christmases on skis, ugly gnomes with illuminated features, chubby-cheeked little angels, paper stars, glass balls. There was something for everyone. The evening ended with everyone singing "Little Father Christmas."

For Mardi Gras, the adults really let loose. Madame Dubois appeared as Mélusine. With a wand in her hand, wasn't she the fairy godmother of the Club? She was charming. Madame Bonenfant was more classically disguised as a doll with a little skirt just covering her behind, anklets, and a large bow in her hair set in tiny curls. She made a remarkably good doll, turning her eyes, closing her lips, and walking in a jerky manner, elbows held in tightly, palms facing forward, really an impressive imitation. She achieved a great success that lightly eclipsed the more discreet apparitions of Elise, dressed as a country maid with a basket on her arm, and Matilde as Princess Mathilde.* No one recognized Mathilde in Matilde. Each of them remained a little obsessed with herself or himself. The men, especially, felt uneasy. Their outfits did not do justice to their prestige. They were afraid of appearing ridiculous. Refons was admired

---

* Daughter of Jerome Bonaparte, youngest of Napoleon's brothers. She almost married Napoleon III but thought better of it. She later married and divorced Anatole Demidov and subsequently became a patron of writers, no matter what their political persuasion.

as Augustus, although they pretended not to recognize him in his costume; Bonenfant tried surreptitiously to pull on his gladiator tunic, which didn't quite cover his thick thighs.... They set to drinking and it all seemed benign; the extravagances were no longer daring.

The evening went on until Madame Dubois' bonnet fell off, the gladiator's epaulettes curled up to his stiff collar, and the drunken doll collapsed. The Judge carried out on his shoulder a sniffling doll, suddenly soft, tender, and desperate. No one wanted to prolong this orgy and they said goodnight on the vision of the retreating underclothes of Madame Bonenfant, who had obviously not foreseen this departure as she was wearing her black, everyday, heavy-duty underwear. They all sobered up quickly, seeing that they had gone too far. They were all guilty, not so much of having drunk too much, but by disguising themselves they had exhibited an immoderate taste for excessive pleasure. Behind their masks, they had come close to the dangerous edge where one invents oneself. They had seen that there was nothing to be gained there.

*

With the sports Michel did no better. He organized a tennis tournament, men's singles that didn't please anyone; as far as the men were concerned, luck was against them. For the women gathered together on the little terrace, each fault was recorded as a personal injury. Watching their husbands running, gasping, sweating, the image they had had of a worldly sport was altered by these miserable actors. The players were no less dissatisfied. They didn't play for fun, or for the group effort, or out of habit going back to their lithe blond youth on the green courts of Sussex or the clay courts of vacations in Biarritz. They played for no reason, or rather out of snobbism, for something easy and beautiful that escaped them.

Michel was blind to the bored children watching their fathers, neither stronger nor better, from the edge of the lawn. He was blind to the wives, who suffered because they were seated and because the men were running, the bitter volley of disdain: You could have gotten that one! Michel was unfeeling when it came to the competitions, a player out of breath confirmed that the ball was out, and as for the logistics, the changing of sides took more and more time. He held them to the point of exasperation, until their weaknesses were visible, until it was no longer a question of being off one's game or being rusty, but one of being out of shape, one of age and clumsiness.

He gave the final blow by organizing a men's doubles. The others agreed to play. They wouldn't be alone in their misery. Ah! To play with a partner meant no longer being the victim only of one's own swing, too hard if the ball goes out, too soft if it dies before reaching the net in the zone where a good shot—how are such shots possible?—becomes a sorry waste. Accuse the other, too close, too far, never gettable, call out "Your ball!" when the ball is already lost, let the weight, the excessive weight of an expensive fault, fall on the one who didn't know, exaggerate if necessary, bring it up to the others, sign the whole movement with the signature of powerlessness and disdain, with a finger pointed at the partner. Yes, they wanted this game to crucify the other, to prove *a contrario* their superiority.

There was a moment of pause when they realized they needed a fourth. Their haste to settle accounts had blinded them to this lack as they agreed to Michel's proposal. Why not ask Beretti to be a fourth? Michel went to summon him from the bar. He had never played? Michel convinced him. All he had to do was pay attention and address the ball; he couldn't miss. He said, Have you ever shot a rifle? Well, it's the same thing. It didn't take more than that to convince Beretti, suddenly excited and dressed in a remarkable outfit of knitted navy blue shorts that looked more like overalls than Lacoste. Their impatience had been such that on the court they hardly noticed the little man in blue. He was strong, Beretti was, hard, quick, tense, unbeatable.

The game began. Bonenfant and Dubois sent a volley of balls toward Beretti. Surprised, he made large swings, missing everything. They were feeling the rising chant of an easy win that makes for happy handshakes at the end of a game. But then everything went wrong. The game was controlled by Michel: Get back, I'll cover you. Go on! Attack! On the left! Holding his racket in both hands, the body almost hidden behind the shoulder, Beretti became adroit, sublime, dangerous. In front, sideways, only his face toward his adversary, dancing on one foot, then the other, bounding across the court, getting everything, sending unexpected volleys, dropping them in, whistling past, deadly shots. Beretti seemed intent on sending shattering explosions into their faces. Instead of trying to make the other player run for the ball, he seemed to want the ball to hit the opponent, to finish him off. Incomprehension, then horror grew over their faces when they understood that in playing tennis, Beretti was at war. It became clear that you couldn't play just anything with just anybody. Better not to play at all. Games were dangerous in and of themselves. They were forbidden to the children, but the children had stopped playing games a long time before.

III

At the foot of the drive Tiffany watched for the van that went around to collect the schoolchildren. Well before it appeared she heard the rumbling of the motor and the crackling of the tires on the gravel surface. Matilde insisted that her daughter wait at the side of the road. With her head still in a story that was too old for her and that disturbed her mind, with her heart still longing for the latest animal collected, with her fingers lingering in the sheep's wool that had been bought under an awning as the animal was prepared to be sacrificed, Tiffany, on these mornings, thought neither of her lessons, nor her breakfast, nor her clothes that she often couldn't find, nor of her hair that she did not know how to braid.

Matilde was always picking up the things her daughter left all over the house. She braided, dressed, found shoes, stuffed into a schoolbag all that she could find that looked like schoolwork, and then she demanded that Tiffany, who was unable to swallow her tea because her throat was in a knot, hurry up. Well before the bus arrived Matilde "sent her off" because "she couldn't take any more." "Tiffany had exhausted her." And Tiffany, at the end of the drive, unconscious of the whirlwind that had propelled her there, the *topee** pushed down to her eyebrows, waited, her hollow stomach filled with anxiety, for the fearsome vehicle that would take her away from what she held dearest. She had so much to do here and so little to do there where she was being taken. So much to do with the sheep that she had not petted enough, with the last page that she had not finished, with the small antelope doe that she didn't know if she would find alive on her return.

In the van, Big Yvonne was already there with her long beige braids on either side of her head, falling on her shoulders, slithering into the gaps between her large chest and her arms. Yvonne spent a lot of time pulling them out, holding them up with sure and quick gestures that

---

* A canvas and cork colonial-style helmet.

showed she was in charge. Even if in the morning she let them escape, as soon as she was in class, she never missed a chance to impose her discipline on them. Her braids knew that they would be tied together at the back with a barrette. Tiffany's braids were nothing like these long soft coils. Short and stiff, so tightly woven that they didn't move, they framed the little face. Watching the perpetual agitation of Yvonne's braids, Tiffany touched her own to reassure herself. She put her fingers into them, just there; you couldn't even get a fingernail in, hard and dark.

In front of the Residence, the van collected the Bonenfant boys and, with the littlest one just old enough to be learning to write, this added to the excitement. The Bonenfant boys refused to get in through the door, but, putting a foot on the mudguards, heaved themselves in through the window, falling onto the seat; it made them giggle. They pulled Yvonne's braids but getting only the most cursory disdain in response they began tapping on the window that separated them from the driver, making faces at him. It was a long ride. They settled down at the windows to insult passersby with gestures and loud remarks. They mixed their imitation of childlike African dialect with the most obscene language they knew in French. What they liked best was to pass a schoolboy, from their own class if possible, Moses or someone else, walking to school. As soon as Big Yvonne, whom this sight drew from her usual silence, announced, Hey, African! (as if all those who walked to school were not Africans), they let loose vulgarities they had forgotten because they couldn't use them at home. They offered these and others they had never used, having only just heard them recently, without knowing if they were really offensive or on the contrary rather mild. They tried them out haphazardly. With all this new vocabulary, the younger one, who was just learning to read, got quite wound up.

Tiffany was very quiet in her corner, doing nothing that could draw any sort of attention to herself from the Bonenfant boys. All things considered, she was just as happy to see them hanging halfway out the window belching their filth. When they pulled themselves back inside to see what effect they had had, Tiffany laughed a contained, sharp little laugh. She knew that the moment would not be long in coming when they would get to her and her heart was beating fast. It would happen when the truck stopped at the small market in front of Alexandrou's shop. This stop had become a daily ritual since Madame Bonenfant, who loaned the van and the driver, took this opportunity to drop off her order with Alexandrou.

In the gray market, Tiffany saw only the old leper woman without hands, without feet, without a nose, able to stand only by leaning on a stick that she held tightly between her forearms. The Bonenfant boys saw her too and they called her over loudly: Come here, come here. You, come! She has something for you to eat, pointing to Tiffany. The old woman ran as fast as she could on her stumps, using the stick for support. She heaved her whole body in a terrible effort. Sometimes the driver had finished and the van drove away under the approaching gaze of the old woman; sometimes he took forever and the leper woman got to Tiffany. The child lowered her eyes. Frozen, dying, she did not want to see, and she heard the sound of the stumps rapping against the window pane, trying to get her attention. With this sound, the world no longer existed.

*

After the market, Tiffany recovered as best she could. Big Yvonne was not much help. At best, if Tiffany's silence and pallor lasted a long time, she said to the boys: You are stupid. And the boys answered her: Stupid, yourself. Arriving at the school, there was no counting on Elise either. Turned toward the blackboard where she was writing the date, she didn't see them come in. She said: Take your seats. Be quiet. Quiet! Take out your notebooks. Draw a line. Write the date. And school started. Terror growled in Tiffany's stomach; her heart bayed. With the pen that she didn't feel in her fingers, she copied a date that she didn't see. Fear beat on her head and ran down her legs; her knees began to tremble. The lesson went on, unperturbed.

To calm herself Tiffany told herself stories; she cradled herself with words that she chanted. The beginning of a fairy tale, a bit of a song for which she didn't know the tune: O Prince, you are malicious, you have killed my white duck. What she imagined grew from the embroidered figures on the hem of her dress. On the gingham set in chain stitch were little houses, a blue river, red fish, primitive flowers. Tiffany looked at them intensely and was sorry that these designs weren't oriented upside down; she would have been able to contemplate them more easily, instead of right side up for people who weren't interested in them.

For Tiffany school was nothing but a succession of tragic events. She had hardly entered her private world when she had to succumb to the thousand abuses inflicted upon her by Elise. Grammar quiz: she remained mute. The soft words of the duck, of the little house and the blue river or Rose Red and Rose White danced in her head. What difference did the past tense of the verb "to finish" make? If she had opened her mouth, she would have said something else! Dictation: she shuffled letters, nothing but letters. Meaning was not in the text but in the quiet she clung to in her head. Mathematics: Where did the letter *h* go? Mathematics with no *h*? How many times do I have to tell you! Spell!

What did you do today? Matilde demanded of Tiffany. She meant of course at school, not on the way to school or on the way home. Matilde wanted to know what Tiffany had done in class as soon as she sat down, all that missing time, already forgotten. Tiffany didn't know what she had done. Like yesterday and the day before, it didn't change and it would never change.... She stammered, dictation, mathematics. Saying it, she felt important because for her mother the *h* was not a problem. But this was not what interested Matilde. She wanted to know if Tiffany had done WELL or BADLY. Tiffany answered, "I don't know." "It wasn't graded." Matilde had to stop there.

Between the sheep that the cook had not yet slaughtered and the little antelope doe that was weakening, that couldn't get up anymore, her feet remaining curled under her white belly, so stricken that she no longer tried to leap away when touched, Tiffany came back to life as if the lives of these two animals already destined to die rested in her hands. She thanked them for existing in songs, in embroidered designs on her dress. She was taken so intensely with them that her dreams came true there, and with one hand on the sheep's neck and the other on the neck of the diminutive doe, pulling the two heads toward her knees, she imagined the end of a new fairy tale.

*

Some sounds could be heard, like the footsteps of the first gardener, who passed by with over filled baskets, and the other one, who adroitly manipulated his machete under the windows to bring the bougainvillea into line. They alone had the right to make noise during the afternoon *sieste*. Matilde and Michel's *sieste*! But having heard them often, Tiffany knew that these noises moved. The kitchen gardener went by quickly and the trudging sounds marked the amplitude of his gait that tramped toward the kitchens; the one trimming the shrubbery, he made a back-and-forth movement, a kind of swinging flight that clicked sharply. The masses of flowers fell on the ground where nothing held them but silence. Today there was a different noise. A noise that pushed, that took hold, a noise that wrapped itself all around the house. Tiffany took enough assurance from this to get up, which was forbidden, and to go onto the terrace to see.

THEY were there, all assembled; they were there as never before, emerging as in her worst nightmares. She recognized them before she could actually see them, and it was only after she had walked to the extreme edge of the terrace that her eyes opened upon all those living wounds, those absent faces, those mutilated hands that were like tree bark, those feet wrapped in rubber, bundled and tied with string. Tiffany looked at them straight in the face from the first step where she felt the sharp ridge under the pads of her bare feet. It took all her concentration not to fall or slide toward them, toward the closest ones who stood there just beyond the fifth step. Tiffany knew that when she was in a hurry, these five steps were nothing; her outstretched legs swallowed them lightly and not once had she ever stepped on the second one, the third one, or the fourth. Today these five steps protected her from the void.

Michel came out and the screaming started. Tiffany didn't understand. She saw only the horror, and then the anger. Horror, shaking with anger. Time seemed to stand still until a leper, apparently the chief, revealed the cause of the riot. He had a large basin brought to the stairs from which two lepers poured out the contents. Pink flesh, bloody, trembling, covered with dirt and flies. With a stick, they spread the ignoble magma on the stone step, as if to show the extent and gravity of their own wounds. When he took up the head of a sheep with white eyes, the hump of a zebu, greasy and yellow, a hoof, an antler, Tiffany understood that it was the meat from the butchering and not their own flesh that the lepers exhibited there. They wanted meat, real meat, not what Beretti had thrown at them once again. They shouted and the flies went back and forth from the meat to their wounds, grazing Tiffany's face.

Michel had cans of condensed milk brought and the lepers threw themselves on it shoving so brutally that some of them fell onto the driveway. Soon there was no more milk and Michel sent for oil, and after the oil, flour. Matilde took corn from the chickens and potatoes bought too dearly from Alexandrou. And the lepers did not leave. Quite the reverse, they waited and waited for someone to fight their hunger, a hunger that had been eating them for such a long time. They kept coming down from the hospital, up from the village. They came out of the bushes, wrapping themselves around the house, squeezing it with the powerful force of their pain. There was nothing left to give away. Michel spoke to them but they didn't listen. Michel said that their very legitimate complaints would be taken care of. They waited. Michel gave his word, guaranteed that it would happen. But the lepers still waited.

Finally, they had to get help; the *boys* had taken refuge in the living room with all the windows closed. Michel tried to telephone the Administrator, then the Judge. It was Beretti who arrived driving a truck straight into the crowd. It gave way. Military policemen got out of the truck with long spikes, and with whips they beat back the lepers, who ran away. All around the house, the bush trembled with feet racing into the woods. Not long afterward, the leaves stopped trembling. The policemen took away the meat. A *boy* stuck his head out the door and threw a large pail of water over the soiled steps. Night fell and the *boys* lit the lamps. Tiffany listened from her bed to the damp darkness dripping with the steps of the policemen patrolling the grounds.

*

The house was not the haven that Tiffany had imagined. It had not protected her from the lepers any more than from the van that collected the children for school, and Tiffany wondered if it were not dangerous to live with adults. Not only did they not provide help when she needed it, but they attracted to themselves, and thus to her, numerous ill effects she could have done without, not the least of which was the revolt of the lepers. She passionately scrutinized their faces to see even a trace of terror that resembled her own. She saw nothing. Michel pouted. Matilde, excited, talked about abundance. Since they understood, perhaps they could tell her, and Tiffany used the recent events as a pretext to talk about the daily encounter with the leper woman that had been going on for several months.

She did not say: The Bonenfant boys frighten me with a leper woman. They call her over to touch me. But she did ask: How do you get it? Matilde, who looked at her disheveled daughter, bare feet and dirty hands, took advantage of this occasion to tell her that it was from going barefoot, from not washing your hands, and that dirt and the fingers in the nose were sure signs of suffering from the dreaded disease. Did Tiffany understand? Tiffany felt her feet curling up and her nose itching. This illness was confused in her mind with the sufferings of the soul. The lepers were bad just as she was dirty and disobedient. In a way it was reassuring. At least one knew where it came from; it wasn't like microbes that came out of the blue, hitting you without warning. Now she had been warned. Still, Matilde's explanation left her unsatisfied, there had to be something else. Indefinitely, she replayed the film of the revolt in her head. More and more it seemed obvious to her that they were hungry and that they had been beaten. The fear in their mutilated eyes faded; the only thing that remained in Tiffany's memory was how fast they had fallen on the unimaginable food, sealed cans, raw potatoes, cereals in the grain, and how fast they had fled into the woods running from the policemen's sticks. The nice policemen of reality became the ogres in Tiffany's story, and the awful lepers and their revolt became the poor, simply the poor.

One morning Tiffany put into her schoolbag a can of condensed milk opened at breakfast, and during the entire trip in the van she held her schoolbag straight up. In front of the small market, she looked for the leper woman and offered her the can. The woman, no longer expecting anything, didn't take it at first, and it was when the Bonenfant boys said "yum-yum" rubbing their hands over their stomachs that she took the tin in her forearms. It was time to go and the van pulled away. Tiffany didn't know if the old woman had eaten. She brought her bread, a large piece, and everything else she could find, including, one day, a Camembert, a rare commodity, because it was cleaner than most. The old woman held out her arms. It seemed to Tiffany that she would never be able to fill the void in the hollow of her arms, joined at the wrists to hold the offerings.

Tiffany wasn't afraid anymore. What was alarming was not understanding, hearing a call for mercy without being able to identify it. Now, she knew: they wanted food. And since Michel had tried to keep them away from the house by giving away their reserves, Tiffany made friends with the old woman by feeding her.

*

Moses and Tiffany continued to ignore each other in class. To see them, one behind the other absorbed in their tasks, so different that they didn't read at the same rate or have the same difficulty with a math problem, no one would have guessed that they were indispensable to one another. Did they even know it themselves? Their accord was so great, so deep that neither ever doubted that what the other did would suit. They never waited for each other; at the moment when one might have had to wait, the other always appeared. Between them there was a coordination as deep as the gestures of love.

On Thursdays, Tiffany climbed out the window of her bedroom, slipped through the giant ficus trees, so yellow that they competed with the sun. She sneaked along the path saturated with dust, with light, with heat. While she was walking, wherever she went, he emerged from a bush, from behind a tree, from the mouth of a shadow. Tiffany didn't slow down; he sped up and they went along together. In the beginning their friendship had been only this walk, quick and silent, this joint flight, this passion of each for the other, roughed in together side by side. It was a walk toward something in the distance, a physical need, a consilience. For there was tenderness in being there together and in being each one's other, point and counterpoint.

They had discovered The Place and had sniffed out all its resources: the carcass of a pickup truck, completely fleshless, eaten away, abandoned. The bush had swallowed it and a tree that had grown up through what remained of the motor had fixed it to the ground. They had not seen it immediately and if it hadn't been for the glint on the windshield in the branches, they wouldn't have noticed it. The abandoned vehicle was sticky with moss, with plants growing in the cabin; they thought the tree that ran right up through a hole in the hood splendid. They weeded the inside. Moses cut several branches so that the doors could open on their hinges; they disconnected the running board. They could climb in and close the doors. They possessed a house. It was their ship.

They were not frightened by a nest of snakes that had made a home in the pickup's only seat. It was Moses' job to pull them out with a stick and to crush the twisted nest. They tied the doors shut with string. Moses took the wheel in his two hands. He didn't try to turn it but stayed immobile, his eyes fixed on the foliage that crushed up against the windshield, streaked with cracks. There was still a rearview mirror; it was Tiffany's first mirror. She looked deeply into her own eyes; they were gray with little points of gold. Large. Behind the sadness, spears of rebellion.

Now that they had taken possession the time of their occupation began. Tiffany brought fountain pens, ink, and packets of prescription paper:

> Captain-Doctor MURANO
> Doctor to the Colonial Troops
> Former Resident at the Hospitals of Bordeaux
> Croix de Guerre

They wrote, fountain pen poised at the ends of the fingers. They dipped it too deeply into the bottle and covered thumb and index with ink. They learned to write backwards, upside down, from right to left. They put all their passion into dictations.

Tiffany dictated while Moses wrote. Since Tiffany had no texts, she invented sentences appropriate to this barbarous exercise. There was a definite tone for dictation. There could be no everyday words, only difficult expressions, traps, homophones. The verbs had to be in difficult tenses; everything that was not the present was difficult for Tiffany. Finally, the meaning had to have nothing to do with reality, so that from the first words the pupil would feel lost: How will I write that? Tiffany tried to put the anguished impression of a freefall into words.

Furnished with these principles and several painful experiences that lay in her memory, Tiffany composed for Moses dictations that she thought impossible: The Mulhouse storks circled for a long time over the bronzed tips of the lime trees. On the sawhorses of the wedding table, Marguerite placed the buckwheat bread and the soup boiling with slivers of garlic...and so on with "they were made to sing," "physiognomy," "mathematics"...until she ran out of traps because Moses never asked her to go easy. He would never have stopped Tiffany to ask her how to spell "Mulhouse," which he wouldn't have been likely to know. Neither would he ever have asked her to slow down. It was all part of the game, to dictate as fast as possible so that the writer could not take notes. The point was to make the writer despair. Tiffany didn't want to make Moses suffer, only to play the game for real, in its smallest details. These dictations were not corrected; Tiffany would have been incapable of finding errors. She didn't read what Moses had written; she was happy to plant a huge zero in the margin, underlining it twice. Sometimes she added, VERY POORLY DONE. Moses accepted without a word this sanction associated unfailingly with the functions of authority that Tiffany performed. They never knew that Moses wrote the texts perfectly, without a single error.

*

Books appeared later in the pickup truck. Tiffany brought them to supplement her imagination. She dictated texts like: Yes, he said to Philinte, who had come immediately upon learning of the difficulties his friend had suffered and who forced himself to be calm, showing him the failures that such calumnies had brought. Yes, I am going. Call a halt to the case? No. No. I would rather lose twenty thousand francs and buy with this sum the right to hate human injustice forever. You cannot, despite your customary indulgence, deny that my anger is justified.... What case was this? Why this formidable sum of money? Moses, who had chuckled at the "calumnies," at the "customary indulgences" wanted to know more. There was in this text a unity that he was unaccustomed to finding in Tiffany's wild imaginings. They read *The Misanthrope* in the version *Molière for Children*; they read every word. Then Tiffany brought *Stories and Tales by Corneille* and *Stories and Tales by Racine*.

Moses loved Corneille; he pretended to be Sévère, Horace, Cinna. Tiffany preferred Racine. There were so many queens and kings, so many princesses, so many gods. She loved Iphegenia but soon preferred Eriphile. The surprise ending touched her deeply. They no longer sat hunched over the same book, but side by side, their backs against the rails of the pickup, their knees up to their chins. They read intensely, following with a finger so as not to skip a line while looking at the illustrations: Britannicus crowned with roses and lying on a bed had let the contents of a goblet spill onto the ground; Athalie like a malevolent fairy spreading out an endless royal cape; Esther crying at the feet of Assuerus with his pointed beard. When she grew tired of reading, Tiffany revived the pretty blackness of the shiny pictures with a finger dipped in saliva. Britannicus' goblet, Athalie's cape, and Assuerus' beard began to shine like so many symbols of death. With her index finger, Tiffany traced among the three images the line of trouble.

The gods whose shadow haunted the plays revealed themselves to be both more monstrous and less fatal in the light of the *Golden Legends* of Antiquity. The two children adopted certain ones: Jupiter for the thunder, Hermes for his winged feet, Diane and her "gazelle".... But Moses asked too many questions: Why were they dressed that way? Where did they really live? Where were they now? Tiffany could not answer. It's old, she said. Moses wanted to know more: What did Jesus have to do with it? What place did the Son of God have in the realm of the gods, all of them sons and fathers of gods? Tiffany was supposed to know. They were white, white gods, like her. Legend and theater became synonyms for history and life.

Tiffany felt very Christian when they read *The Marvelous Story of the Martyrs of Uganda*. As a future martyr, she pardoned Moses, a future persecutor. It had been true, so it would be true. More than anything, the fatality of the real affected her. The real was the only value they granted to literature. It's true because it is written, pleaded Tiffany. If it's true, then it is magic, responded Moses, who swung between a banal reality of survival and magic. And if magic impressed Tiffany, reality seduced Moses. Magic was happiness or beauty; reality was courage and glory.

They agreed however that Robinson was better than anything else in terms of literary perfection. They read *Robinson Crusoe* and convinced themselves that in their situation they needed matches, a rifle, and goats. With their heads together they gobbled up *Robinson of Pempei*, *The Swiss Family Robinson*, and finished up with *The Robinsons in the Mountains*. They had found in this book everything they wanted. Moses became Gaspard and Tiffany was the admirable Nelly. They memorized the book. Using a borrowed vocabulary, they expressed between them a tenderness they could never have dared share in their everyday lives.

*

Moses' village was that of his ancestors, not just the village of his father and grandfather, but going farther back still, the village of the father of his father and of the father of that father, almost to the time of the spider and the hyena when the animals could speak. Tiffany was surprised that mud and straw held up better than the castles in history books. Moses told how this village was the first village, the village of the birth of the tribe, a long time ago...it was exactly the same...not this one but the same mud walls, the same straw on the roofs. It was a good village, but then the illness had come. The people slept and they died. So the sorcerer had said that it was under a curse. The ancestors of the ancestors must have had to abandon it leaving behind the dead and dying. They had built another village, farther away, near the river for water, a good location, really good, that one.

And the illness had come back. They had gone farther away, once, twice, three times in the space of a single lifetime, always more or less close to the river and each time the illness had chased them away. One day, it was in the time when his father's father was still a child, while looking for a new location, they had found a place that the bush seemed to have spared; it was cleared, there were traces of huts and fires. The oldest among them remembered being children in this place. They had returned to the first village, brought there by the water that made them ill and by the water sickness, they had come full circle. The successive abandonment of all that had gone into their history had brought them nothing, unless it was to demonstrate the permanence of unhappiness and the weaknesses of human efforts. Moses' grandfather and his father had abdicated once and for all in the name of the village.

It was a marvelous and cruel story like the legends of slavery. There had to be a hero who would win the battle for the closed space guarded by Evil, a magician or a sage, someone who conjured the evil spirit, who would wake the sleeping village after a hundred years. If Moses was proud of being born in the cradle of his ancestors, he was even more proud of being the one that destiny had chosen. He told Tiffany the fabulous story of his birth, when one after another sorcerers had made predictions, the conjunction of a moon with five branches and the baobab tree that had opened from its middle, with a stunning scream. All during the night of his birth, while his mother was supported by the older women, prodigious signs kept appearing around the village in an unheard-of series, like a meteor shower before a storm.

Together they did magical things, such as collecting feathers to tie them up in sevens, modeling statuettes of mud, cutting wood into the form of a cross, mixing their own hair with animal hair, finding round and square stones, walking with the left foot always in front. Little things that meant nothing but that persuaded them of their magical nature. Moses, because he knew it, Tiffany, because she felt better in the magical than in the real. She felt very powerful since the world had opened up to her a story beyond what could be seen, a story that concerned her secretly. Whether Elise asked her to read page seventeen (seven was good) or eighteen (eight plus one made nine and nine was bad), it made a difference. She read well or badly according to the number that she had recognized beneath its innocuous appearance and interpreted as a magical sign. The number had told her even before she began to read. If sometimes she made a mistake, it was not the sign that was at fault but her interpretation.

Since Moses had initiated her into the magical secrets of things, Tiffany was fascinated by the smallest details of her life; she did nothing without a marker, usually a number. She counted her steps; she counted the lines in her notebooks; she counted the stars and the white stains on the back of a jerboa, the petals of flowers as long as there were more than five. She counted on her fingers; everything indicated good or ill. It was good to have a reason for being.

*

Paradoxically, water was scarce in OUREGANO. The river that ran all along the plain, red and gray, the rains that beat upon the earth for days and days digging deep ravines that filled with water, the leaves green and full of sap, the water holes around which women gathered, did not approach the kind of water Tiffany desired, clear water, transparent water, blue water. There was of course the water in the cistern that supplied the house with rainwater but it was forbidden. It had taken a very hot day during the *sieste* when her parents were absent for Tiffany to risk it. The water was tepid and didn't bring her as much pleasure as she had thought. The shouts of the cook, who had seen her on the roof, did not leave her the time to rethink her first impression.

Water for playing was what she wanted; there was some at the Bonenfants'. The Judge had had a cement basin built, covered in a blue paint that peeled under the fingers. They had pretentiously called it a swimming pool. The water was refilled by the water carriers; in the morning it crawled with tadpoles in all stages of evolution and toads that died on the bottom with their feet splayed. Madame Bonenfant had invited Tiffany: She may come whenever she likes. She didn't go because she must not "disturb" and because the water was "putrid." How could it putrefy, this immaterial substance that was the color of the sky, itself immaterial and filled with huge clouds? The water in the pool vibrated with the rhythm of the sky and the clouds running up there where it made soft, smooth waves, in a tender, dreamlike stream.

Moses taught Tiffany that water drew nourishment from the earth. After the heavy rains made the river overflow its banks, an immense lake of steel poured forth, so dark that it reflected in the sky, tarnishing the azure with its gray shadow where clouds no longer floated. The river had staked a claim on the sky. Everything that was ultimately hollow, honey-combed, potholed, rutted filled with water and held it. And the sky re-flected these points of darkness, black stars of the daytime. You didn't have to go far to find this water; it was everywhere, on the tennis courts, behind the house, at the bottom of hillsides. It was thick water that stayed in the hand, spreading water, clumped, syrupy, brown water that looked downward and dissolved the melting earth.

The water of the first morning of the world, the virgin water of life went directly into the earth, without froth, without end, without shellfish. It had to reinvent all the cycles of species, to conceive the first plant, the first animal. Even the toads hesitated at its edge. Tiffany and Moses went in. They were curious, a little indecently even, to feel the grasses of the embankment that they knew so well or the roll of familiar pebbles under their feet. It was a journey in darkness, in the creation of the underground world. They went in with their elbows in the air, tapping with a foot, quickly reassured. This water was womb and bed, voluptuous tenderness and sleep. They squatted to feel it up to their necks. Their eyes opened onto an upside-down world, a geography of lakes and estuaries where the tall black trees had lost their magnificent manes.

And so that was water to them, emptiness, happiness. Their pleasure was taken in silence. No squeals, no words to say that they were happy with this caress. They didn't jump; they didn't throw water into their faces; they didn't dive. They had gone in little by little and slipped into a succulent sensuality that could not be expressed. Closing their eyes, they stood still. No, crouched down, they did make a gesture a long time after the thick water brought each one back to the other who had moved (the touch of the water was very precise on their bodies), the gesture of a far-away caress. Becoming heavy, taking on color and occupying the earth, water existed. And the children, in the hollow of the overflowing pool of water, communed with the universe and with eternity.

*

Time passed over the inundated earth. The sun had forced away the shadows; the water receded, leaving a crust of salt on the edges of the marshes. Already humps of earth emerged out of the water that now occupied only the deepest parts of the holes. It gave the countryside a tortured physiognomy that the long period of floods had carefully erased and that ordinarily the leaves suffocated. The water disappeared, soaked into the earth, sucked up by the sun. Moses and Tiffany saw the vanishing, as if by enchantment, of what had been so real and, more than real, had been true. The animals had reappeared. They chased the toads from the puddles. Moses captured a small caiman that had ventured too far from the river.

It wasn't very large, fifty centimeters, or perhaps forty. Tiffany had, it seemed, carefully measured it. From the nose to the tip of the fine, streamlined tail, it was fifty centimeters, practically a monster. It was a yellowish gray, cold, insensitive to the caresses that Tiffany gave it very gently with the back of her hand in order to feel more deeply the unknown matter of the animal. Moses held it tightly, squeezing it with his hand by the throat and the tail. Reduced to impotence in this way, the caiman's only sign of life was the black line across the pupils of its gray eyes. On the ground, it would be no fun at all; it had to be used in the water, to see how it swam or how it tried to get away.

They set off to look for a puddle neither too deep, nor too wide, in which they could try out the animal. Moses went in up to the waist. Tiffany waited, nervously. When Moses had checked out all points of the swampy pool, they proceeded to float the animal. Moses held it very tightly at the neck; with a flash of the tail it tried to escape. This earned it an immediate reprimand. Ah! So that was the thanks they got! It wanted to get away! Don't let it go! Don't let it go! shouted Tiffany excitedly. They tied the muzzle with string, and the rest of the line served as a leash. What a good idea! Impressed by the animal to which so many prestigious stories were attached, Tiffany had not imagined that it could be treated like any common beast, like a wild pig, like just anything.

To try it out, Tiffany went into the water that didn't even come up to her back; she took the cord and "made" the caiman swim. They made it dive a long time "to see" what happened. The animal was like wood, apart from its little clawed paws that agitated convulsively and the tail that beat against the water, it did nothing. Tiffany extended a finger to touch its eyes; she withdrew it quickly. The animal had real eyes. In the water, not far from the caiman that no longer amused them, Tiffany and Moses had found another game. They touched their own eyes. It took great strength of character: keeping the eyes open as the finger advanced. Whoa! Only the caiman was capable of that.

They left the water. They continued on, not knowing where. Tiffany carried the caiman under her arm, against her body. She grew accustomed to the coarse or pearly contact of the animal, depending upon whether it was the dorsal ridge or the stomach that rubbed against her skin. From puddle to puddle, they carried it to the river because they didn't want to keep it and yet they didn't want to abandon it just anywhere. It's a baby, Tiffany said, pinching the paw joints; the skin was still supple. Moses didn't answer.

*

The vast glimmer in that night sky had nothing to do with lightning. It was not a flash that went away quickly but a pulsing light, dying and coming back to life. Rising red tongues of forest fires, tongues of light from outside that danced inside on the walls of the bedroom. It was this that was disquieting: it stayed; it penetrated; it heated. The redness in the room, the shadow that lit up the bed, the light that disappeared on the face. And it began again: the bed went black; the face lit up; the heat poured over the walls, here, there, always present. The heat! And the noise, it was like a big, refreshing storm, the noise of a violent wind in the trees, the noise of the forest's power, of a lashing rain, it was all reassuring. Except for the ceaseless whistling of the flames, the roar, the crackling, flashing everywhere in the pyrotechnic heat.

Matilde came to get Tiffany. It was time to abandon the threatened house. On the porch, Tiffany was surprised. This fire that seemed so near was still far away, beyond the tennis courts. It was red and black, yellow near the top; it had appropriated the sky and the ground, and in the center of the grounds was their house. The distant conflagration threatened, penetrating, licking, sucking, devouring. Matilde was afraid. They were watching from the terrace, reassured because it was over there; they could see it from afar. Her eyes belied a wakening understanding, the skin of the face, the ear, and above all the feeling of fear. The eyes said that the fire was far off, that it would turn to the left, that it would spare the orangery and the house, thanks to the barren slice of the tennis courts. And the eyes were right. The fire went high and straight up the other side of the courts; it nipped at their heels but it didn't come any closer.

The emboldened men fought it at the edges, beat it back with sweeping strokes of dead branches, insulted it, and the fire retreated like a wave folding in on itself. The men pushed it farther. They occupied the abandoned space, advanced and challenged it again and again, meter by meter. They followed it, tracked it, sending it to die far away where other men waited their turn to push it back. Shouts were heard high above the fire's roar; it rolled on, beating the same calcified trunk, the same reeds already flattened, which it brought back to life as it passed over. The night belonged to the men it had freed; it had given them space, ash-covered earth and all its wildlife. The fire that had passed that night was the fire of the men of Africa. Only those who had not mastered fire were afraid.

The bushfire was part of a hunting ritual; it was not an accident but lit point by point along the geography of the hunt. The men no longer went into the bush for fear of getting lost; they destroyed it, and the wildlife of an entire area was brought into their nets in a single night. One night of hunting in the year, the night on which everything burned. Afterward there was nothing left; they went back to sleep until everything grew back and was reborn. It was a festival of fire, the festival of life that revitalizes and dies. It was the proof of man's ascendancy over nature that all year long suffocated and broke him, and over the animals that ran from him and condemned him.

Tiffany did not perceive her mother's fear or her father's anger, the fear and anger of all the whites who had assembled. In the deepest part of her being, she felt the miracle of this fire that had started without being announced, like a Christmas no one expected, the first Christmas, a festival that wasn't a birthday, a day that was not a commemoration, an event without being a celebration. It was new, and therefore true, rich. And it was magic because the village, all the villages, had run after the fire that spread into infinity. The men who contained it had an absolute power. It was marvelous, that was all. While the men who directed other men worried, agonized, collected their belongings, made ready to capitulate, the men who commanded the fire saved everyone using a technique that was no longer the hunter's; it belonged to the soldier and to his mercy. In the morning, the whites saw in front of their terraces that the trees were still green and there was, perhaps, a curtain of high grasses. They had had a bad dream; they had believed all night that they would have to leave. But they were served their tea, their orange juice. For them nothing had happened. On the white sleeve of the *boy*, there was a little bit of gray ash; Tiffany brushed it off with her hand.

Part Three

I

Under the pretext of helping with the placement of students at the Mission, Madame Bonenfant had loudly insisted that female personnel were to be hired for the bar and to wait tables. The proposition was greeted with mixed feelings: A woman! What an odd idea! That's never been done here before, not even to mind children! Men were preferred. Women were soft. They lacked initiative. They were incapable of learning. They had in fact never even been seen close up. Wives of the *boys*, small-time merchants in the market, women at oxbow lakes, submissive women.... It was not so much African women that Madame Bonenfant wanted to promote as the products of the Dutch Mission. She wanted to dot every *i*. She didn't mean those women; she meant the ones in white dresses who embroidered so well and who would not know how to stir a sauce without a wooden spoon in a copper pot. No need to take a real African woman; there were the mixed bloods, the daughters of Alexandrou, for example.

Great! What a great idea, one of Alexandrou's daughters, of course! They knew the father, so they would be doing him a favor. It was normal that the proprietor would want to place his offspring. He didn't ask for this; it was a surprise. From the lot they had chosen a Marie-Rosalie, who had reached the perfect point of maturity, the point at which, at the Mission, she could only start to forget what she had learned. She was past thirteen and getting on. She had a clear, appealing look about her that gave the impression of openness. What more could be asked? Alexandrou agreed; this one or that one, was there a difference? As a matter of fact, there was no way of knowing whether he knew who was meant when he gave his blessing since he had not chosen her name. Thinking he was donating another one perhaps, he gave this one. He never knew who worked at the Club.

Marie-Rosalie wore out her white dress behind the bar. She rubbed the glasses vigorously, digging the towel into them, checking them in the light for spots, starting over again. She was learning. The *boys* swept, Beretti served, and Marie-Rosalie wiped the glasses. Fear of doing her job badly consumed her like an incessant noise in her head. She was incapable of any gesture other than the one Beretti had taught her when she first arrived. She had taken refuge there, seizing greedily the two objects that had been put into her hands as if it were through them that she was connected to the Club, to the life that she led there. All her timidity, her anxiety, even her fear were expressed in the plaintive squeak of the towel in the glass.

Life went on in the barroom. At first, Marie-Rosalie was amazed by the hubbub, the joyful exclamations, the noisy voices, the loud conversations, punctuated here and there by an order called out to Beretti. She let herself sink into this audible background from which she occasionally recognized a word: truck, meat, forest, Mission, Residence. These very clear images shone at the back of her retina; the very materiality reassured her because most of the time the members of the Club said nothing real but only chanted tunes of varying degrees of power. When, in the middle of all this conversation, an order was barked out, Marie-Rosalie blanched and turned toward Beretti, completely terrified. In this way, speech broke through all obstacles, agreeably if she understood, disagreeably if the word reached her not through her ears but through her body, shivering.

Beretti was a great comfort to her; he made the transition between the outside world, which he did not yet let her approach, and the world of before. He pushed her, spoke to her in a scolding tone, gave orders and expected them to be carried out without so much as a "please" or a "thank you." If need be, he kicked her in the behind, calling her "stupid ass." All this was as good as to say that Marie-Rosalie, born in Alexandrou's store and polished at the Mission, remained a HALF-BREED. There was nothing more frightening for her than the assigned identity that inhabited her from the other side of the bar where she didn't even dare take off her "tennis" shoes.

*

Marie-Rosalie came out of her shelter for an overturned glass, a broken bottle, an important event that wouldn't wait. The need at the table had to be urgent for Marie-Rosalie to interpret it except in fear. She had arrived running, her tea towel in hand; she had dropped to the floor, which she rubbed among all the broken bits of a glass, risking injury. Madame Dubois called her to order: it was not the floor that had to be sponged first, but the soiled table. What was she thinking? Marie-Rosalie lifted her arm and, still crouched on the floor, wiped the edge of the table. The Club members saw the balled-up towel, dingy with the dirt from the floor, going back and forth over the wood, a clenched hand holding it tightly, a head bowed. No! What a klutz! exclaimed Madame Dubois, laughing.

So Marie-Rosalie got up and for the first time they saw her up close; that is, they noticed the white dress that was too short, torn in several places, the uncovered thighs, and inside the armhole that was coming unsewn, the swelling of a breast. She was tall, a little heavy perhaps. Dubois raised his eyebrows, nodding his head in a gesture of appreciation that, combined with a grimace, rendered his expression comical. Bonenfant didn't want to be left out, and with his hands, he imitated the weight of a lovely bust. Marie-Rosalie looked at these gentlemen making gestures that she didn't understand. She had made a mistake; it was the only thing that counted. Would they pardon her? They didn't seem too angry since they were laughing among themselves. Even the ladies were amused; the gestures mimed by the gentlemen gave them fits of coughing.

I give up. I give up, clucked Madame Bonenfant. She can sew; she has been trained in home economics. Look at how she applies herself. Look how she wipes the table. Oh! No, I swear! Impossibly thick! They are hopelessly thick. No longer interested in Marie-Rosalie, they had gone on to something else. Marie-Rosalie knew by the sound of their voices that there was no longer any danger; it was the usual soft rumbling. She took enough courage from this to return to the bar, her dirty towel in hand. The voice of Matilde stopped her in her tracks. A sweet voice that uttered agreeable, simple sounds: Hospital, dresses, tomorrow. Marie-Rosalie was happy.

Matilde handed the child her skirt with the purple flowers, the yellow top that went with the black dress, a bright red scarf, and some high-heeled pumps. Marie-Rosalie put them all on at once. What a hit she made, with the skirt open at the back, the top badly buttoned, the feet squeezed into the too-small shoes, the scarf wrapped around the head! Matilde arranged, kneaded, pressed. Around Marie-Rosalie she made the gestures of Matilde on Matilde. In the waist that she tried in vain to close, she held the tiny waist of Matilde, in the shoes the small feet of Matilde, under the blouse, the breasts of Matilde. Playing with the amazed young girl, Matilde was intoxicated with herself. Looking at her grotesque reflection in the clothes that didn't fit, she remembered having been very pretty in them, very, very pretty. A crazy regret took hold of her, a wild excitement, the certain drama of having been. She gave Marie-Rosalie a green handbag: With that you will be perfect! And she sent her off: Go on, you're fine like that. Go. She didn't even give her the time to change, and the young girl, filled with happiness, went out in her extraordinary hand-me-downs.

While making her way to the Club, Marie-Rosalie accomplished her metamorphosis; she removed the shoes and placed them with the green bag on top of her head. She tied the red scarf around her waist as a belt, pinned up the skirt that was too long to show some leg. She walked like a large flower, unknown to the mass of earth and grasses in the country-side, luminous. She was lost in the colors that played on her: she liked the motion of her leg lifting the violet gauze; she liked how the belt made the yellow stand out. Doctor N'Diop was walking toward her. He too was fascinated by the bits of cloth that burned in the light. He stopped; it was a woman, the first. She looked up; he forgot the red, the green, the violet, and the yellow. All the color was in the brown amber, the earth red, the transparent shell, the golden honey. He felt a great joy, a great sadness. He knew no more. He was going to die.

*

To put his hand under a skirt, to let his fingers run along the length of thighs while the forearm holds up the fabric, a gesture of defense, and the same again. To take the edge of the skirt in his fingertips, to seize it with his whole hand, to lift it, knead it, and squeeze the flesh. A pleasure Beretti had never known. The black satin pants of little Vietnamese girls, the open thighs of whores, he had never seen anything as exciting as the ample skirt that Marie-Rosalie wore against her bare legs, never seen anything as provocative, never anything that made him want this much to take, to rape. The fabric concealed nothing; on the contrary, the legs were free beneath it, free and open. He could see them very well when a gust of air flattened the gauze against the stomach, marking both stem and calyx. Beretti couldn't stop himself pinching her behind the bar, caressing her buttocks with a quick almost breathless pat that held her for a moment under the dress. She pulled away just enough to release the gesture. He made another attempt, harder this time. He had not had enough to satisfy.

In his room under the grinding ceiling fan he pushed her onto the bed, her skirt turned over her head. The air lightly moved the thin fabric that gently touched the child's face, like a reassuring pat. By the light of the violet material, Marie-Rosalie was less afraid. Well, afraid as usual, like when something unexpected happened or was about to happen, for example when Monsieur Dubois demanded another whiskey or when Monsieur Bonenfant's car braked in front of the terrace. Underneath the skirt she couldn't see anything. She felt Beretti's hands on her and that reassured her. She gave in to the rough hands that she knew, opening up a little under those hands, the golden hands of Beretti. It hurt, suddenly, very hard, just once. She began to struggle. It was too late. The dress ripped. Beretti groaned, crying, Whore! Whore! Bitch! Pig! He was not happy. He let her go. She saw the blood stain on her skirt, measured with her fingers the tear in the purple gauze, and she cried out loud, really cried, with anger.

A pair of pins repaired the damage. Marie-Rosalie was glad that the rip had been under the belt because by wearing the scarf a little lower it could not be seen at all. The blood showed up only a little darker on the violet. You couldn't wash this sort of fabric. The color would melt away in your fingers if you dared to get it wet. She was still crying a little, but even in that there was a bit of pleasure, the pleasure of burying her face in the lovely color, of being reborn there, hungrily.

Each day Beretti took a nap. Marie-Rosalie learned to spread out on the bed, raise her skirt over her head, to protect both the skirt and her face, the docile Marie-Rosalie. Beretti made love with a woman without a head, deep inside a gauzy corolla, a sex. He didn't make love with Marie-Rosalie: he didn't play with her; he took her. Every day, he did it again. He couldn't stand it. He just had to have her. He swore each time that he would make himself look at her, but it was impossible; when she was on the bed, he dove headlong under the skirt.

The skirt was very dirty now. When Matilde went to the Club, she didn't recognize it; Madame Dubois had to point it out. But Matilde did not see the dress of outer petals and the tall girl-flower that wore it. For her, Marie-Rosalie had passed from looking like a clown to looking like a grubby gypsy vagabond, a sad caricature of what she, Matilde, had been. The dress had been a trifle; *her* beauty was elsewhere. In this way her existence didn't depend on such material contingencies; it just was. And yet it wasn't anymore. It was all rather difficult to understand. Madame Bonenfant said over and over that they were all dense. Madame Dubois said that something would have to be done about hygiene. Matilde said, very softly, that she would give her something else; it wasn't so awful, the death of an outfit…

N'Diop was haunted by the memory of the marvelous woman he had met by chance near the Club the previous week. He knew all about her. Her name was Marie-Rosalie, she had been with the Sisters, and she worked at the Club. A wealth of details. He would never forget her, not in OUREGANO, not in his memory. He couldn't manage without her. It was simple: go by the Club to see her again. He was still mining the first encounter, but he wanted to see her again, urgently. Not yet. The memory warmed him. She existed. She was near. His mouth was dry; he succumbed.

*

She was waiting at the side of the road; he did not recognize her. Yet it was her, with her flashy hand-me-downs, only distorted. There was no more magic in the painful composition of her outfit. Ridges, folds, sequins hanging by a thread, on her feet high heels that didn't fit. She had dampened her hair to flatten it against her head. In her hand she held the green bag in which she carried nothing. She seemed younger to him, and slightly defiled. It was almost without pleasure that he held out his hand to help her climb into the pickup truck.

He didn't ask himself where he would take her. It was obvious, everywhere. She went so well with the countryside, born of it, vibrating with light, dark under the leaves, transparent as the water, fresh and warm... He drove. Since the truck was meant only for tarmac, he took to the road and drove fast enough to avoid the disequilibrium of the undulating surface. He was near her yet he didn't see her, completely taken as he was by the effort of driving and the memory of her that he preferred. The truck drove through the dust; they looked straight ahead, seeing nothing. At the airport, there were no airplanes. Nothing to show her.

He remembered a logging site, now deserted. They headed out. They walked among the sleeping trunks that the rainy season had half buried in red clay. It was hard to walk; she took off the high heels, wiped them, and carefully balanced them on her head, mussing her hair. He felt a burst of tenderness for her that had nothing in common with the adoration he had experienced on the first occasion. He pitied her a little with her borrowed clothes, her large useless bag, and the gesture as old as time of protecting the shoes, of carrying them. He wondered if she were bored, wandering in the middle of the chunks of wood, so crowded. It occurred to him that she had perhaps never gone for a walk, and his heart ached. Marie-Rosalie had never done anything for the pleasure of it, and walking was for her only a means of getting from one place to another, as fast as possible. He felt incapable of teaching her the freedom of gratuity, the idea of doing nothing, of feeling the wind, of looking into the distance, of going nowhere...

They headed back. They drove along the African village's muddy periphery, packed down with hunger, with misfortune, with its hundreds of naked women who like Marie-Rosalie had never gone for a walk, with its men who had never experienced anything for no reason at all, with its children who had never dreamed. They crossed the center of the village and the deserted area of the little market. There was no café, no cinema, no place to dance, no shopwindow with displays. There was only the road, the same road going to the same places. So he took her to the hospital. He didn't look for excuses. He had tried to explain the airport to her, the wooded park. She didn't speak. He couldn't even speak to her about herself, couldn't tell her how he marveled at her. He said what he didn't feel because he wanted to please her, that she had pretty clothes. Marie-Rosalie answered that it had been Madame Murano who had given them to her.

N'Diop's room was similar to Beretti's. Marie-Rosalie moved easily between the bed arranged as a sofa, the table, and the chair. She sat on the bed, kicked off the high heels, which she had put back on for what it was worth. She gazed at the books. Already N'Diop extended his hand to take up the volume on which the girl's eyes were fixed. He was delighted that she was interested, amazed that she had noticed. He didn't ask himself if she had read anything other than her A-B-C book, if she had ever owned a book. He wanted to be the one to tell her, wanted her to understand through the music and the images, wanted her to enter with him into the domain of the dream or into the realm of negritude that was forbidden them outside. He chose a poem with a trembling hand: no, not that one, this one. When he had decided, he turned toward her to prepare her to listen, to present the passage to her. She was spread across the bed, her skirt carefully pulled over her face, thighs open; she was waiting.

*

Beretti watched in front of the Club for Marie-Rosalie to return. She got out of the pickup truck, fearful, plastering herself to the door. When she judged herself to be out of reach of the foot and the fist, she ran to get inside without thinking that sooner or later Beretti would get to her. By leaving N'Diop, she abandoned her only hope. Beretti approached the doctor and, hanging on the window, he belched his threats, vomiting insults: This filthy nigger would see, he'd just see, the shit, the bastard. Ah! He'd see all right! And then: Get the hell out! But he had one more insult, and that one, he would not spare him. N'Diop put everything he had into starting the engine, putting it in gear and getting away. Beretti ran alongside, screaming, screaming again and again.

So that was it! N'Diop oscillated in a movement at once tender and cruel between pain and revolt. He felt tears on his cheeks and a sob in his throat. Everything was fixed in his memory, the monstrous shoes on feet that were meant to be bare, the shameful disguise, the open thighs. They had all had her, the debauched child. They had all sullied her, each one of them. The Bonenfant woman and the Murano woman were guiltier than the reprehensible creature who took her every day. His heart ached. He discovered that he loved her differently than he had through the stunning memory of their first encounter, the echo, and the reflection of poetry. He loved her for herself and for what was eternal. He loved her for what had been irremediably taken from her. She had been given a false job, false clothes, a false lover, and she was happy. What else had she known, born into a false family, subjected to a false education. She was the victim of this inverted situation, a hundred times more than the village merchants, a hundred times more than the sick in the hospital, a hundred times more than any other servant of the colonizers. The rape of Marie-Rosalie had been carefully orchestrated from the beginning. From among the others, a child chosen for this miserable destiny, apprentice to the whites, soiled since her birth. By her birth!

It occurred to him that this evening she would be unhappy, beaten certainly, raped again by the awful little man who would show her in this way that he could hold his own against a Negro. He hadn't touched her? Doesn't surprise me, an impotent, a degenerate. So much the better, this'll show you, you'll see.... Kidnap her? He was ready to. But it was more involved than taking her from a sadistic old man or even a group of Europeans in OUREGANO for whom the girl was their proof that integration was possible. They would show her off all over: You see, we're making progress! He would have to separate her from herself. Would she give up Matilde's dresses, the glasses and the Club, and even Beretti's desire (all that existed, she was learning it daily) for love, for happiness, and for respect?

What remained real in the person of Marie-Rosalie? He saw again the lighthearted step of the first day, the way she carried these objects on her head, lovingly. What was he thinking? These were nothing but images, and the worst kind! What a counterfeit of the truth! Oh, Marie-Rosalie who polishes the white people's shoes! Oh, Marie-Rosalie who bows before Beretti's every wish! She was no longer anything. There was only her amber skin; her tender honey-colored eyes carried the mark of the white man. And him, who was he to judge her? What was his truth? Wasn't he making in his own way exactly the same gestures as Marie-Rosalie? He had bought his suit; no one had made him. And worse, he had paid for this and plenty more. How can the merchant be resisted? The bow tie, the shirts with French cuffs, the English shoes—all bought at a price, a terrible price. She offered her body out of fear and habit. He offered himself every day out of cowardice; he closed his eyes out of weakness. And so she was happy! He swallowed his revolt. What was there about this revolt that was nobler, more respectable, this revolt that led to nothing?

*

She had spent a whole afternoon with a Negro! They must have really gotten it on! His was big? How big? Big enough to suffocate you, isn't that so? Well, he, Beretti, no longer wanted anything to do with Marie-Rosalie. It was as simple as that. He would tell Madame Bonenfant. He didn't hit her. You see, you see? I'm not even hitting you. I don't want to get any diseases, not me! And don't touch the glasses either! Stand there with your hands in the air, and don't lean on the wall, Pig! Marie-Rosalie was crying. She hadn't done anything bad, she swore it. Liar, shouted Beretti. Bitch! So he read you poems in his room! I'll bet! Because, you little slut, I don't give a fuck who you screw, but nobody takes Louis Beretti for a fool. No one!

Marie-Rosalie began to beg to be beaten. Afterward, that would be the end of it. Hit me, hit me, she begged. Beretti refused. It would be too easy, and what was this? At the other end of the room, Marie-Rosalie mimed her earliest gestures of love, gestures of submission. On her knees she begged Beretti, raising her arm, and her open hands formed the face that she had never touched, in a caress of adoration. Beretti wanted her to stay that way. It was more than he could have asked; seeing her so submissive fired his imagination. To forbid her to touch the floor with her knees, the feet if necessary! He threw a scrap of bread at her to make her eat it off the floor. She took it and ate it. He did it again with a bit of chicken; the meat in its sauce remained stuck to the floor. He yelled: Lick it up!

The passivity of Marie-Rosalie had no limits then. To this degree, it was not normal. He remembered a scene that had made an enormous impression on him. One of his sisters had been suspected by their father of having sex with a neighborhood boy. She would admit nothing. Their father had ended up dragging her to a midwife to have her examined. He could still hear the screams of the girl, her pleading. She would have accepted anything to escape the examination, including death. In the end, she had proved to be a virgin.... No one had understood. And what if the same thing were to happen to Marie-Rosalie? The thrill of arousing absolute terror in a human creature. He told her he would forgive her, but first he would have her examined by Doctor Murano.

N'Diop saw the car in front of Doctor Murano's office. Beretti dragged Marie-Rosalie toward the consultation room, her head hanging down. He feared the worst. She was ill, hurt even. He waited, sick with anxiety, for her to reappear, not even thinking that she could be hospitalized, that is, that she would be returned to him. It did not occur to him that he might be allowed to create or recreate new images that would absolve her, that would return her to life, that would no longer be the life of before. N'Diop didn't hope that they would give Marie-Rosalie to him, not even in this way. He imagined her only as tied to the whites, lost to him forever.

Beretti had to be sure of himself to ask Murano what he was asking. The girl had gotten into trouble; he wanted to know if there would be consequences. What did he mean? A pregnancy? An illness? Or simply lost virginity? In any case, there weren't that many ways to get into trouble. Murano asked Marie-Rosalie to undress. She protested, trying to be modest. Nude on the obstetrical table, she looked into the face of Murano. It was the first time that, lying on her back, she saw a man over her. She began to cry. Murano said she was no longer a virgin. Beretti was overjoyed: For sure, she's been getting it on with your assistant!

Matilde couldn't get over it. Marie-Rosalie was no longer a virgin? She wasn't even fifteen years old! And she had trusted her! Had she given her clothes to a slut? Disgusting! To think that the clothes she had worn touched this body openly, freely, it made her ill. It wouldn't have taken much for her to take everything back. Make rags out of it all, anything, but not to dress Marie-Rosalie.

Murano was confused, amused, and he was working up to being angry. So N'Diop was putting on airs and sleeping with a child of fourteen or even thirteen. At the first chance he got, he would give him what for. Actually he was not unhappy; he had leverage now. Authenticity? I'll show you authenticity!

They imagined scenes! In his career as Judge, Bonenfant had seen others. It wasn't fair to blame N'Diop. These girls were hot to trot. He had seen some who…at twelve, at ten, and prostitutes at eight years old. Really something! But what is this all about, Madame Bonenfant was saying. At eighteen she knew nothing about life and at twenty she hardly knew much more. Tell them, Jean. She didn't want to brag about her purity. It was a challenge to the Ladies, who had remained a virgin the longest, and to the gentlemen, who had, all of them, been the first! The Virgin Mary was fifteen when she gave birth, Dubois said quietly. Elise shivered.

*

The world knew the meaning of a little girl sacrificed, taken and drained. The universe knew the mystery of her short forehead and her ample skirt. Marie-Rosalie stood alone in the past, in the future. N'Diop couldn't even say that he was different from other men in thinking of the young girl as a private shelter, as happiness, as a dream.

Marie-Rosalie was everywhere. Hundreds of Marie-Rosalies came to the pediatric consultations, little girls with the backs of their heads shaved, in dresses that were too large and bare feet. And N'Diop was the father of these little girls. The grave and tender father who held them as if in loose handcuffs, like birds whose bodies one daren't squeeze too tightly, boneless hands without tissue, just a warm touch, feather light. To hold them, he had to take them by the wrists, linking them to his own fear, for N'Diop was afraid of the evil that floated over the heads of these children riddled with fever, and like the father who brought them in, he didn't dare shake hands or touch the forehead. Oh little girls, ungraspable in their illness.

Marie-Rosalie was everywhere. Her image could be seen on the body of every woman who came to give birth, a light-skinned baby between her legs. The shortened breath of Marie-Rosalie could be seen between the parted and dried lips of the woman, and the large brown eyes with the deep, dark iris in the woman's eyes that cannot even close in exhaustion.

Marie-Rosalie was everywhere, grave and broken in the unsexed old women, the tightly pulled hair, the *pagne** tied around the torso over the deep fold of sagging breasts, the hollowed bones of the thorax, and the bird's hands becoming birds' claws. The shriveled softness of these old women's shoulders was the horrible companion of age. They had gone mad, these old women. A horrid voice screeched for who knew what reason.

He imagined a tender embrace; the curve of his arms would stifle their suffering. Save Marie-Rosalie to save them all. Feed Marie-Rosalie to feed them all. Calm her and make her rebel, to be within her in order to be among them, to dissolve, to take root. The little girl in between. Marie-Rosalie as destiny, that is, as a reason. A force drove him toward her as if the world would start over with their mixed breath, as if the happiness of others would grow from theirs. Marie-Rosalie, madness surely, necessary, absolute.

And now all OUREGANO threw her absence up to her. It was not, as in the beginning, to know quietly that she existed and to wait for her, trusting in the laws of chance at a crossroads, sure to put a hand on her because once before that had been possible. Still, if ONCE, when she had been unknown, uncalled, she had emerged warm and lovely, violent and tender on his path, what would he be today when he claimed her with all

---

* A length of cloth about one meter by two meters wrapped around the body as a skirt or dress.

his power and all his folly? Come! She would appear, truly, still more beautiful, still more tender, still more.... It was the law of desire. Who would doubt that so violent a force would not be acted upon? Everything happens; only weak desires lack the strength to seduce us. It was not against destiny then that one must turn, but against oneself, against the illusion of desire that we take for truth, for authenticity, which alone creates miracles. Desire, again and again, and this desire that was madness was too weak for Marie-Rosalie to hear. It went no further than the doors of the hospital, no higher than the bundled tops of the banana trees. A desire that did not have the strength to go as far as four kilometers...

In front of the door that opened, he closed his eyes standing motionless at the crossroads. He waited in the neighborhood of the Club. With his eyelids tightly closed, with his hands, wringing with the power of an embrace, at least enough to accomplish miracles, all N'Diop's violence went into this rigid immobility, into the silence that tore out his tongue, into the obsession that took over his soul. He could have died turned toward her, irresistibly.

*

Marie-Rosalie's submission unleashed all of Beretti's violence. The feeling of power was so strong that he could no longer make allowances; he lost all control. What with keeping tabs on Marie-Rosalie everywhere she went, one day he realized angrily that he was reduced to the perimeter of his bed, of the Club. In the kitchen he terrified the *boys*; it felt good to instill fear. But the Club protected its inhabitants, in a manner of speaking. Fear without surprise was no longer fear. The domestics learned very fast to accommodate their anxiety. They made it ordinary by enclosing it within time. The *boys* discovered that there were only two bad moments in the day, Beretti's awakening—before he had fully regained his head in order to organize the usual unrelenting hunt—and at dusk just after the first whiskey, swallowed very fast behind the bar followed by a second drink, taken more slowly, before the members of the Club appeared. The rest went by. Oh, there was the odd moment when the sweeper made a mistake, a similar moment for the cook, and for the launderer. But they waited; they had learned to pace themselves.

Marie-Rosalie, in her way, combated the fear Beretti inspired in her. From the first signs of anger she approached him, glued herself to him, defending herself from his blows and his screams with her body. She was less vulnerable closer to the body of the pitiful fellow than farther away, with her arms firmly around his body, her hands hanging on his shoulders until they clawed his flesh. This manner of holding on more and more tightly when he tried to use his knee to get her off him gave the appearance less of the terror and flight they expressed than of erotic excitement. At last, Beretti's body gave in. It was true that the vile man never looked at the terrorized eyes of the child. He felt only the heat of the embrace, especially where the frantic hands had torn at his flesh, where the breasts, flattened against his chest, enflamed him, enflamed his sex, swelling always against the skirt and against her screams. He mistook fear for desire and he said to the girl, weakening but already quiet because she knew very well what was happening: You want it? Okay, you, you...

Marie-Rosalie was an accomplice to the depth of anger Beretti could only reach in sex. She accompanied him when he went hunting with his headlights, when the Club was closed, at night, going after any sort of prey. And the pickup that roared about in the darkness with its high beams on, the better to surprise something, was a large raging animal suffocated with hatred.

The night passed by the doors and if it had not been for the noise of the motor that Beretti gunned and the massive jolts of the track, Marie-Rosalie could have believed the car was standing still. She thought herself trapped in darkness, in the vast blackness. Deep in the cycles of the night, she regained a bit of self-control, felt a wavering flame—her heart, her soul, her despair? She felt it come back to life. No longer seeing the world, at last she listened to herself. She made no large discoveries. She didn't ask herself about the meaning of her life, or about the nature of the people around her. She didn't reflect. Only dense weariness invaded her. She gave in to fatigue. She could now tell that her neck hurt, and her back. And if Beretti were quiet, she might even close her eyes.

It was not the night that terrified Marie-Rosalie but the day, and more than the day the yellow light, the white light of the headlights that Beretti flashed to make monsters jump out: the huge trunk of a purplish tree or a bloodless one that twisted toward unimaginable foliage, dark, moving shadows, terrified flights, phosphorescent red and green eyes, startled animals, turned toward the automobile, the jaw opening ready to scream, the shock of nighthawks flapping against the windshield with their vertiginous violence. Everything was horrible, the fluttering of night butterflies, the agitated coils of a snake torn to pieces, the black water of the grumbling river. They got back in the morning drunk with terror, with blood, exhausted.

*

It was on one of these nights that destiny was accomplished. N'Diop was in his car about a hundred meters from the Club, awaiting not so much Marie-Rosalie but the vision that would make her appear, bring her closer, into the real. When Beretti's door opened, the dome light lit the face of the young girl, turned toward him, hardly a few meters away, the length of his arm, the distance needed to take her into his embrace and hold her. The light made her appear paler than she was, her eyes on the other hand seemed larger, darker, holes in the night, as if they didn't exist, exposed to the void. And if N'Diop got up and approached Beretti's truck, it was to look more closely at these eyes, to recall the dream and the reality, to erase the clouds that floated in these deserted pools, to flood the night, to dissipate the shadows. The eyes of Marie-Rosalie were too real however; they looked to him as if in a nightmare. Blind child.

Between the two vehicles came Beretti. Now he knew what he had been tracking all these nights, with Marie-Rosalie at his side: N'Diop! Anger didn't overwhelm him: face-to-face with this man he hated, he felt suddenly, strangely calm, almost serene. He had to get worked up, though, to bring all his power to this resentment. Before he could let loose his fury, the presence of N'Diop brought him pleasure. Who else could give him the pleasure of hand-to-hand combat? He would have liked the other to be on his guard, aggressive, his fists up, dancing on his heels, ready to fight to the end. What irritated him was that N'Diop paid little attention to him.

N'Diop's face was tense. He advanced with his hands in front, like a sleepwalker protecting his fall, moving toward Marie-Rosalie, his hands held out to the young girl. As soon as he was within reach, Beretti struck him hard; he reminded the other of his presence. N'Diop did not defend himself; he only staggered under the punch and fell. His face altered by unimaginable horror, he lay on the ground by the car. Beretti kicked him here, there, again and again, harder and harder. N'Diop crawled toward Marie-Rosalie. Beneath the pickup truck he raised his arm to touch the young girl, with a movement both desperate and ridiculous. How did he think he was going to reach her, the cab was too high, the windows closed. His hand groped for the door handle, hanging on as if sunk into dead eye sockets, N'Diop let out a scream he didn't recognize, a shriek that was a scream of death.

The scream fired Beretti's anger. He attacked the body lying on the ground with all his force. N'Diop no longer knew his body. He closed his eyes, feeling only the freshness of earth and the warm life that drained out of him. With Beretti's foot digging at him relentlessly, lifting dust in his face, he choked. He understood that if he couldn't breathe, it was because he was inhaling the earth; it entered his nose, his mouth. Like the zebu that Alexandrou assassinated each week, N'Diop's body settled into the soil. He could no longer spit; he no longer wanted to. The blood that poured out of his head had caked in the dust; he tasted the deep flavor, this intimate mixture that he recognized. He felt just enough peace to bring his arm slowly up in front of his face, dragging it along the ground, in the enclosure of sleep, voluptuous and eternal hand-to-hand combat.

The truck lurched as Beretti angrily turned on the ignition. N'Diop lay inert in the shadow that covered him, making him disappear, not in pain or broken but languid and overcome. Beretti put the engine in gear. He wanted to break this gentle expansion, this gesture of love. He threw the truck forward. N'Diop's body reared up, its life expelled. The vehicle backed up and crushed the cadaver. Stars shone brightly on fragments of the body.

II

Dubois lifted the sheet that covered N'Diop's head, wanting to see the face of a man that death had taken by surprise. There was nothing remarkable in the obscured features, already erased. Death was nothing. At least, nothing visible. N'Diop was no longer N'Diop. Dubois was about to cover the cadaver again when he finally saw what death was. The shrinking of the tissues, the eyelid embracing the curve of the ocular orb, stuck there, and under the upper lip, barely visible, the pearled surface of an incisor.

Was this the death that he watched for, evening after evening, from high on his terrace, death of the sun, death of the day, the death of noise, of smells? The death of a man, a little less flesh, more light and more noise. N'Diop was dead, touched, though he had not expected it, removed, beaten, annihilated. A man was dead. Nothing marked the event save the fear that floated all around, a fragile fear, a fear that had to be dissipated. This sort of thing happened and it would be a shame to upset everyone over something that this body had accepted without resistance. Maybe he lay bruised, mutilated under the sheet, but it did not concern him any longer. The face of the dead man knew nothing of what had happened to the living man.

Death had to be allowed its chosen one or its victim. Let it take him far away, away from memory, away from fear and sadness. Let it set him up the best it can. Let it neutralize the cadaver, no memory, no emotion, no tears. N'Diop's death had the color of sacrifice; it wasn't necessary to spoil it with monstrous human manipulations. No trial, no guilty party for N'Diop. Guilty of what, by the way? Life must not come back, not even once, to disturb the corpse. Dubois would do all in his power to see that nothing happened.

On his terrace at dusk, the murmur of N'Diop's death covered all the other noises. In this way death encroached on his life, submerged it with a gentle insistence. N'Diop's face came to brush against his own, and he felt in the gust of wind the touch of the shroud. He would have preferred that everything keep silent, that everything leave him, abandon him, to be forgotten in turn. He couldn't remember N'Diop alive; had he ever met him? Seen him around? Perhaps, but he didn't recall when or where. He had lost all memory of him, except this face. It penetrated him; it was inside him and he could not see it. Dubois closed his eyes and forgot the wind, the shadow, and the black clouds. He no longer kept watch through the night; he was absorbed, tenderly, marvelously absorbed. He accepted it.

When Beretti came for the mail, Dubois gave him the report, and since the other was questioning with his eyes, he told him to open it. Beretti read that all was well: The death of Doctor N'Diop was deplored. It was an accident. The report of the Judge and the certificate of autopsy would be sent as soon as they were available. Beretti said: Thank you, Sir, for being so understanding. Dubois looked at him, speechless. Understanding? Him? He had never been understanding! Beretti was mistaken if he thought for an instant that he had been considerate. It was death and death alone that he was sparing in the whole affair. He didn't want death to come into something a man had done. It was presumptuous of Beretti to believe that Dubois had used his influence. No, he was profoundly, truly innocent, the fool. He did not offer him a drink. For the first time, he had completed his report on time. He could go, wait up there, where men do not die at the hands of other men—they simply die.

*

When Beretti came into his office, Bonenfant didn't look up. He just mumbled: Since when don't you knock before you come into my office, Monsieur Beretti? He had deliberately made the "Monsieur Beretti" sound comical. And before the other could defend himself, he added: What do you want here, Monsieur Beretti? He smiled provocatively, keeping him dangling and then plunging him into terror. By smiling didn't he indicate that this was not a smiling matter? Beretti stammered that he was there to collect the statement, that it was Monsieur Dubois who was waiting for it so he could send it with his report, that the mail plane left this evening, that...

With that Bonenfant exploded. He didn't give a shit about the Administrator; the mail could leave when it wanted. He had not finished; he didn't give a damn about the plane. He had work to do and he would do it. He answered to no one. Justice did not have timetables or geographical limits. Isn't that so, Monsieur Beretti? You cannot escape Justice; it takes its time but it always gets you.... So that was it: he knew about the other, the mechanic in Niamkey! He was done for. He wouldn't even have the right to a suspended sentence. But how long had Bonenfant known? Did the Administrator know? Beretti forgot about N'Diop; he saw only the body of the shop assistant lying on the ground. He didn't want to pay for that. He held his tongue.

Bonenfant began to play with him. He returned intensely to his papers, looking for this, checking that, and from time to time, so that Beretti would not know that the Judge was doing other work, he occasionally posed a question: You were in the war? No. Indochina? No, Beretti had never been to Indochina. The Legion? Beretti had never been in the Legion.... Jack-of-all-trades in a bar in Marseilles? Pimp? A little. A lot. He was something to see, this fellow, yellow-bellied, weapons on the ground, naked, more than naked. The Judge returned to his papers, time passed, and it was no longer time for the mail. The plane would be taking off soon.

Beretti decided to take the plunge. He hadn't meant it. His Honor knew it since he knew everything. It was the heat of the moment; the girl belonged to him and not to the other fellow. He hadn't been able to stop himself. She was a virgin. He explained how he had taken her one afternoon. The story spilled out of him. She had been pure and she turned out to be the worst of the worst, a real slut; he hadn't resisted. With such a lamb, he couldn't stand for a nigger taking her. A bitch, a child. It wasn't important, a filthy bastard nigger, and besides he had been drinking, and then it was just his temperament, just the way he was. Louis Beretti was like that. The Judge looked at him, amused. How he loved these moments of pure truth that are no longer totally true because the accused always added something more while holding something back. Beretti admitted a crime of passion, a racial hate crime, an alcohol-induced crime, an unbelievable crime; it was a lot for one man. Bonenfant knew it was true, deeply true, and false at the same time. What did they hide, what did they protect, so many of these confessions?

Beretti had not limited himself to just killing N'Diop; he had beaten him, tortured him. Perfect, this Beretti, absolutely perfect. The Judge was not at all disappointed. Immorality to this degree demanded a certain admiration. Rapist of a child, executioner, coward, and pathological liar, amazing! The Judge knew that he would dismiss the case because he could do nothing else. It wouldn't do to ask for trouble. OUREGANO would remain quiet. And he couldn't do anything but support such a scoundrel. For Beretti, crime paid. Beretti was pardoned of rape, torture, crime, and cowardice. Go in peace, Beretti. No, wait, just a bit more terror. You can't take any more? No more, really? Bonenfant took out of his folio the report that declared the criminal innocent and signed it.

*

Michel remembered a drunken legionnaire who, after having annoyed a group of diners at a Saigon restaurant, jumped fully clothed into a swimming pool, much to the displeasure of the management. Although everyone commented on the bad manners of the soldier and mocked his drunkenness, a distinguished officer, another legionnaire, perfectly lucid, jumped into the pool as well. He had spoken the same language as the soldier. He had convinced him to come out of the water. The story went that the next day the officer had had the soldier thrown in the brig and even flogged. So many legends of this sort beat about in his brain. That had taken guts. He admired the officer for his style first of all but also for his almost theatrical sense of solidarity with his men. They were from a world other than that of civilians and idlers. Next to them they were united because none of the men who dined at flowered tables so much as came up to the ankles of a soldier, even drunk, and it was important that the soldier not lose face in front of the others. On the other hand, military hierarchy remained in place: the soldier had to be punished by the commander, but within the realm of the military establishment for having put at risk the "face" that the officer had saved. The soldier respectfully accepted the punishment inflicted on him.

For "legionnaire" Beretti, Michel felt himself to be the soul of this officer. He didn't want Beretti condemned by civilians for a civil crime. Because ultimately, the murder of N'Diop, with its obvious passionate overtones, was no more important than the soldier's drunkenness. This murder was a little matter of a piece of ass. A man had died, what of it? You cannot go after the girlfriend of a fellow like Beretti and expect to get away with it. This poor N'Diop, it had to be that he had no experience with this kind of man, that he had insulted him perhaps, or that he had thought his chances were even, or even that he didn't know that wars are fought in the hearts of men. Men, real men, they existed still! Here's proof! And it was not this heap of civilians, the Dubois and Bonenfants, who would understand this, unless he, Murano, weighed in on the subject in a decisive manner. No, he would not let a man be humiliated in the name of Justice where Justice was not concerned. Beretti was purified by the war, blessed by the courage to kill, outside the laws of those who had risked nothing. Murano was ready to plunge into the depths of the crime, to bring him out, to excuse him in the eyes of public opinion. He would speak to him later of morality, of their morality. As for the others, it was none of their business.

The body of N'Diop was horribly mutilated. The truck had run over him, first across the stomach and ribs that it had crushed into a bloody purée. Then it had come back, obviously in reverse, attacking the thighs. The face was intact. Doctor Murano saw only this face, the features of a patient who died at the wheel of his car, the steering column embedded in his chest. The "accidental" accident, the stupid mistake, misfortune, chance, destiny. He almost pitied N'Diop, so stupid to die like that. But it was his own fault: one didn't drive if one didn't know how to drive; one didn't drive drunk; one didn't drive alone with no one to go for help in case of the kind of accident in which one bled to death. *Vixit* N'Diop.[*]

Captain-Doctor Murano welcomed Beretti onto the battlefield; he

---

[*] Literally, 'N'Diop had lived.'

thought him pale. The idiots must have begun to tease him, the stupid administrators, and he felt humiliated for him who had been humiliated. Beretti had not a word to say. Captain-Doctor Murano announced coldly: Due to his accident, Doctor N'Diop died of a crushed thorax. The hemorrhage had been instantaneous. The causes of death were obvious and excluded any need for an autopsy. Beretti seemed so beside himself that Murano didn't have the courage to tell him what he had promised himself he would say; he let him go. Beretti had the urge to click his heels in the air. But he could only think about the other one, the Judge: What a jerk, that Bonenfant, what a jerk! Well, this would shut him up.

*

OUREGANO was not prepared to celebrate death. Now that the whites of OUREGANO had to face the death of, if not one of their own, at least someone close—culturally speaking of course—they were uncomfortable. Death in OUREGANO spared the whites; it left them time to kick the bucket elsewhere. You could always hang on till the Wednesday flight, perfusions, transfusions, camphor, caffeine. Ice on the forehead, hot water bottle on the feet, continuous cardiac massage so that on the plane the heart would keep going. You see, it's beating. You see, still breathing. No one had died in OUREGANO. It was something to be proud of. Thank you, Doctor, thank you, Monsieur Administrator, thank you, Monsieur Pilot. The windsock is full. Be off with you now.

At OUREGANO, white death had to be reinvented in honor of the Negro, N'Diop, as if death were a question of social progress, of intellectual success. N'Diop, the Negro, had the right to a bourgeois death. That was all so far away. They searched their bad memories, the days after which they had said: Best not to think anymore about it. You can't live for the dead. Get hold of yourself, Mama; he's fine up in Heaven. She has suffered so, the poor dear; it's a blessing. He's better off dead; he wouldn't have wanted to live like that. She had wasted away so. What hell for her daughter, I'm telling you! Go on, you are young still, go on and live.

What would he have done if he hadn't died this time? He would have lived, two, three more years, and then he would have died all the same. Faced with eternal yearnings for the crown of glory, they persuaded themselves that they should not pine too long. Faced with death, they persuaded themselves to live. Faced with absurdity and madness, they invented a reason to accept it. Faced with terror, they roused themselves to feel joy and even pleasure: The widow, it was good for her to begin to think again about a little morning satisfaction. It was death and they talked about life. It cost them deeply. There was not much gaiety in life, but it was more pleasant than death.

When someone died, there was the brief visit of the priest, everyone was pleasant, sanctified oils and palms, extreme unction of course. Afterward came the worst, dressing the body, dinner jacket, evening dress, formal overcoat, hat and shined shoes, the Legion of Honor on the button-hole, and off you go, into the casket. Close up the lid? So far, so good. Then the mass, absolution, candles and crowns, silver tears and matching chasuble, incense, holy water.... Yes, yes, exactly like that, it was just the same! And then the grave, the cords, the sermon, the dirt, the flowers on top of the dirt, and the cross on the flowers. All packed up! Perfectly, nothing forgotten? Oh yes, the condolences. That's where the shoe pinched. Who was the victim here? The doctor who had lost his colleague, the Administrator who buried a citizen? The bourgeois community was touched as a whole. They would not shake hands.

Madame Dubois and Madame Bonenfant entered N'Diop's room; they opened the armoire, unearthed the suit and the English shoes, the bow tie and the shirt with the French cuffs. If all goes well, we'll just get him done in time, if you get my drift. Worse yet, there were no coffins in OUREGANO. One had to be made, quickly, very quickly. Elise took care of it. She went off to find her carpenter; they'd make it out of mahogany, the lucky dog! The cabinetmaker was surprised; he wanted a drawing. On a plank of wood, Elise scrawled a parallelogram that narrowed at the end. She had never seen how a coffin was made. She was a bit muddled; large at the shoulder, narrow at the feet, that's it. The carpenter thought it strange. The main thing was to hurry—even if it was approximate.

No silver tears? No black surplice at the Mission? No matter. White would do for the service, the color of death in China, the color of something somewhere, whatever was customary.... The most important thing was to leave nothing to the imagination, to do everything by the book. As for the cemetery, well that was another story. All was nearly lost. What is the point of having a burial if you cannot bury? What did the Africans do with their dead? They had no idea. Here, there, everywhere! Where they could. The Mission absolutely refused the use of its garden and its Dutch compost. At the hospital, at the foot of the flagpole then? And in the name of what, I ask you! burst out Michel, who thought they were making too much of it all. Monsieur Dubois decided the matter. He created a cemetery for OUREGANO out of an acre of land. N'Diop would be the first.

*

The four nurses carried the coffin. It threw a shadow over the chapel and the white people turned, their eyes following the slow swaying of the cortège. The nuns intoned the Miserere; clear voices responded. They were all there, the Marie-Joséphines, the Marie-Christines, the Marie-Urbaines. They were there as so many Marie-Rosalies on the first day. A new dawn, a new relay, for what? Just as dark, just as fervent, just as young, and just as innocent of their destiny...

The oblong box rested on two stools in the aisle between the Dubois' row and the Bonenfants' row, facing the priest who descended toward it. Dubois could not take his eyes off it, the barely hewn wood, the naked cross. N'Diop was nothing in there, and the ceremony which he followed in spite of himself meant nothing. It would never bring him back, not in their memory and not in their faith. There was no God to spare here, and there was certainly no God for N'Diop. It was naked, this coffin underneath these unclothed prayers, beneath these hollow chants, surrounded by this cult without any objective. It slipped into oblivion; no tear would prevent it from going, no memory, nothing. Naked death. And God without men could do nothing either.

Bonenfant looked at the pitiful cortège and felt the truth torn from his heart. There was only one victory, only one, a single triumph: life.

Because N'Diop was dead, Bonenfant exulted in his entire threatened life. With so much evidence, he was thrilled; he was the strongest because he had survived. And his mind wandered away from N'Diop, wandered to all those he knew who had died: his father, dead, his grandfather, dead, and his uncle, a certain teacher, a certain friend and classmate, the dead in the war, and all the dead from before. He didn't know why he was a bit ashamed; his mind triumphed over Napoleon, Caesar, Attila, all dead. Vercingétorix, dead. Louis XIV, dead. They had meant nothing to him, this lot, but they remained in reserve in his schoolboy's conditioned memory. N'Diop had meant nothing to him either. There was nothing in this feeling of victory that smacked of resentment; it was a pure victory, a victory over no one. An inalienable right, indestructible. Live, and let die!

N'Diop's coffin was the logical end to his long adventure. It seemed perfectly clear to Elise, now that the body had received absolution. She had believed that events were unrelated. She had awaited a child. N'Diop had treated her. She had lost the child. He was dead. It was all linked. The story had been written for a long time. She had been so tense the past few months, fighting fate, believing she could influence destiny with all the strength of her love and her hatred. At the end of the day she would have liked to rest, to sit down with her arms hanging at her sides, to surrender and to say: Lord, I am nothing. You are everything. Forgive me, Lord, for my pride, for my prayers, for having believed for a moment that I could prevail. He was dead, the child assassin, and in her extreme fatigue, she felt no pleasure, only a deep pain. It was not N'Diop under the lid but THE BODY. He had given his son for our salvation. HIS ONLY SON, THE ONLY SON. Oh! Lord, I don't want to. She couldn't give him that. She begged with bits of prayers, pieces of the Gospel, fragments of parables; she pleaded in the name of her love. Broken, Elise sobbed on her chair.

Madame Bonenfant looked approvingly over her work: this casket, this chapel, and these singing girls. Whatever had been the religious sentiments of N'Diop, she had brought him back to the right path, perhaps not quite on the right hand of the Father, but within the immediate vicinity. The important thing was not that he was dead, but that he had been saved, and the priest had confirmed this. Absolved against his will,

N'Diop had been saved. She had been efficient, she had worked hard for the Savior. She knew he would recognize her for this and so many other things. Madame Bonenfant was assured that God would look upon her with clemency in the future. She had never sinned against Hope, not her. She had never imagined Despair, the suffering that spits blasphemy, Charity that screams revolt....

*

Now that N'Diop was no longer dead but deceased, legally, medically, and religiously, the inhabitants of OUREGANO could breathe again. In death subjugated, put in its place, or simply caught in the nets of habit and custom, there is nothing terribly remarkable. They could think about themselves, because the passing of N'Diop, reduced to the most banal dimensions of death, touched them individually. Normally it is the family who shoulders the largest part of the burden of mourning, wearing it on their clothing. See how the veiled widow sails by like a schooner and then, along the length of the rest of the cortège, watch the grayish black, turning white, turning blue; it's the bit of mortality that the mourners adopt, just the smallest part. Accompanying the deceased to the place where they will abandon him, they let themselves be touched by death, brushed by it, leaving a glove, a scarf, an armband, a tiny button! But they also leave something of themselves.

All along the cortège there are tears, fewer at the back, more in the middle, passionate tears at the front. It is not the dead man who is mourned. He was always very happy to be well out of it—and none too soon. He had so many good reasons for passing over to the other side. What is mourned is the moment shared with him, a life, a childhood, or a simple card party where he had made a fourth. That was he, the poor fellow! They feel a sense of amputation from his life, from his childhood, from the bridge party that had meant so much. Everything the deceased had touched becomes important, and those who had made even the smallest concession for him find themselves sanctified. And there are always more of the living around the deceased than during the time when he was forcing himself to hang on, ill, old, injured, powerless, condemned. It's that they want their part of the mourning, their share of heroism, their portion of respectability, their ration of the sensational. They do it *alla romana*,[*] leaving something of themselves but in return they want a reward and they take it, shamelessly, amid the tears, the ashes, the irremediable, the damned.

In this way, the death of N'Diop had something for everyone. You had only to see the ladies kneading the edges of their head scarves to be convinced. They didn't know what they had lost, they still didn't know it, but it would come to them, as with tears; all you had to do was to think about it. Madame Dubois had nothing in common with this doctor, African in more ways than one. Their paths had crossed on the back of Brigitte. Nothing to make a fuss about. Madame Bonenfant tried desperately to evoke the pain of the operation her cook had borne, but it was the latter that she pitied, not N'Diop. And yet...and yet...there had been something...but what? It is not possible to meet someone condemned to death with impunity, without some trace remaining. Deep in their humanity, they had lost a little of themselves. They remembered intensely. N'Diop's hands were trembling over the syringe, N'Diop's gestures were unsure handling the tweezers. He lowered his eyes, breathing heavily.... He was intimidated! That was it, they had found it. What they had lost today was N'Diop's intimidation, their superiority over him. Reassured, they pulled themselves together. They too could be in mourning.

Matilde had lost nothing. She felt the death as she had felt the loss of her beauty. N'Diop existed much more in his coffin than he ever had before. Dead, Matilde saw him at last. She had consoled herself for the lost image of herself as beautiful in faith; she had to believe in something outside herself. She rejoiced that the dead man was dead. She thought of God as outside all reality, not in the constant intervention between herself and Him of a poor person, a sick person, an unfortunate person, a relative.... Between God and herself, there was only one death whose shape the casket wiped out after covering its face with a mask. This was the link, the fragile pathway from the material to the void. Matilde's

---

[*] Roman style.

thoughts vanished as they rose toward the Lord like so many iridescent soap bubbles so fragile that they burst, nearly all of them, before reaching God. Matilde was in mourning from the bottom of her soul. She was no longer sure that she was sad.

*

There was nothing left but to clean out N'Diop's room, to condemn him irremediably to non-existence. The ladies of OUREGANO undertook to do it. There was very little in this room, but enough that these ladies felt the heavy shiver of death. They broke every important rule of propriety and modesty. But they were forced to be there. They pounced on the armoire first of all, ready to toss everything into a box using the tips of their fingers. Off you go, into the trash, the plague ridden, the remains of the dead man! And when they came to the clean laundry, they opened up the shirts "to see." It was crazy to throw all that out; it could be of use to someone. They looked at the collar and cuffs to measure the wear, and under the arms, and in the absence of the others they would have sniffed the fateful places to see if there did not subsist a murmur of life, a forget-me-not of sweat.

N'Diop's laundry spoke of his life in simple, almost miserable terms, a solitary life drained of color from the undershorts washed all balled up in the sink, frayed like pilled knit sweaters, stained, heavily stained—above all, worn. And the ladies examined even the crotch: Are these still presentable, these shorts? They formed a bad opinion of N'Diop's intimate life which came back to cut off the official life, just by-the-by. There were one or two short-sleeved shirts of African cloth, a traditional outfit, a *grand boubou*[*] that Madame Bonenfant unfolded and held against herself to see what she looked like in such a thing! The tone was sure, no longer a question of disgust but of pleasure. It was the frank camaraderie of burgeoning drawers and exposed armoires.

---

[*] A *grand boubou* is a traditional costume for men, with wide pants and a large, flowing gown, often embroidered around the neck and sleeves and down the front.

They exclaimed over the smallest things, holding up another shirt by the sleeves—What amazing shirts he had, N'Diop! He collected them or what?—and tearing it from each other until, puffed with laughter, they let it go. Madame Dubois abandoned them to take charge of the desk. She opened the drawers; there were a few scattered papers. A portfolio. A photograph. But it was hard to tell if it was a young girl or a woman. She stood very tall on the threshold of a hut; near her was a child of three or four, out of focus as well. They tried to guess the secret of the photo. Where was it taken? Not Dakar, surely? Let's see, let's see! His mother, his sister, his wife, HIS MISTRESS, THE BASTARD! Village marriage? They don't even know each other; they're betrothed in the cradle! What customs! The violent light on the overexposed photograph made a vague halo, like a memory.

They had given up on the clothes and were now pulling out the books, looking at the titles and end pages. The titles to make a judgment, the end pages for the dedication, often so revealing! To my dear N'Diop, for all these years together at William Ponty. For you N'Diop, this book so full of wisdom. With my very best wishes. I hope you will like these poems as well as I do. As for Madame Bonenfant, she had her own particular way of proceeding with the inspection of a book. She took it by the covers and shook it so that it would release its crop of letters, pictures, or bills. She harvested a letter. It was about money, help, aid, clothes for a child, a father who was getting on, a mother who sent her blessing. It was banal.

On the other hand, they really liked the pages written by N'Diop himself. So Monsieur N'Diop was a poet! An African poet of course because for the meter you didn't have to know how to count. And Madame Dubois had tried in vain to work it out: One, two, three, four, five, six, seven, and tapping on the table with the flat of her hand or repeating in her head, one, two, three, four, five, six, seven, eight, nine, ten, eleven, twelve. N'Diop's poems were always off. There were big words, Earth, Africa, Woman, River, and big ideas, Homeland, People, Suffering, Love, Africa again. There were everyday words, calabash, child, millet, fish, and always Africa. What can you rhyme with that word? asked Madame Bonenfant.

III

Shortly thereafter, Elise's hatred of children submerged her like a heavy swell that she could not hold back. Hatred of the child Tiffany especially, because she so liked the OTHER ONE, who had grown in height and wisdom since she had conceived him, educated, reared, and multiplied. She liked all the others, the big Yvonne who was already a woman, the Bonenfant sons who were boys, the younger one just learning to read, the little lamb! And the Africans, because they were blacks. She liked them individually; she liked them globally. She detested Tiffany.

She did not accept in the little girl the side of her that escaped childhood, or so it seemed to Elise, yet fell neither into the category of adult nor into any of the intermediate unrewarding ages. Tiffany was nothing. Nothing. The eyes drawn deeply into a vague face. Nothing, the sharp body in its child's clothes, soiled at the collar or the hem marks of six, eight, ten years, ridiculous with those flowerettes, those rabbits embroidered in chain stitch, Snow White and the house of the seven dwarves. Tiffany displayed only the appearance of childhood.

As for her attitude, one expected a gesture, a sign of submission, an effort that made her a child again. She did nothing so much as try to be forgotten. Elise was sure of it. Since the beginning of the year she had tried to make her disappear. In front, so as to avoid meeting her eyes, behind because in front it became evident that she only looked at Elise, behind the tall Yvonne so as to not see her anymore. But she sensed her everywhere, with her vague eyes, present and absent at the same time, on the moon, elsewhere, half awake, in the clouds, gaping at the crows, inattentive, distracted, scatterbrained.... She had called her all that and even worse, because Tiffany did not react, because she became rigid in the face of adult speeches, indifferent in the extreme. The insults that hit her only bounced off; they returned to Elise still hot with her anger and disdain.

She felt on this morning an enormous freedom, an infinite deliverance, knowing that her anxiety had an object. She had found a scapegoat. She rode Tiffany with a violence of which only those who think laziness lurks beneath exhaustion are capable. Had she been stupid, Tiffany would have been pardoned; suspected of intelligence, where had Elise gotten the idea that Tiffany was not the least bit stupid? Tiffany was hunted with so much spite that it had taken Elise some time to realize what was happening. Elise went after her with so much malice that she was already running out of weapons in the teaching battle against this dunce.

The fight was on then, first at the level of insults: donkey, blockhead, cretin, imbecile, lump, thick-as-a-brick, jug, turkey, so much that the Bonenfant boys learned words they hadn't known. The whole class had a morality lesson in the flesh. All they had to do was watch and listen. What the class didn't learn was that the punishment didn't stop with the words; it went on all morning long and started up again the next day and the day after, every minute that Elise went remorselessly after Tiffany. Elise was clever about how she proved to Tiffany that her stupidity was compounded by laziness. She kept on questioning her and while Tiffany reflected, because of course she didn't answer instantly, Elise made comments that sent the class into hysterics. Take your time. We have all day. Don't rush yourself, of course. Would you like a pillow? Tiffany found no answer. Elise was thrilled. The students took the teacher's side: Truly, Tiffany went too far! Elise gave the answer. Everyone knew that. It was easy! Elise asked the same question again and Tiffany remained silent, her head filled with dreams, the insults of Elise: A donkey was soft, a turkey pretty, a brick reddish, but why a jug? She saw her grandmother's flowerpots, red and blue, and it made her remember a small and tender feeling that took her back, her heart beating loudly, to the pillow that Elise had offered her because she had always preferred the long bolster-type pillows. No, Tiffany could not answer.

Elise did not take the time to savor her victory because she wanted less to prove the irreducible laziness of Tiffany than to remove the child, strangle her, reject her, wring her neck, annihilate her. NO LONGER SEE HER. She yelled, and yelled again, to reach Tiffany, to destroy her at the core of her silence, to break her out of her dreams, to expel her from the place where she took refuge to escape from her. Elise buzzed all around

Tiffany, attacking faster and faster, here and there. She would soon get her, bring her back to childhood, back to the narrow place of terror and dependence of which only adults are masters.

*

This particular week there was a shower of zeros. An ineluctable succession, Tiffany fell from zero to zero. The first, then half an hour later the second had startled her. She had accepted them before with resignation. The faster they came the more she had the impression of being buried in them. Elise, at least, was aware of it because as soon as the exercise was completed, she went for Tiffany's notebook, saying, And a zero for Tiffany! Another zero, poor Tiffany! What do you deserve? What can I put on this trash? Aren't you ashamed? You don't take me seriously! You can't even write! Tiffany felt an oddly bitter taste in her mouth—caramel or tears? But the tears did not fall; she didn't have time to think about it. She was beaten. She couldn't mount another challenge, couldn't swim upstream; stuck, squeezed at the shoulders above the fault, she was drowning. That's how it is to die when you can no longer conceive of reality in its entirety: you go outside yourself abruptly; you go somewhere else.

The zeros opened for her, however, the door to her family. It was out of the question, admitting what had happened. To: Did you have a good day? she answered: Very good, smiling. Once the lie was decided, it knew no limits. And to keep it up, it meant a lot of lying. Did you make any mistakes on the dictation? Not one. Her clear eyes looked straight into her mother's. And your math problem? I was the only one to get it right. Tiffany knew that success came through the failure of the others. Tiffany had taken a long time, but in the end she had done well. Ultimately, there were two types of student like the two types of memory, those who learned quickly but soon forgot, and those who took longer but who learned solidly. Obviously, Tiffany belonged to the latter category. Matilde gloated. She had always believed in Tiffany. Remember, she said to Michel, I told the teacher right from the beginning when she wanted her to repeat a grade. That's my girl, said Michel. What luck, Tiffany, do you realize, you will be able to go into the sixth grade, to take Latin, English, and after that Greek! Spanish! Calculus!

It was fun being a good student; it made you the pet of the family. You were loved, respected; there were secret admiring glances. They asked what you were reading as if this would influence your studies. How did you get to be so good? Matilde had an opinion on everything. A child who reads is naturally a good speller. Tiffany had the child's version of Racine on her knees. What are you reading, Darling? *Iphigenia*? That's good, my pet, good work, baby doll. They spread it around: Imagine how surprised I was to find her deep in *Iphigenia*! Very good, Tiffany. You'll see when you know Greek, you'll read Euripides in the original. It's so much better! Iphigenia could not be read alone, as singular, indivisible.

If it hadn't been for Elise's scathing attacks that rubbed her nose in her laziness, her vile handwriting, her slow wit, her absent memory, Tiffany would have quickly found her parents' purring monotonous. But here was Elise, who could no longer stand her, and the whole school knew it, and none of them would miss a chance to spread it all over OUREGANO. At this time the military policeman, the now-and-then father of Big Yvonne, the Bonenfants, and perhaps even the Dubois KNEW. So the situation was temporary. Conscious of what was coming, Tiffany looked at the sweet face of her mother as if at something forbidden. She had managed to open it, to light it from the inside, to animate it. She had never seen anything as lovely.

The fatal hour sounded one evening at the Club. All the way from the street, Tiffany had seen the Refons' van. They were all there. When Elise appeared, her face tense, Tiffany looked straight into her eyes as if at a challenge. Elise advanced toward Matilde, and Matilde, who was so happy to be able to talk about Tiffany's progress, and in public no less, moved toward Elise. They met in the center of the room, under the overhead fan. Who would speak first?

*

When they came back, they were silent. Nothing seemed less like the end of the world, and yet, it was the end. Tiffany wanted a moment of reprieve, but on the point of escaping she became reluctant, seized by tender thoughts. Things were good with them when you knew how to extinguish the anxiety, leaving on a small night-light, just enough to breathe; things were all right in the car that hurled along the savanna. And, as if by accident, they saw giraffes, a bouquet of giraffes only a hundred meters away. Michel did not stop and Tiffany turned to watch as long as possible. The noise of the automobile had alerted them; they had begun to gallop quickly away, slowing as they reached the edge of the light, the large red sun that was setting.

I saw giraffes! I saw giraffes! Two big ones and a little one. They have soft eyes, soft horns, soft skin. I want to sleep with the giraffes, curled up between their legs and the necks. A last instant of happiness. Impossible. The car stopped. She would have to get out and walk under the white lamp. And then the shouting began, a torrent of screams. How close she was. How close to the danger of their words! Matilde was crying. What humiliation! How could she do that, to her! She didn't deserve this. The tone of the schoolteacher! And the Bonenfant woman who weighed in with her remarks, and even the Dubois woman knew about it! She howled, sobbing with rage. Michel would not let them show such disrespect to her. No nurse would have dared treat her this way, and the brat had made her a laughingstock. She must have had a good time all this week. But the jig was up. Liar, loafer, pervert, hussy, wicked child. She would see! She would see!

No, Tiffany had not laughed. She had felt good giving them in just a few words so much pleasure. On the other hand she didn't feel responsible for all this angry unhappiness. They could abandon her. She was not happy with them; they were not happy with her. All their dissatisfaction came from her. Why was she obliged to do things for which she had no talent? She would have liked it if one of them had approached her saying, We're getting rid of you, like Elise had said in class: I wash my hands of you. She would have felt a space of freedom instead of the insufferable embrace that their pain imposed on her. She was in danger here; fear came from inside this house, which was suddenly and definitively intolerable. She wanted quiet. She was angry at this mother who carried on, bemoaning her fate endlessly.

The next day at school, Elise held forth on children who did not work well and who lied about it, an inexorable vicious circle. The whole class looked at Tiffany and Tiffany looked, as she had never done before. Moses' eyes rested on her, full of compassion. They read each other's eyes, the anger of the little girl calmed in the large dark eyes, so sad, of the little boy. Elise finished by saying that she was going to try to bring Tiffany back onto the right path, and this she would do only because Tiffany's mother had begged her to. She asked them to take out their notebooks. Solemnly, she took the pages of the previous week and ripped them out of Tiffany's notebook. The string that held the notebook together hung loose, the leaves badly torn out beginning to curl up. She dictated. Tiffany did not take up her pen. She crossed her arms on the desk and tried to sleep. She would have managed if Elise had not made her get up and if she had not thrown her out. She said: School is for working, not for sleeping. And she added: You thumb your nose at me! Well, my girl, I am stronger than you.

In the courtyard, there was only dust and the shadow of the hibiscus bushes with their fat flowers spreading softly, gently over the shiny foliage. They were all very strong. Did she dispute this? But she didn't want them anymore. The idea of them held nothing more for her. Since they would not abandon her—just the opposite, they were always there holding her by their side—it would be she who would leave them. She would leave OUREGANO; she would go to The PLACE; she would go anywhere, anywhere there were no adults, either good or bad. She wanted quiet, the perfume of flowers and the gentleness of the animals.

*

Leave for good? Are departing and letting go the same as leaving? And the feet that carry you, if they flee, do they leave for good? Urgency and risk do not necessarily mean the finality of leaving for good.

Tiffany departed, fled even, but she left nothing for good. It's not until later, in a sheltering place or in the course of time, that one morning you recognize the precise moment that you left your house, your parents, your childhood. The back turned, the feet going forward, the chin on the chest, the hand that closed the door, seem like so many bits of proof that you left for good. And then you remember the faces in the last moments. Rarely sweet and sad faces, solemn, but faces swamped in banality, deluded faces.

For children like Tiffany the door does not close in violence or the sharp trajectory of an angry rebuke. When this happens the child cannot leave anything; care is taken to make sure she sees all the anger and to heap on the recriminating screams until her resistance is extinguished and a knot forms in her throat above a quivering chest. Pulled by an elbow, the head forced up, she must be the spectator of her crime. She is shown the evil, the pain; she is told about the war and plenty of other things that are too old for her to understand. She is given a family version of all the horror in the world. The father wounded to the quick by the zeros, the mother reduced to spluttering by the schoolteacher's revelations, the gambler who has lost everything on the notorious bet called a child, the lover betrayed. In an instant the child sees what is hidden from her in the weekly magazines, *Détective* and *Paris Match* combined! *Noir et blanc* and *Aux écoutes!** It is not until everything has returned to its former mood, when the adults get back to their own images now more exaggerated than ever but still saying the same things, that the child can open the door and leave for good.

A mother, you leave while she is quietly lingering over a cup of lemon tea; a father, you leave when he is busy looking elsewhere. The blue tablecloth and the white plates, the day-to-day details, you leave for good with a terrible feeling of urgency that the physical appearance of these things does not explain. Terror has no need of the present; it has absolute recall. And on this morning, the mother is no longer the mother, never again; the father will never again be the father. The tablecloth will never again be blue and the plates were never white. The day-to-day things are full of traps. Screams can slip in between the footsteps of the

---

* Gossip magazines featuring celebrities and their troubles.

boy who is clearing the table. Anger can spurt out at the mere chink of a cup on its saucer. Terror slumbers in the smallest of objects, in the slightest gesture. It is a screen between the world and Tiffany. On this morning Tiffany leaves nothing because she sees nothing. Fear had laid its hand over her eyes. Tiffany was blind.

Leaving was making all the usual gestures, folding her napkin, picking up her book bag, taking her *topee* off the hook, putting it on her head, tightening the chin strap at the jugular; it was going down one, two, three steps. It was looking down the road at the van, feeling impatient and then running as if to catch up. Leaving was reflecting on actions never before considered, taking their measure, their nature, giving them only what they deserve, no more. It was difficult to play at being when that self would never again be. After the turn in the road where the van should have stopped, everything became easy; nothing more was needed to liberate joy and fear at the same time, run, throw away the book bag, pull off the chin strap, and if the dress didn't go too it was because it was impossible to abandon everything at once.

Leaving was catching your breath, planting your feet in the dust, and tracing a path through the trees. It was becoming an outsider. Tiffany had brought nothing with her. Her eyes looked differently at different things, her legs took her to different places, and her hands, so awkward, plied with perfect tension the branches that obstructed her passage, a quick and exact movement that permitted progress and at the same time hid its evidence, for Tiffany avoided breaking the branches, holding them just enough so they would return to their places, elastic, behind her. Leaving, it was departing for another place; it was being otherwise.

*

Hiding, making no noise at all, waiting and trembling in fear of being discovered. Tiffany's first day away from her father's house. Shelter and peace, which is what The Place was, soon showed its deficiencies: not far enough away, not deep enough into the vegetation, and every movement splintered the air. The Place was no longer The Place because games and dreams no longer lived there. Was this defending the Palace of the Ladyfingers against a ravenous ogre? Would Snow White have been found if she had not taken refuge in the house of the dwarves? Hiding wasn't enough; it would be necessary to disappear, which was impossible, or die, which was possible. Tiffany, lying down on the floor of the truck bed with her eyes closed, heard screams.

Tiffany was listening, listening again to everything that growled inside her and that made her suffer. Matilde's frenzied shrieks, without rhythm and without modulation that keep rising rather than receding. Michel's thick shouts, rough and deaf that go on and on, a long exhalation of screams, and Matilde's screech that rises in the inferno of Michel's shouts. The screech that exhales life, climbing, tortured by Michel's hollering, always louder. Rising perfectly. It breaks the voice but Michel's shout holds it back, aborted; it stays there in mid-air, takes another breath on throwaway words. Sad observations. It fires up again. Such exclamation! It staggers, catches itself, rises again, Michel's shouts supporting it. They growl, a bass sound. The earth opens onto the piercing mountain. The snow peak of Matilde's scream takes hold of the clouds. The castle of the queen of the night protected by enslaved monsters. The clanging chains and perfect eyebrows of the witch.

The screams of dogs tell simple stories: love, the hunt, impatience, and, if you listen, you can hear what they say. If the scream is deranged, the threat is unparalleled. Magic, divine intervention? What ghost has passed by, what bubonic volcano exploded? You listen, you look. You blame yourself for not understanding. It's a reasonable fear. The scream of dogs, the horrible scream of dogs is reasonable. The mad dog that chews its tail as it screams is reasonable. Men are afraid of what the dog is feeling and what they cannot see. When the screams of man go mad, it is absolute horror. This scream has nothing reasonable about it. It says nothing true; it says nothing magical. It speaks mad things. Yes, truly mad. It's not about hunger when Matilde screams against Michel. It's not about love, Matilde's scream linked to Michel's. It's not about fear, Matilde's scream that buries itself in Michel's. Tiffany did not understand the dislocated sound of ambition, of success, of deception, of wounded pride, of frustration, of lack.

Tiffany knew when an animal was going to die. A bird had its feathers all splayed out, its eyelids open, blue, the eye white. A doe's muzzle drooped and she was tame, a sudden abandon, because she doesn't become tame until the very last minute and to feel her next to your skin, to hold it against your body, in your arms, you have to accept that she is going to die. The last moments of a doe tamed by death are the saddest, even if you deny it to yourself by feeding her grass: Hey, she's eating! When she dies, the grass will be found on her tongue. The little gorilla crosses his arms, refuses a banana you offer him. He pouts as hard as he can. He swings slowly back and forth. He makes himself dizzy until he falls at last. How does a little girl die when she wants to so badly? Tiffany didn't know.

*

Night fell. Tiffany settled into the cab of the truck. She was not afraid; she had wanted to sleep here. She had anticipated this moment so intensely that nothing surprised her. The rustling of the foliage, the cracking noises, the tree-night under the night sky, a little hungry, hungry for something cooked, something warm, something sweet, and something salted. Hunger in the night like an indefinable excitement, one eye open to see what happens. A happiness tangled in fear. A sadness, a little spongy, like at the end of a sobbing cry when calm is returning and the force of the heartache is gone. Tiffany didn't miss anything. She was comfortable here. She wasn't happy, however. Freedom was for dreaming, not for living. There were a thousand things that held her back there, everything she had overlooked because it was insignificant. The pickup truck contained everything essential; she could drink, eat, sleep, read, write if she wanted to.

What more did she need? She didn't know, the indispensable, what could not be taken away, a territory, space, discoveries. The noise of the *boy*'s steps in the living room, the smell of smoke from the oven in the morning, the red and white of the armchair's slipcover. It was not Matilde, and it was not Michel, but something that included them and at the same time refused them even as it created them. They had no place there: it was called home. It was warm bread, a watered lawn, large baskets of vegetables, the call of the parakeets in the birdhouse, the braying of the donkey, peaceful sounds, rich smells, bright colors. It was the cycle of food and sleep. The ballet around the table that is set, that is cleared, shaken tablecloths, wrinkled tablecloths, washed and ironed tablecloths. Clean dishes, dirty dishes, clean dishes.... The ballet around the lanterns: kerosene, matches and red teetering light, matches and white light, and the intense noise of the acetylene lamps, brown faces, pale faces, sudden night.

Time stopped here the entire night, lost its duration. What sign would awaken her, the one that had slipped behind the shadows? How empty nature was, empty of regular palpitations, of domestic preparations. Dawn peopled itself at the house and prepared Tiffany's stirring. Muffled sounds, careful gestures, a caress into which erupted the sound of a pot falling on the floor. Clumsy! What silence would heave her to the edge of sleep, what noise would throw her into the light? And her day, once the fears that had submerged her had dissipated, how would it go, now that the pressure of returning no longer inflamed the course of time, now that she was free and alone?

Go for water or light a fire, read or collect guavas? What would inspire action, desire or boredom? Tiffany suspected that it would be boredom as is always the case when dreaming is done. The wonder of the walk to the nearest oxbow lake, the one she would use when the time came. The wonder of the stores of tinned foods, they represented a meal, a day of life, a day of freedom, a day of solitude. But today there was no walk to the water hole. It was a long way when you were alone; it was a long way when you were free. Tiffany turned over in her hands the round can of *paté*, the flat can of sardines, the oblong can of corned beef. Tin cans sealing in a taste too familiar, little hopes in tin cans, sad, rich realities. Life could not be fed from these oils. Besides, Tiffany had no can opener. In the Garden of Eden, the Surinam cherries were bitter and the guavas green; in the Garden of Eden, the mangos grew too high up. And when Tiffany opened a papaya, the warm odor of the flesh on fire made her uncomfortable. This is how the world of adults overcomes children. From their birth, they attach them, line by line. In this way, for them freedom has no more meaning.

*

Here is Michel, here is Matilde
Monsieur Dubois, Madame Dubois
Ah! Moses, Ah! Moses...

Monsieur Bonenfant and Madame
Monsieur Refons, Madame Refons.
Ah! Moses, Ah! Moses...

The policeman, Big Yvonne
Beretti, Marie-Rosalie.
Ah! Moses, Ah! Moses.
Ah! Moses in front of them all.

    Beretti advanced in front of the parents, in front of the Administrator, in front of the Judge and the policeman. He seized Tiffany by the arm and held tight so she could not get away. He crossed the four steps that separated the little girl from the people of OUREGANO. He showed them he was a volunteer, that they were not dealing with an ingrate. He had set out to find her and he had brought back the lost child. The four steps he had crossed in the grass, they represented the distance of absence, all that separated France from Africa, impossible contact between Negroes and whites, irremediable rupture between adults and children. He was a hero, Beretti; the white people all gathered on the other side waiting for the little girl to be delivered to them. What! No dash of the mother toward the child! No action on the part of the doctor to verify the health of the young patient! No questions from the Judge that would lead them to conclude that the little girl had not been raped! Elise did not cry out: My little one! They silently delegated all their powers to Beretti, who used them. In front of Tiffany, he was the father, the mother, the judge, the policeman, and the schoolteacher. He was woman and man.

    Tiffany did not see the group and didn't feel Beretti's hand that took hold of her high up, well into the shoulder; she looked only at Moses. He had turned her in; he had guided them to her. He had given her only a day and a night, just enough time to lose her fondness for solitude, not enough to inhabit it and to tame it. She didn't blame him. She would have gone back to the house in any case; she had no other choice. But she discovered that she had never counted for him; that is, she had counted only as far as school was concerned, science, power, and, one day, access to the world of white people. If he had said nothing, she would have cost him everything, but since he had spoken up, he saw his dearest hopes confirmed, the future little N'Diop. He already had a choice place, next to, in front of. He was the guide and the companion; he was not yet an equal...

All of a sudden, OUREGANO was enriched by one Negro. They reclaimed Moses. They made a good deal. Moses possessed all good qualities and he was young. For everyone, the white people that is, Moses had a name. He existed with his absent father, his interchangeable mother and his brothers whom he didn't recognize. Madame Dubois said: Moses. Madame Bonenfant said: Moses. And the schoolteacher no longer said: You, over there. He became a worthy student; he would earn the Certificate of Primary Studies. OUREGANO would open the door to Dakar. Was it Monsieur Dubois who had first mentioned William Ponty? Moses was happy in the world where people had names like in books and occupied precise functions, respectable people. He had had enough of his anonymous world that was nothing. Here everything had a consistency; everything was organized for an ideal order. Courage did not have to put up with hunger, death, illness; it appropriated the sweet names of education, labor, work, miraculous names, the names of marvelous stories.

Tiffany thought it was Big Yvonne who had denounced them. A real tattletale, that one. Madame, Tiffany was always playing with Moses! Elise questioned Moses; he didn't want to answer. His silence hid something. The Judge would make him talk. Bonenfant threatened him, hit him; Moses said nothing. Matilde was told; she cried in front of him. Monsieur Dubois would have him expelled from school; Monsieur Refons agreed. Moses was afraid, he was crying, and he admitted everything. Now he was ashamed. And if Tiffany were mistaken, if Big Yvonne had nothing to do with it, and neither did Elise? Moses must have seen that only one person counted in OUREGANO, and it was not Monsieur Dubois, the supposed top of the hierarchy, it was not Beretti, compromised by the murder of N'Diop, and it was not the parents who would have recovered their wayward child without making a scene. The most important person was the Judge. And what if Moses had gone to find Monsieur Bonenfant, alone, like a grown-up? What if he had said he had just heard about Tiffany's disappearance, that he knew where she was, that he could only tell it to the Judge, because the others would not have paid any attention to him? He would have been humble and submissive, his little conscience torturing him.... He would have expressed himself in perfect French. No, Moses would not have encountered ingratitude.

*

Of all the adults who had come to find her, it was her mother that Tiffany hated. All the more so since it was for her that Tiffany's heart had begun to beat in the first place, with the scream "Mama," the scream that is forever stuck in the throat, our only animal scream. Tiffany had uttered her "Mama" the way people say "My God!" the way people say "No!" She had said it like an old man, like a woman; she had not said it like a child. Matilde had of course misinterpreted it; how is it possible to think that a child calls out for you because she hates you, that the heart that is pounding is terrorized by disgust.

Everyone had loved this "Mama," and Matilde had been secretly flattered by it. Tiffany had confessed to her fault in public and absolved her mother at the same time. They would have to place the guilt elsewhere, with the father, who had never been much of a father, and with the schoolteacher, who lacked psychological understanding. But they were not accused of anything. It was not their fault. If soldiers now had to babysit, or schoolteachers to diagnose minds! Tiffany was the only guilty one. The "Mama" had saved Matilde. She was neither with Tiffany nor with the others but in a place apart, untouchable, sanctified by the Love of the Child. She was THE MOTHER, the only wonderful thing in the world because it was understood that children always love their mothers, no matter what.

Tiffany detested Matilde. It was the only passion that inhabited her, her only vitality, her only reason to live. Hatred accompanied her from morning to evening in small, furtive actions, all destined to avoid contact with Matilde. Tiffany kept well out of Matilde's reach, away from her mother's cheek. How it made her sick, this room with its covered bed, its armoire with the hem of a dress caught in the door. And the sugared odor of perfume in the bathroom, which Matilde had just sprayed, or because the heavy crystal perfume bottle had been left with its faceted stopper off, was intolerable to her. And Matilde's voice, distant, near, in the room, outside, made her skin crawl.

In the days that followed her capture, Tiffany tried to avoid her mother. She reversed her earlier steps when her feet had led her inevitably to follow Matilde, in a kind of lovers' *pas de deux*. Now Tiffany fled the places where her mother was likely to go. She needed the same cunning as before, the same hearing, the same sense of the hunt to guess where the young woman was going, but she made use of her senses, unencumbered by love, to flee the former object of her passion. Inversely, Matilde, who had been touched by her daughter's flight, sought Tiffany out. She wanted as much to keep an eye on her so that she wouldn't run away again as to make the most of the situation, before childhood was completely finished. Matilde called Tiffany and Tiffany answered, "Yes, Mama," while turning her back. Matilde did not call again; she wanted less to see the child than to know she was still somewhere in the house.

At the table Tiffany stopped eating. The pieces of meat remained in her mouth. That little unconscious motion that expedited food into the throat, Tiffany couldn't remember it anymore. She sat there, stupidly, chewing and rechewing, waiting for it to come back to her. This new problem was all the more troublesome since it attracted Matilde's attention, Matilde's voice, Matilde's eyes, and Matilde's hand, which took the fork from her fingers saying, Let's eat, it's good, the way all mothers do. Tiffany saw the hand over her plate, a tanned hand with white nails, translucent dead tips and clipped cuticles, and near the moons a bit of leftover, badly dissolved red nail polish. This hand begged, anxious to show that at the end of the fork there was something appetizing. As if she were calling a dog to dinner, she stirred the food to tempt her. Tiffany's mouth closed less to refuse what it was offered than to keep from throwing up what she had already swallowed. Tiffany was very pale, breathless, faced with her mother's hand. So the hand abandoned the fork and approached the face of the child. It touched the forehead and Matilde, like all mothers, said: You don't have a fever, do you?

What could no longer be resolved between the child and her parents was resolved between the parents and the society of OUREGANO. They all agreed on one point. Tiffany could not stay any longer among them. Her gaze endangered the other children; her attitude defied the adults. They decided that she would leave. Grown-ups have a solution to hide their defeat: it's called boarding school, a convent. The child would be cared for, reared, disciplined, educated. It would certainly be better than the present situation. She would be sent in the name of a serious education. There is always a large garden, flowers, perfect and maternal schoolteachers. It's not prison, and you get to go out every Sunday. They would select one of these establishments for Tiffany. The only thing left to discuss was the location. Madame Dubois wanted it to be in the Paris region; the Bonenfants preferred Lyon because they had a cousin who had taught there. Matilde remembered that her parents were near Bordeaux.... Already she was weakening....

They now imagined Tiffany exclusively in navy blue, her braids tight and neat. She would brush her teeth every morning and shine her shoes. They saw her in the sixth grade, *rosa*[*] the rose, the War of the Gauls. Tiffany playing volley ball. Tiffany decorated with the medal for good behavior, for accuracy, and for orderliness, all in one. Tiffany in line wearing her beret. Tiffany at church, the Mass and Salvation. Tiffany in the dining hall, eating everything. They imagined these scenes and delighted in them. They loved her this way. They were ready to forgive her for what she was because of what she would become. She was touching, Tiffany, as a serious little girl. She was lucky! The ladies shared their memories of boarding school, and the Institution of the Legion of Honor ceremony, which Madame Dubois had experienced, gave a note of glory and high tone to the common convent to which they had decided to send Tiffany. In the future, there would be balls for Tiffany with the young men of the best universities. She had become a slightly stiff young girl,

---

[*] Latin.

very distinguished, not too pretty, serious, and smart. Perhaps a polytechnician* or a scientist would one day come her way...

Since Tiffany seemed not to comprehend, they told her how happy
she would be there with all the other little girls, how it would be to experience the autumn crocus (saffron meadow flowers), winter and
snow, spring and cherry trees in bloom. There, in France, cows had
calves and chickens had chicks. They described for her the sea that she
would not see, the countryside where she would not walk, the mountains
that she would not climb. They told her about their own past, their lost
happiness, their forgotten childhoods, their mutilated youth. That was her
future.

Around Tiffany's neck Matilde slipped a sign on which was written:
Marie-Françoise Murano. 9 years old. Institute of the Teaching Sisters.
Slaughterhouse Road.† X. France. Tiffany was so occupied by the cardboard that decorated her chest that she paid only distracted attention to
the last moments she spent in OUREGANO. At the airfield, they were all
there, but behind the kisses she recognized no one; they had never kissed
her before. Her departure gave her a disturbing feeling that was above all
the fear that she would have to stay. Best to get it over with. Beretti
handed the mail to the pilot; Tiffany climbed aboard. The others stepped
back. She saw them once the plane began taxiing out to the runway; they
were pitiful, huddled together. She saw them again as the plane was
gathering speed in the opposite direction, the distance making them indistinguishable, one from the other. Tiffany could no longer tell her

---

* A polytechnician is a graduate of one of the *Grandes Écoles* founded by
Napoleon. *Polytechnique*, a very rigid military school, is similar in terms of its
engineering curriculum to the Massachusetts Institute of Technology in the
United States. They want discipline for Tiffany.

† *Rue des sanguinaires*, in the original. "Sanguinary" or perhaps "bloody"
might have done here, although the latter seems gruesome as a street name and
the former a bit erudite and therefore unlikely in a small town. As is explained
in *Propriété privée*, the sequel to OUREGANO, the street is named for the slaughterhouse (*abattoir*) at the end of the road. There is also reason to associate the
nuns of the school in *Propriété privée* with the activities of the slaughterhouse.
There is even a scene at the end of *Propriété privée* that repeats the scene in
OUREGANO in which Michel checks the meat before it is distributed. "Sanguine"
also means hopeful, a note of irony on Constant's part, undoubtedly.

mother from Madame Dubois, or Monsieur Bonenfant from Albert Refons. Together they made a magma from which extended the tentacle of
an arm waving good-bye, as though it were being swallowed up. She saw
them one last time as the plane gained altitude and made a half turn
above the field. Little white dots, like the first sign of rot on meat, tiny
white feeder fish. Nothing special.

The trip was not long. Stopover, change of planes, a stewardess led
away a docile little girl. Tiffany was lost in the contemplation of her
name, her age. First, her name. It was good to have this honest first
name, a real first name for a little girl; it was good and it was reassuring.
Suddenly she was someone with an identity, a little girl like hundreds of
others. She liked even the commonness of this first name, and she
chanted to herself the litany of its saints. Françoise, *framboise*. Françoise,
gerboise.* Françoise. Delicious. Tiffany didn't mean anything. Tiffany
was nothing. She had been called that because she didn't exist or to make
her not exist. It was pleasant to get out of her thing-name and to put on
her person-name, like Brigitte, like Gaston.... And it was touching to be
nine years old, surprising even. She remembered only being seven; she
had never been eight. Eight had been OUREGANO, and she had already
forgotten. Suddenly, she had become a big girl; suddenly, she had aged
two years. Extraordinary journey. The night had invaded the huge cabin
of the airplane. There was music and light, and then darkness. Glued to
the small window, Marie-Françoise looked at the streaks of clouds. She
didn't know to what skies they belonged but she recognized them; they
would never leave her. In her arms she squeezed the cardboard sign that
brought her back to herself.

The mothers came and went. They carefully placed the folded
clothes in the cubbyholes and the last moments with their children
smelled of lavender. They spoke of the Wednesday shirt, the Thursday
panties, the Friday socks, and the Saturday collar. The little girls had an
entire week of clothes, scented and motherly, the stages of a caress that
started sweetly on the back, dropped lightly over the buttocks, a tickle on
the little feet—Stop! You're making me laugh!—and then they put their

---

* *Framboise* means raspberry; *gerboise* rhymes with it and means gerbil or
jerboa, a possible reference to the pet killed earlier in the novel.

arms around their necks to take them back to school; it was Sunday. Tiffany wondered how to get her clothes up onto the shelf she had been assigned. Climb on the base of the armoire perhaps, hold onto the door with one hand and toss them up? She had not finished when a nun came to inspect. She opened Tiffany's cupboard and looked at the sloppy pile of shirts, the balls of socks, and the collars that were losing their intimidating celluloid. Well, well, we have a messy one! Miss Murano, you are a mess.

She was left in the dormitory. Fifty beds, twenty-five on one side, twenty-five on the other, separated by an aisle. Next to each bed, a stool. A rectangle, a square, a rectangle, a square, all the way to the end, a long way, to where the white washstands stood. All the blue quilts in the room rising up, it made a heavy swell in the room, a choppy, overpowering sea. Tiffany felt sick; she vomited on the blond sand of the parquet floor, a starfish splatter. The day was dawning red. Tiffany remained glued to the spot, not knowing whether to go toward the bathroom or into the hall to ask for help. She had to be pushed aside to clean the floor with bleach. A nun, on all fours, scrubbed. The mark was imbedded permanently, whiter on the wax, designating Tiffany's place for years to come.

SELECTED BIBLIOGRAPHY

Works by Paule Constant

Balta. Paris: Gallimard Folio, 1983.
Confidence pour confidence. Paris: Gallimard, 1998.
La fille du Gobernator. Paris: Gallimard, 1994.
Le Grand Ghâpal. Paris: Gallimard, 1991.
OUREGANO. Paris: Gallimard, 1980.
Propriété privée. Paris: Gallimard, 1981.
Sucre et secret. Paris: Gallimard, 2003.
Un monde à l'usage des Demoiselles. Paris: Gallimard, 1987.
White Spirit. Paris: Gallimard, 1989.

Translations in English:
The Governor's Daughter (*La fille du Gobernator*). Translated by Betsy
    Wing. Lincoln: University of Nebraska Press, 1998.
Trading Secrets (*Confidence pour confidence*). Translated by Betsy
    Wing. Lincoln: University of Nebraska Press, 2001.
White Spirit. Translated by Betsy Wing, Lincoln: University of Nebraska
    Press, 2005.

Critical Works

Adamson, Ginette. "*Un monde à l'usage des Demoiselles*." *Rocky Moun-
    tain Review* 63 (1989): 1-2.
Christmann, Ellen. "Untersuchungen zu Paule Constant: *OUREGANO* und
    Propriété privée." Master's thesis, Johannes Gutenberg-Universitat
    Mainz, Germany, 1983.
Fisher, Claudine. "L'ailleurs d'*Ouregano* de Paule Constant." Paper pre-
    sented at the Conference on Continental Latin American & Franco-

phone Writers, Wichita State University, April 7-9, 1988.

Karlsson, Britt-Marie. "Illusion et réalité dans Balta de Paule Constant." Master's thesis, University of Goteborg, Sweden, 1988.

Miller, Margot. Introduction to *Trading Secrets* (Confidence pour confidence) by Paule Constant. Translated by Betsy Wing. Lincoln: University of Nebraska Press, 2001.

———. *In Search of Shelter: Subjectivity and Spaces of Loss in the Fiction of Paule Constant.* Lanham, MD: Lexington Books, 2003.

———. "The Matropole: Anxiety and the Mother in Paule Constant's Fiction." *The French Review* 77, no 1 (October 2003), 102-111.

Pichot-Burkette, Brigitte. "L'œuvre romanesque de Paule Constant: Polymorphie et unité dans *Ouregano.*" Master's thesis, George Mason University, 1999.

Rye, Gill. "Lost and Found: Mother-Daughter Relations in Paule Constant's Fiction," *Women's Writing in Contemporary France: New Writers, New Literatures in the 1990s.* Edited by Gill Rye and Michael Worton. Manchester: Manchester University Press, 2002, 65-76.

———. "Reading Dialogues: Exploring Interactions between Text and Identity in the Fiction of Christiane Baroche, Hélène Cixous and Paule Constant." Ph.D. dissertation, University of London, University College, 1998.

———. *Reading for Change: Interactions between Text and Identity in Contemporary French Women's Writing (Baroche, Cixous, Constant).* Bern: Peter Lang, 2001.

———. "Time for Change: Re(con)figuring Maternity in Contemporary French Literature: Baroche, Cixous, Constant, Redonnet." *Paragraph* 21, no. 3 (November 1998), 354-75.

Willging, Jennifer. "Chrétienne's Colonial Misadventures: Echoes of Céline and Duras in Paule Constant's *La fille du Gobernator.*" Hybrid Voices, Hybrid Texts: Women's Writing at the Turn of the Millennium. Edited by Gill Rye, special issue, *Dalhousie French Studies* 68 (fall 2004), 57-67.

See also: http://www.themillers.org/margotmiller/pauleconstant.html

Margot Miller holds a Ph.D. in French literature from the University of Maryland. She is an independent scholar and lecturer, specializing in contemporary women writers. She teaches at the School for Advanced International Studies, Johns Hopkins University, Washington, D.C.

Claudine Fisher holds an *Agrégation-ès-Lettres* in English and a *Doctorat-ès-Lettres* in French. A specialist in twentieth- and twenty-first-century literature, she is a professor of French at Portland State University and Honorary Consul of France for the state of Oregon.